CONTENTS

THE LAST SPIRAL

A LEILANI KEALOHA
HAWAIIAN THRILLER

Book 3 of the Leilani Kealoha Trilogy

BY

CHUCK MORGAN

CHAPTER ONE

A New Wave of Crime

Waikiki Beach looked like it had survived a very polite hurricane. Tourists in mirrored sunglasses clustered behind lines of yellow tape, craning their necks for a better view. Two officers in dark blue tried in vain to herd them back, but each time one group retreated, three others edged forward, drawn by the promise of drama on their vacation. A woman in a neon pink tankini sobbed into her phone. Kids gathered shells from footprints left by tactical boots. Somewhere, the faint sound of a ukulele drifted over the sirens.

Detective Leilani Kealoha parked her battered city Explorer in the spot that wasn't sand and locked it out of reflex. The salt in the air made her T-shirt stick to her skin. She ran a hand through her long black hair, twisted it into a bun, and slid on her mirrored aviators. Her eyes flicked over the scene, and she absorbed the information the way a local absorbs the ocean, without thinking.

The armored car sat canted on the bike path, its nose deep in ornamental grass, and its wheels dug into churned-up sand. Its doors yawned open, twisted in a way that suggested explosives, but not a hint of fire. Leilani noted the precise angles, the clean seams where the metal had peeled. This wasn't some back-alley meth job; this was surgical. There were two armored guards on the curb, both breathing but pale, their shirts speckled with sweat. An EMT hovered over one with a blood pressure cuff. The other cradled his own wrist and blinked at the blue sky as if expecting it to explain things.

Leilani walked through the perimeter, ignoring the officer waving her towards the press tent. She ducked under the tape, sidestepping an overturned beach umbrella, and greeted the patrol sergeant with a nod. He looked like he hadn't slept since the last luau.

"Morning, Sarge," she said.

He grunted, eyes narrowed at the chaos beyond the cordon. "You picked a good one, Lei."

She smiled. "You know I like the classics." She scanned the armored car. "So, what's the story?"

Sarge shrugged. "It's got style. They waited for the pickup at 10:00, but the truck never showed up at the scheduled hotel. Instead, it was rerouted here to the beachfront. The company says it was an internal call, but their dispatcher swears nobody put it in. Five minutes after arrival, boom. Guards out cold, driver tased. And the haul." He shook his head. "Clean. Not a dime left."

Leilani scanned the path. There were empty money bags in a neat row by the car, as if someone had left them out for the trash. No sign of a firefight, no spent shells, no blood except for the superficial scrapes on the guards. "Any witnesses?"

"A couple. Nobody got a plate, but they say three guys in black masks, moving like they had rehearsed it. Out in sixty seconds. They left behind the uniforms." He held up three clear evidence bags. Inside each was a folded black jumpsuit. "This is the third hit in two months. Looking like more than a coincidence."

Leilani picked up one bag and flipped it over. The material was thick. "The other two, any connection?"

"Different carriers, different districts. Same style. Fast, clean, smart."

She grunted. "Yeah, it's a classic." She set the suit down and stepped away, walking the crime scene with slow, deliberate steps. The sand was hot through her shoes. Forensic markers stood in the footprints of the thieves, marching toward the parking lot.

She followed them, eyes trained on the chaos

around her, but her mind was looking for patterns. Near the pale blue wall of a hotel's pool cabana, she stopped. Something black and inky sprawled across the pastel stucco.

A spiral six inches across, spray-painted with confidence that made her scalp prickle.

Leilani crouched, the world narrowing to the glossy swirl of paint. It was a perfect curve, almost hypnotic. She reached out, stopping an inch away, feeling the faint chemical heat still rising from the paint.

She'd seen that symbol before. It was drawn at the four resorts that had been robbed. All high-end jewelry. The second time was at a casino that got hit for fifteen million dollars during a poker tournament. Both cases were solved but not closed. They were the work of crews set up by the Mastermind. An elusive criminal who was combining crime and ancient Hawaiian culture. And so far, he hadn't been caught.

Her stomach tightened. She stood, snapped a photo on her phone, and again with her work-issue digital. Two shots for insurance. She lingered, tracing the spiral with her eyes, forcing herself not to get lost in the what-ifs and whys. This was not the time.

A junior officer hovered, uncertain if he should interrupt. "Detective? They're asking for you at the truck."

She nodded, tucked her phone away. "I'm coming." As she turned, she let her hand rest for a heartbeat over the spiral, not touching but close enough to feel the arrogance in it.

The armored car was a few yards away, sunlight bouncing off its dented flank. She ducked under the open back door and avoided stepping in the powder they'd used to dust for prints. The inside was bare, the money shelves stripped down to metal ribs. She imagined the crew, fast hands, gloved, counting seconds as they moved. She pictured their boots tracking sand and sweat and the reek of bad aftershave. The spiral was for her; she was sure of it. Or not her, but anyone who could read the signs.

She kneeled near the driver's seat, the upholstery still warm from the sun. She ran a finger over the console, looking for residue. A smear of something gritty, ash, or beach dust. She collected it in a plastic vial and labeled it. She returned to the curb to study the guards. The EMT looked up as she approached.

"Both stable. Shock, possible mild concussion. No lasting damage."

"Can I talk to them?" she asked.

He hesitated and stepped back. "The one with the wrist, he's lucid."

Leilani crouched, catching the man's eye. "Do you remember anything?" Her tone was soft but precise, the kind that got people to listen.

He nodded and winced. "There was a noise, a hiss. My partner dropped first—" He faltered, eyes glassy. "They were already inside. It was like they appeared out of nowhere. One of them had, like a wand? Black, with a needle on the end. I felt the prick, followed by nothing."

"Taser or dart. Did you see faces?"

He shook his head. "They all wore masks. They didn't talk."

"How much were you carrying?" she asked.

"We were carrying two point five million. We made one stop before we got hit, so reduce that amount by one hundred fifty grand," said the guard.

She thought about that. No words, no names. Intention and a big payday. It fit the pattern.

She thanked him and stood, watching as the paramedics led him away. Her mind worked through the possibilities, rejecting the simple ones. This wasn't about the money, not really. Not with this kind of showmanship.

She walked to the spiral, pulling her phone out as she did. She zoomed in on the photo, blowing it up until the pixels bled together. There was a single dot at the center of the spiral, almost invisible, but perfect. Deliberate.

Leilani let herself exhale. The city would call

it another heist, another black eye for the banks. But for her, it was more than that. It was a message, and it was personal.

She thumbed through her contacts, hovering over a number she hadn't called in months. She forced her breath to slow. Not yet. Not until she had more.

Instead, she returned to the perimeter, snapped more photos, made notes, and asked the questions that made people uneasy. All the while, the spiral lingered behind her eyes, pulling at memories she'd spent months trying to smother.

By the time the scene cleared, the sun had started its slow drift toward the horizon. The beach was already reclaiming its territory; kids building sandcastles near the tire ruts, lovers posing for selfies in the golden light, and the ukulele player singing about happy hours and rainbows.

Leilani watched them, wondering how many had noticed the darkness that had swept through their paradise this morning. Wondering how many would care. She stepped over the crime scene tape one last time, the echo of the spiral tugging her forward, and drove off into the heat shimmer, the case file already unfolding in her mind.

By the time Detective Kealoha returned to

the tape line, the media had sniffed blood. She stepped through the cordon, sidestepping a swarm of microphones and cell phones. The press was like pufferfish: all noise and bright color, easy to ignore but liable to poison the unwary.

The junior officer who'd hovered earlier hustled to her side, eager for direction. "We've got a witness, Detective. Two big ones. The tourist saw everything, and the hot dog guy says he caught the start of it." He fumbled with the clipboard. "You want statements?"

"Get their information and write everything they say. I'll record their statements as well. I want to hear it raw," Leilani said. The officer nodded, running off like a loyal retriever.

Leilani rolled her neck, popped her jaw. The adrenaline from the spiral souring her insides. It would take more than hot coffee to fix that. She headed for the palm-shaded tables where the witnesses waited, hemmed in by tape and an officer with a look of terminal boredom.

First up was the tourist. He was as easy to spot as a cruise ship in the harbor. Sunburned, six-four, and wrapped in a button-down shirt covered in pineapples and leering hula girls. His name tag (from some self-important corporate retreat) was still pinned to his chest. He looked up at her with watery eyes.

Leilani offered a steady smile. "Hey there. I'm Detective Kealoha. Mind if we talk for a minute?"

He tried to stand but gave up halfway. "Please. My wife's at the hotel. I want to get back." He kept wringing his hands as if trying to strangle the fear out of his fingers.

"Take your time," she said, sitting across from him. "Just tell me what you saw."

He sucked in a breath. "I was walking here; my wife walked to the hotel. She had a stomachache from eating too much shrimp. That's when I saw the truck pull up. I wondered why they were stopping at the beach. There are no stores or anything, and I doubted the hot dog guy needed an armored car delivery. A black pickup truck pulled up, and these guys, three, four, it all happened so fast, they ran up. They moved like I don't know, like soldiers?"

"Like they rehearsed it," Leilani said, prompting.

He nodded furiously. "Exactly. They knew where to go, where to look. I tried to shout, but nobody else noticed until the bang."

Leilani leaned forward. "The bang?"

The tourist bobbed his head. "Yeah, like fireworks. Not huge, but loud. Something popped behind us, near the snack stands. Everyone turned to look, and." He snapped his fingers.

"Those men were already inside the truck. One of them had a gun, I think. I mean, it could've been a toy, but he waved it around and everyone hit the sand."

Leilani kept her voice level. "Did they say anything?"

His face was blank. "No. Not one word. I thought it was a joke, a show, but it wasn't. They emptied the truck, got into a black pickup, and —" He gestured helplessly. "Gone. Vanished."

She nodded, jotting the essentials into her notebook. "Did you catch the license plate?"

He shook his head, cheeks flushing with shame. "Sorry. I was too busy looking at the sand."

"Don't worry about it." She softened her voice, before switching tactics. "What about the pickup? Anything unusual?"

"Shiny. Really clean. Like they'd washed it."

Leilani made a note. "Thank you. You did great." She slid him a business card. "If you remember anything else, please call me. This officer is going to have you read your statement and sign it, and thanks again."

She moved to the next witness, a local vendor with skin the color of rich coffee and hands stained from a lifetime of handling hot dogs and sticky rice. His nametag read KELO, and he gave

Leilani a grin with one gold tooth gleaming.

"Detective," he said, in the tone of someone who'd seen a dozen dead bodies and half as many carjackings. "You want the entire story or the highlights?"

"The facts," she replied, settling in.

Kelo obliged. "I was prepping for the lunch rush. Next thing, boom, a little firecracker, nothing major. Enough to make tourists duck and scatter. I look up and see three men in black jumpsuits sprinting for the armored truck. They didn't waste time. First guy covers the guards, second, and third pop the doors. They toss bags like they're tossing poi, all in sync."

Leilani asked, "You said they tossed bags?"

He nodded. "Yeah. Not money, at least not at first. Looked like they were after something specific." He shrugged. "Money came last."

That was new. "You sure?"

"I've seen plenty of idiots go after cash before," Kelo said, "but these guys, they didn't care about the coin bags, throwing those in the black pickup. A Ford F-150. Pretty new. The odd thing is it didn't have any plates. They grabbed the cash first."

She scribbled a note. "Thanks, Kelo. Anything else stand out?"

He shrugged. "Nah. Unless you want to know

who's got the best spam musubi on the block."

She allowed herself a half-smile. "Rain check. I'm going to have one of these officers take your statement and have you sign it. You can keep working until they can get over here."

She shook his hand and walked to the scene, replaying both interviews in her head. The pattern held. Military precision, efficient violence and a knack for timing. But they were looking for something other than cash. She would need to check with the company and find out what else was in the truck besides the money?

She strode to the path, where the pickup had parked. The sand bore two deep ruts, cleanly spaced. No tire marks on the pavement, too smart for that. But in the sand, faint tread patterns overlapped with the waffle print of a thousand tourist flip-flops.

She crouched, the world shrinking to three feet of packed sand. Her phone camera snapped shots from every angle, while her fingers teased a piece of the metal free from a clump of dried mud. She tucked it into an evidence bag, eyes scanning for more. She spotted a fleck of blue paint clinging to a grain of sand, probably from the armored truck, but worth bagging anyway.

Behind her, the junior officer returned. "Detective? Sarge wants to know if you're done.

They want to move the crowd."

She looked up. "Hold the line for another ten minutes." She pointed at the sand. "Get forensics over here and have them comb this patch. Nothing gets stepped on, understood?"

He nodded. "Detective? What do you think, these guys, the ones that hit the truck? Is it them again?"

Leilani didn't answer right away. She brushed the sand from her knees, stood, and looked past the police tape to the line of hotels and the endless blue of the Pacific. "You ever hear of the Ouroboros?"

The officer blinked. "What?"

She pointed back at the spiral painted on the wall. "That symbol. It's an ouroboros, means something that feeds on itself. Comes back over and over."

He nodded, not really following.

She almost smiled. "It's them. Get forensics on the tire marks. Pronto."

The officer jogged away, and Leilani turned her attention to the evidence in her hands. The pattern was clear, and yet the department would say she was making leaps. She let herself stare at the spiral, and sensed the old anxiety twisting in her gut. She knew she was right.

The scene was already winding down.

Tourists checked their phones for dinner reservations, the beach boys called to each other about surf conditions, and a line of garbage trucks crawled along the access road, prepping for their nightly run. In Honolulu, nothing stopped for long.

Leilani bagged the last evidence, recorded her notes, and stepped back. She considered calling her mother to hear a voice from before things got complicated. But work came first. It always did.

She let her face relax as she gazed at the ocean, the rolling blues and greens, the waves pulling at the shore and let go again. It never changed. Neither did people like the Mastermind. She walked the perimeter, determination steeled by habit and by hope. She walked to the water, her calm place.

Waikiki's beach was still warm, the late sun leaving every object coated in honey. The evidence team loaded their last bags into the van, but the line of police tape stood like a bright boundary between the messy facts of the morning and the curated beauty of the world beyond. Detective Kealoha paced to the water's edge, rolling her shoulders. She dug her toes into the sand, phone out and thumb poised, and dialed the number she'd memorized months before.

The phone rang once.

"Torres," the voice came, sharp and clipped over digital static.

"It's Leilani," she said, watching the water smooth out over the reef. "Are you sitting down?"

A soft snort. "Is this about your armored car?"

She cracked a smile. "That, and the spiral they left on a public restroom wall. Same as the Kakaʻako job and the Kalihi van. This time, the target was the vault compartment. Must have been something of value. They took all the cash and coins. In and out, less than sixty seconds."

Isaac Torres was with the FBI. He was brought in last year on a joint task force for what they called exotics, the sort of crimes that didn't fit the usual criminal mold. He was smart, careful, and way too good-looking for someone who wore a polyester badge. Sometimes, he was the one person in the Bureau who listened to her theories. Sometimes, that was worse.

"Tell me you got a print," he said, not quite daring to hope.

"No prints," she said. "They wore gloves. But we have tire tracks, a pickup, a newer model Ford, no plates, and a witness who says they ran a diversion at the food carts. Same playbook as before. They're learning, Isaac. They're getting better."

He was quiet, with the hiss of background noise on the line. "And the symbol?"

"Perfect spiral, fresh paint. The center dot is new. I think it's deliberate."

"You're sure it's them," he said.

"I'd bet my badge on it," Leilani replied, and found she meant it. "This wasn't a heist for the money. Not only the money, anyway. They headed straight for the safe, cleaned out everything and left the guards breathing. This was surgical. This is a message."

She listened to him breathe, a measured inhale. "The Mastermind?"

"Either he's back," Leilani said, "or someone's learned his tricks."

"Do you want me to come down?" Torres asked.

She looked out at the horizon, where a paddleboarder traced lazy arcs in the water. "Yes," she said. "We'll need the manpower, and the locals are already spooked."

He hesitated. "You okay, Lei?"

She squinted into the sun, watching the reflected glint off the high-rise windows. "I'm good. Tired of chasing my tail. You'll be at the airport by nightfall?"

"I'm on the next flight out," he promised.

"We'll crack it, Leilani. Don't lose sleep yet."

She ended the call and let the phone hang at her side. She let herself exhale. For a minute, the waves drowned out the noise in her head. Torres had finally accepted a mainland promotion after he realized Leilani was married to her job. She liked the attention, but she understood she didn't need anyone in her life right now, and she was good with that. She had been sad to see him leave, but since he had gotten shot twice while working with her, she thought he might have needed the break.

The world behind her kept spinning. Children ran, oblivious, into the surf. A couple in matching aloha shirts kissed under the banyan tree, totally unaware that the concrete still stank of ammonium nitrate and fear. Crime scene tape fluttered in the breeze, barely holding back the tide of vacationers.

Detective Kealoha tucked her phone away and squared her shoulders. She strode up the beach, back toward the spiral, back into the chaos that never quite left this island. The pastel wall glimmered with fresh paint. The spiral was there, black and perfect, and waiting for her.

She bared her teeth in a quick, fierce grin. Paradise didn't get to keep its secrets, not while she was watching.

CHAPTER TWO

Family Tensions

The first sign of trouble was the light. A thin band of gold spilled under Kai's bedroom door, flat and unwavering, cutting a line across the faded wood floors. It was nearly nine p.m. and the house was dark, the way Leilani preferred it after a day like this. She'd expected silence, a humming fridge, the lonesome slap of palm leaves on the roof, or her mother's snores from the back room. But here was her son's defiant lamp, holding vigil against the black while her mother banged around in the kitchen.

Leilani locked up behind herself, triple-checking the bolt before sliding her badge and keys into the shallow dish on the sideboard. She peeled off her department windbreaker, its armpits salt-stained and reeking of adrenaline, and left it to wilt over the back of the couch. She ignored her stomach's reminder, filled a glass of water, kissed her mom on the cheek and padded down the hallway, bare feet silent on the battered planks.

She stood outside Kai's door for a long beat, listening. He was supposed to be asleep; the morning would come early, and ten-year-olds needed sleep the way surfers needed waves. She heard no video game beeps, and no whispered narration of the Pokémon saga. Just the faint, steady rustle of paper.

She nudged the door open. "Detective Junior," she said, voice at half volume.

Kai startled, glancing over his shoulder. His face glowed with both the lamp and a wild energy that made him look like he'd been electrocuted by his own imagination. His hair, still damp from his bedtime shower, spiked in all directions. He wore his favorite board shorts and a T-shirt two sizes too big; the collar stretched from being pulled over his head in a hurry.

He grinned at her slyly. "Hey, Mom. I'm, uh, working on something."

"I see that." She stepped inside, and her mouth went dry.

The wall above Kai's desk had been transformed. Last week it was plastered with surfer stickers, vintage Marvel comics, and one picture of Kai wiping out at the beach. Tonight, it looked like the operations tent of a small but ambitious intelligence agency.

Three maps of Oahu had been taped together; their surfaces stippled with marker dots and laced with red yarn. Newspaper clippings, the heist at the Bishop Museum, the jewelry store smash-and-grab, and today's armored car robbery, were thumbtacked in overlapping sequence. Between them, Kai had scrawled notes in green Sharpie, some legible ("suspects look same = team???"), others written in the cryptic shorthand of a ten-year-old prodigy ("X marks = clue?" "Waikiki hit #3—order??"). A printout from the Honolulu Police Department's public page had a big circle around the word SPIRAL, underlined twice. A tiny Post-It near the edge read. "If they never get caught, are they the good guys?"

Kai turned back to his desk, which was littered with a scatter of crime scene photos (badly photocopied from the internet), a police scanner borrowed from Leilani's gear bag, and a half-empty box of sour gummy worms. He was cross-referencing something in his notebook and didn't notice her move closer, eyes scanning the wall.

Leilani didn't say anything. She was going to say, this is too much, or why don't you draw superheroes, or I love you, but the words caught in her throat, a fishhook of pride tangled with something darker. She noted the crazy tangle of clues, at her son's wiry frame hunched in the glow, and sensed a chill she didn't like.

Kai finally glanced up, and the grin returned. "Did you catch the robbers yet?" he asked, like she might have bagged them and brought them home in a doggie bag.

She snorted, the tension breaking. "Not yet. They're quick. The grown ups are having trouble keeping up."

He straightened; his face flushed with excitement. "I think they're using tunnels," he said, voice low and conspiratorial. "There're all these old lava tubes under the city. See?" He pointed to the maps, where he'd traced a crazy zig-zag of routes from Waikiki to Kaka'ako. "If you rob a bank or a museum, you could get away without ever being on the street."

Leilani crouched next to him, eye level now. "You think that's how they did it?"

Kai nodded, solemn as a priest. "Also, they never hurt anybody. They're careful." He hesitated. "But that doesn't mean they're good. Right?"

She observed her son, his eager face, his eyes that always seemed to reflect a little more than they took in. "It means they're smart," she said. "And being smart is good if you use it to help people." She hesitated, searched for the right lever to pull him back from the edge. "Detective work is hard. Sometimes, it's not fun. It gets inside your head and makes everything else fuzzy."

He wrinkled his nose. "I like the fuzzy. It's like a puzzle, and I'm good at it."

She felt the smile, though it didn't make it all the way to her lips. "I know, kiddo." She ruffled his hair. "But you need sleep to be smart. The best detectives need a break."

Kai rolled his eyes but closed his notebooks anyway. "I'll finish tomorrow. I already have two more ideas."

"I believe it." Leilani watched him, torn between wanting to erase all this and never wanting it to change. She pulled the rolling chair back and gestured for him to crawl into bed.

He did eventually, after lining up his pencil, his notebook and the scanner exactly where he could reach them the moment he woke. He burrowed under his sheet, leaving one leg sticking out like a buoy.

She switched off the desk lamp, hovering in the blue shadows. "You know, not all detectives have a wall this cool."

He grinned, barely awake. "I bet the robbers have one, too."

"Mom," he said. "Nana said I can help at the hula booth at the cultural festival. Is that okay?"

She smiled and mussed his hair. "Alway's Kai."

Leilani closed the door most of the way, letting the glow from the hallway seep through. She wandered into the living room, with the ghost of a smile on her lips and something larger on her shoulders. She paused at the dinner table, looked at the sticky dish left for her, and finally took a bite.

The house was quiet again, but the line of light still glowed beneath Kai's door, refusing to be snuffed out. She sipped her water, savoring the chill against her throat, and let herself hope that he'd always find answers to the puzzles he chased. Or, at the very least, that she could keep him out of the darkest parts of the maze.

At nine, their kitchen glowed with the promise of family. The overhead bulb cast everything in a buttery light, and the battered linoleum was still sticky from when Kai dropped a jar of honey last week. The table, scored with decades of knife marks and glitter-glue disasters, overflowed with plates. Food was Naalei Kealoha's weapon of choice. A bubbling pan of chicken long rice, sticky purple taro and her famous lomi salmon, cold, and salty and alive with diced tomatoes. The air shimmered with ginger, garlic, and the warm, sweet rot of ripe papaya.

Naalei stood over the stove, arms folded under her generous chest, humming an old mele under her breath. She was short and round, her hair coiled into a silver bun, her expression equal parts tenderness and tactical awareness. Wearing her faded muumuu, she radiated authority, the kind that could hush a room with a single look.

Leilani sank into the chair facing the stove, fatigue leaking from every limb. She accepted a beer from her mother, cracked it, the cold fizz chilling her throat. "Thanks, Ma," she said, voice rough.

Naalei shot her a look. "You look like you've been wrestling pigs all day."

"Close enough," Leilani said. "Is this the part where you interrogate me?"

Naalei set down a bowl of poi and sat beside her, resting a heavy hand on her shoulder. "You work hard," she said, like a proverb. "Eat in peace."

Leilani caught her mother's eye, shared an unspoken conversation, something about genetics and curses and how family history always circled back around. Leilani scooped food onto her plate, watching her mother out of the corner of her eye. "Some crimes, they're more than the money," she said. "Sometimes, people are chasing something else."

"Like what?" asked Naalei.

She shrugged. "Attention. Glory. Proving

they're smarter than everyone else."

Naalei was quiet, processing. "But you'll catch them, right?"

"That's the job," she said, changing the subject. "Kai told me the cultural festival is coming up. He said you want him to help with the hula booth."

Naalei's eyes sparked, the smile small but genuine. "He's got a good 'ami. Takes after the old blood. He told me nobody does hula anymore. It's all TikTok dances," said Naalei.

"I told him you can do both," Naalei said, tapping his nose with a calloused finger. "You dance for your ancestors, you dance for your friends."

The kitchen quieted, but the silence was uneasy. On the wall, a faded photo of Leilani's late father watched over them. In it, he wore a police uniform and an enormous mustache, his arms wrapped around both his wife and a much younger, gap-toothed Leilani. Around the frame, a lei of dried ti leaves had turned a somber brown, but the memory was bright as ever.

Naalei laughed, reaching for her necklace, a small, carved pendant on a leather cord, weathered smooth by years of touch. "It's important to keep the past where it belongs," she said. Her eyes were far away. "Not to let it chase you into the future."

Leilani listened, and her mother's words echoed the silent refrain in her own head. She almost asked about the pendant, why it mattered so much, what story hid behind it, but let the question drift away, swept aside by the comfort of her mother.

Leilani helped clear the table, rinsing plates as her mother packed leftovers. The house was warm and safe. She let herself forget for one moment that anything could wait outside.

As if summoned by the ghost of her own paranoia, her phone vibrated on the counter. She checked the screen. HPD's main number. She dried her hands on her jeans and answered.

A dispatcher's voice, clipped and urgent. Another hit, this time on the Windward side. Same signature. No injuries, but the pattern was clear; the spiral was back.

Leilani's jaw tensed. She caught her mother's eyes and saw the understanding there, grim and ancient as the black stone of Koko Head.

"I have to go," she said.

Naalei nodded. "Be careful," she said. "And come back before dawn. Your son has a dance to practice."

Leilani smiled at that, kissed her mother's cheek, and walked to the bedroom door to look at Kai, her living puzzle, her best unsolved case.

"Goodnight, Detective Junior," she said.

Kai saluted, already slipping into dreams. The night waited outside, humid and hungry for answers.

The shift was instant, an old muscle memory. She closed her phone and set it down, pulling on her jacket. In seconds she became something else, not Mom, not daughter, but the steel wire that held the island's secrets together. She slipped her badge into her pocket, clipped her holster onto her belt, and checked her keys twice. Her hands worked in silence, each motion economical and practiced.

Naalei appeared in the doorway, lips pressed in a hard line. "Another armored car heist?"

Leilani nodded, not breaking stride. "Looks like it. Near Waimanalo."

Naalei crossed the kitchen in three steps. "Let me walk you out," she said, and Leilani understood the code, adult talk, not for young ears.

They stepped into the night, the air soft and salty. The moon was a thumbnail, not enough to see by. On the porch, Naalei caught Leilani's arm, her grip surprisingly strong.

"These cases you chase," Naalei said, voice low. "They're getting more dangerous. The men behind them are not thieves. They are something else."

Leilani offered a smile. "You think I can't handle it?"

"That's not what I said." Naalei's eyes flashed. "You're strong, but some things in this world are bigger than what you see. And not every monster bleeds when you punch it." Her hand moved to her pendant, thumb stroking the bone until it shone. "There are old connections here. Things you don't know."

Leilani shook her head, bemused. "You mean family secrets? Or like ghosts?"

"Both," Naalei whispered. She glanced back at the door. "It's why your father left the force early. Some lines are better left uncrossed."

A spark of annoyance flared in Leilani's chest. "If there's something you need to tell me, say it, Ma. Don't wait till I'm knee-deep in trouble."

Naalei hesitated, eyes distant. "Not yet. Please. Be careful. Come home safe to your boy."

The tenderness in her voice nearly undid Leilani. She pulled Naalei into a quick, fierce hug, and stepped back, all business.

"I will not let anything happen to us," she said. "Promise."

Naalei nodded, but her mouth was still a straight line. She watched as Leilani jogged down the driveway, slid behind the wheel of her rusted

Explorer, and started the engine.

Through the windshield, Leilani caught one last look at her mother on the porch, framed by yellow light and the thin arms of the plumeria tree. Inside the bedroom window, she glimpsed Kai's face, half in shadow, half in hope, all hunger for the story.

Leilani let the image burn into her mind. She put the Explorer in gear and drove into the night, towards the spiral that waited, hungry and patient, somewhere beyond the curve of the island.

Back on the porch, Naalei didn't move. She stood there long after the headlights faded, one hand on her pendant, the other held out as if to steady the world.

Inside, Kai returned to his bed. He checked the red threads and maps one more time, before crawling beneath the covers, eyes wide open, staring at the ceiling as if waiting for the next page to turn itself.

The house stood quiet, poised between old secrets and the trouble yet to come.

CHAPTER THREE

Patterns Emerge

The overhead Lights in the HPD conference room buzzed like angry wasps, spitting out harsh rectangles of light that made everything and everyone look both overexposed and sleepy. Detective Leilani Kealoha slouched at one end of the battered table, arms folded, as the display of case files and financial spreadsheets advanced steadily in front of her. Her partner for the night, Special Agent Isaac Torres, perched at the opposite edge, eyes red, tie crooked, feet propped on the nearest chair like he was daring someone to tell him to sit up straight. They'd been at it for five hours, but judging by the caffeine stink, neither planned on quitting soon.

Between them, the conference table resembled a crime scene of its own; yellow notepads scribbled with timelines, piles of printouts, and a leaning tower of subpoenas. Somewhere under the avalanche, there were three foam coffee cups with Leilani's lipstick prints in progressively more desperate shades of mauve.

Isaac Torres stabbed a pencil at the third cup, pinching the bridge of his nose. "You know," he said, "when I took the temporary transfer to the island, I pictured surfing and shaved ice, not the world's longest math class."

"Welcome to paradise," Leilani said. Her eyes didn't leave the evidence board. She was affixing a new set of glossy 8x10s to the board. Three different armored car robberies, and each crime scene marked with that signature spiral. The black paint practically leaped off the corkboard, pulsing under the weird office lighting.

Torres dropped his feet and grabbed the case chronology, running his finger along the latest entries. "Three jobs, six weeks, no overlap in crew, no forensics, and not a decent eyewitness."

She countered: "But the pattern is tight. They all hit in the morning, right when the couriers are at their most routine. No injuries, minimal collateral. It's like they're showing off."

"Arrogant or careful?"

"Does it have to be either-or?" she said. She plucked a photo and set it in the middle, the Waikiki Beach hit, where the spiral had been sprayed on stucco with almost surgical neatness. "The one constant is the signature."

Torres took it in, nodding towards the crime scene timeline. "That's the other constant. Every time they strike, someone on the Mastermind's old list walks."

Leilani allowed herself to smirk. "If I didn't know better, I'd say you were developing a theory."

"I'm developing a migraine," Torres grunted. He fished in his jacket for Advil, shook two tablets directly into his mouth and chased them with old coffee. He grimaced and pointed at the stack of financials. "You think we're missing a money trail?"

She shrugged. "Always. But I also think this crew doesn't need the cash. It's about leverage."

Torres bristled. "They're already making the HPD and the FBI look like amateurs. What's left to prove?"

She met his eyes, a challenge. "Somebody's paying to keep certain cases from sticking. But what if the robberies aren't to humiliate us? What if it's to create chaos during court cycles?"

He chewed on that. "Like they're weaponizing our own schedule against us?"

Leilani gave him a slow nod, sweeping her hand over the charts. "First job hit during the jury selection for that corrupt cop trial. Second day of sentencing for one of the bigger fencing operations. And today, three hours before the plea bargain hearing for a banker tied to the Mastermind. You see it?"

"Distraction," Torres said, voice lower now. "Not for us, but for the DA, the courts, and the witnesses. Pull the city's attention every time something sensitive is about to go public."

Leilani pressed a knuckle to her lip, tracing the lines on the board. "They're orchestrating the city. Like a conductor with a baton."

Torres stared. "You ever wonder if the Mastermind's actually dead?"

She was still. "I've wondered."

He stood, started pacing the room's perimeter, his hands digging into his suit pants. "FBI's been sitting on this one for years, hoping the network would eat itself. But here we are, and someone's sharper than ever. It's like the brain survived, but the body didn't."

Leilani's scalp prickled. "You ever get the sensation that we're not the only ones watching this wall?"

Torres grinned. "Always. Which is why I'm supposed to be in D.C. next month, not getting sand in my socks with you." He dropped back into the chair. "My boss called. Two weeks. That's my window, or they yank me off."

She shot him a look. "So, we don't get to save

the day; we get to play chicken with the feds?"

Torres rolled the pencil between his fingers. "Unless you've got a shortcut to case closed that doesn't involve a time machine."

"Better," she said. "We've got tomorrow's court calendar and at least one criminal out on pretrial who'll draw the Mastermind's attention. It's a start."

He cocked an eyebrow. "Are you willing to bait them?"

She grinned, teeth white and sharp. "I want to see if the spiral shows up before lunch. And if it does, I want to be there when the paint's still wet."

Torres shook his head, but she knew he liked the plan. "You're the most optimistic person I've ever met in a crime lab."

"That's what happens when you grow up watching your family get bulldozed by every white-collar predator on the island," she said. She wiped her hands on her jeans, before organizing the files into a new pile. "But I'm not giving up on this. Not tonight."

Torres let the silence expand. "My cousin tried to open a surf shop in San Diego. Lost it to a chain in a month. Spent the next year getting high in a storage locker, before the bank remembered to repo the boards." He caught her look and smirked. "Point is, sometimes the system is rigged. Sometimes you have to be smarter than the people who set the rules."

"Or at least more stubborn," Leilani said.

"Works for you," Torres replied.

They shared a moment of friendship before the lights flickered again and the building's AC coughed, sending a blast of cold air through the already frigid room.

Leilani pulled her phone and started scrolling. "Here. Circuit court, eight a.m., Judge Kumiko. They're sentencing Junior Lim for grand theft, and rumor has it the guy was connected to the old gambling ring."

Torres checked his notes. "Lim's the guy who knows people but never leaves a trail. You think he's on the list?"

"Either as a target, or as a message to whoever's next. If the crew's going to hit, they'll do it while everyone's attention is on the courthouse."

Torres checked his watch. "I'll bring the donuts. You bring your lucky pen."

She fished the pen from behind her ear, brandishing it like a dart. "Ready for action."

He grinned, eyeing the evidence board one more time. "You really believe we can catch these people?"

Leilani thought of her son, asleep under a collage of clues, and of her mother's ancient warning about old ghosts and deeper connections. She met Torres's gaze, her voice like iron. "Yeah. I really do."

They packed up the paperwork, locking the big stuff away for the night, and left the photos up on the board as a warning to anyone who might pass by at midnight. Leilani lingered by the door, glancing back at the spirals, at the endless rows of case files, and at the island map stabbed with red pins. There was a pattern there. There was always a pattern if you were willing to look hard enough, and long enough, and care enough not to quit.

Outside the glass, the city glowed with the last dregs of neon, the sky dark enough to swallow secrets but bright enough to give up a clue or two to the right eyes. She let the moment settle, closing the door behind her, the latch snapping with a crisp promise.

Tomorrow will be another long day. But it seemed like the case was finally cracking.

The HPD evidence lockup was a cinder block coffin, painted brown and windowless, air perpetually soured with dust, toner, and the sweetly rotten undercurrent of ancient copy paper. Isaac Torres elbowed through the door with a grunt, bracing it open for Leilani, who ducked in behind him. She let the door thunk shut with a sound like a judge's gavel. Inside, the stacked metal shelving squeezed the aisle down to a single-file corridor. Every flat surface was haunted by cardboard boxes, gray envelopes or the occasional bin of tagged jewelry with a sticky note clinging to it for dear life.

Leilani's sneakers scuffed the linoleum. "I love what you've done with the place," she said. "Is that a murder from 1982 I smell?"

"Probably," Isaac said, eyeing the bins. "But don't get distracted by the classics."

She'd been here before, dozens of times, but always felt the tickle of nerves. No cameras, only a single security panel and the knowledge that whoever had the key was either a saint or already under Internal Affairs investigation. She scanned the nearest shelf, eyes hunting for the familiar bright orange tags of unprocessed evidence.

"I think the missing link is in the old court records," she said. "The cases the spiral crew hit were all in limbo or evidence suppression. If someone's engineering this, they'll want to wipe the files before the appeals."

Torres nodded, scanning the aisles, his voice

low. "Which means there might be a second set of books, something not entered into the official system."

She grinned. "You're learning."

They fanned out, Leilani working from the left, Isaac from the right, both shuffling boxes like professional burglars. A year of joint task force work had taught her how to spot a box that didn't belong. Most of the file bins were battered, Sharpied, and re-taped a dozen times, but one near the bottom looked almost new. Smooth sides, the HPD logo still crisp, and the date written with a ballpoint rather than a marker. She crouched and slid it out. The dust underneath was less than a week old.

"Found one," she said.

Torres kneeled beside her. She opened the box, her hands careful. Inside, there was a thick stack of financial reports, but beneath it, wedged between two manila folders, was a hardcover ledger. It was old—edges bruised, binding split and the paper inside a faded yellow. No markings on the cover. A spiral, inked by hand, black and precise.

Torres exhaled. "That's either a trap or a treasure."

She flipped it open. The ledger was columns and columns of names, dates and dollar amounts in tidy red ink. Every page was annotated with case numbers or initials, some crossed out, others double underlined. It took all of twenty seconds for Torres to jab a finger at a familiar entry.

"Judge Aranello. Paid off the week before he quashed half the evidence in the Castle & Sons bust. That's almost ballsy."

"Look at the sums," Leilani whispered. "Fifty grand for the judge, twenty to the prosecutor, two to a cop on evidence duty. That's a payroll."

They paged forward, moving faster now. Every entry was connected to a name they'd seen on court calendars or in old headlines. Some dates were paired with crime scene addresses or with the home addresses of witnesses who'd gone silent.

Torres's knuckles whitened on the desk. "This is bigger than we thought. These are federal, state, and private security guys, all in the same log."

"Someone built a machine and made sure it could eat anything," she said.

She set the ledger aside and rooted through the box. The Manila folders were case files, most of which were already copied to digital format, but these contained the original exhibits, including Polaroids, handwritten statements, and chain of custody sheets with multiple signatures. She pulled one, noting the signature on the evidence transfer slip. It was familiar. She flipped to the bottom.

"Look," she said. Torres leaned in. The signature was identical to one on the first page of the ledger: Judge Aranello, but in different pens, months apart.

"They kept their own receipts," he said. "But why risk it?"

Leilani thought about it, lips pursed. "They didn't expect anyone to get this far. Or this is their insurance, in case one of the buyers gets cold feet."

They dug deeper. One envelope had a Post-it stuck to it. Pending—IA Only. She ripped it open. Inside was a thin stack of typewritten pages with the heading. Corrupt Judiciary—Internal Affairs. A list of names, cross-referenced with court dockets and police case files, some with stars or exclamation points beside them.

"Someone flagged these judges months ago," she muttered.

Torres scanned it, eyebrows up. "Looks like IA tried to follow up but got stonewalled. There's a note about evidence sabotage."

She turned to the last page. There was a coffee ring, dark and unmistakable, right over the signature block. The name underneath was "J. Kumiko," the same judge presiding over tomorrow's Lim case.

Torres whistled. "You think they know they're on the list?"

Leilani shrugged. "Doesn't matter. If the Mastermind's crew is trying to burn the evidence, they'll be coming for this room next."

They scanned the rest in silence, gathering what they could. Leilani's hands worked the camera on her phone, snapping pictures of every relevant page, every damning name. Torres double-bagged the ledger in a brown evidence envelope, using his phone to text a few select images to the joint task force server.

They were nearly done when the lights blinked. A faint metallic click sounded outside, like a lock being turned, and all the overheads snapped off at once, plunging them into syrupy darkness.

For half a second, there was only their breath and the sound of the building's old servers. With a stuttering whine, the emergency lights flicked on. The bulbs were set low, casting everything in a blood-red gloom. Down the aisle, the red glow turned the shelving into a funhouse of shadows.

Torres straightened, spine rigid. "That wasn't expected," he said.

Leilani checked her watch and reached for her radio. There was a burst of static and nothing else. She keyed it again. "Kealoha to dispatch. We're in Evidence One, need status on building power."

Nothing but white noise. Torres fished his phone out. No bars.

"You getting anything?" she asked.

He shook his head. "Dead air. And this room is a Faraday cage. Old buildings."

They exchanged a look. Leilani grinned as her heart jumped into a higher gear. "Like the old days, right?"

He snorted. "Except I didn't have to duck gunfire back in Quantico."

They slid to the end of the row, peering down the main corridor toward the door. The red lighting made every movement seem twice as sharp, and Leilani felt her pulse in her palms, her feet, and her temples. She started forward, crouched low, hugging the boxes. Torres mirrored her, his free hand wrapped tight around a canister of pepper spray.

They made the door in five quick paces. It was locked from the outside. Torres rattled the handle, giving her a half-smile. "Hope you're good with lock picks."

"I'm better with paperclips," she said. After a moment's rummaging, she produced a small lock-pick kit from her pocket. She bent to the lock, hands steady despite the adrenaline.

It took a second. The lock snapped open. Before they could push through, a shadow moved on the far side of the glass. Leilani tensed, glancing at Torres, who mouthed. "Wait."

Footsteps padded down the hallway, unhurried, like the person owned the building or had all the time in the world. A faint whistle, a fragment of some old Hawaiian tune, echoed off the cinder block. The shadow passed the glass, lingering for a breath. Before disappearing.

They waited until the silence was solid and eased open the door. The main hallway was empty; the overheads were still dead. The red strobes at each exit and the flicker from the evidence room were all the light.

Leilani's phone buzzed once, screen lighting up her face. One new text, from an unknown number.

Stop digging, Detective. Next time, it's personal.

She showed Torres the screen, and he muttered a curse in Spanish. She pocketed the phone.

They moved as fast as they could, sticking to the walls, clutching the envelope. The entire building was as quiet as a morgue. They burst through the door, Torres blinking against the dark. The air outside was sharp and clean, almost cold after the suffocating box of the evidence room. They kept moving until they were clear of the building.

Leilani checked the time. One minute had passed since the blackout started.

Torres glanced at her, his expression grim but alive with purpose. "We moved from investigation to open war."

She grinned. "You ever try to out-stubborn a Hawaiian woman?"

He laughed, holding the envelope. "Not yet, but I'm game."

She nodded, turning towards the city, the next step already forming in her head.

Behind them, the courthouse glowed in the darkness, a fortress full of secrets. Somewhere inside, the next move was already in play. But for now, they had proof and hope.

She let herself absorb that before tucking the evidence under her arm and heading for her battered Explorer, determination burning in her like a brand. Tonight, they'd survived. Tomorrow, they'll hunt.

CHAPTER FOUR

Ghosts from the Past

Halawa Correctional Facility loomed out of the Koʻolau foothills like a slab of unfinished business. The twin towers of concrete squatted behind four fences; each stitched with razor wire sharp enough to fillet a hurricane. Most locals pretended Halawa didn't exist, but everyone on Oahu knew the stories. Leilani drove past the last checkpoint, ID hanging from her mirror, and parked beside a squad car that looked like it had been stripped for parts by its own mechanics.

The parking lot was hostile, no shade, no flowers, a windbreak of ratty palm trees, and the steady scream of the highway. She took a breath and braced herself, knowing the inside would be worse.

The lobby was all bulletproof glass and burnished linoleum. A single tired fan oscillated behind the counter, barely moving the air. The intake officer looked up, saw her badge, and grunted. She'd called ahead, but the prison made homicide detectives wait. There was a flavor of disrespect here, built up over decades of power games and ruined reputations.

She signed her name on three separate clipboards. A second guard patted her down with the boredom of a man paid by the hour and walked her through the scanner.

"Detective Kealoha," he said. "No electronics past this point. If you get shivved, yell loud."

She deadpanned. "Just like home."

A sergeant with a face like a woodcut led her through two more steel doors, and down a corridor that reeked of floor cleaner and scorched Spam. The guard told her nothing. No small talk. They passed cells where men watched TV or looked at the cinderblock, some faces blank, others raw and bleeding emotion. Nobody spoke.

The last door clanged open onto a windowless interview room. The furniture consisted of a bolted steel table and two chairs. A digital recorder waited, blinking its single red eye.

Leilani sat, resisting the impulse to tap her foot. The chair was cold and unsympathetic.

On the other side of the glass, there was a shuffle of chains and a mutter of voices. The door buzzed, opened, and in shuffled the reason she was here, former Honolulu Chief of Police Janet Tokuda, escorted by two guards and a nurse with a Band-Aid mustache.

Tokuda wore the orange jumpsuit like a dare. She had thick wrists, now cuffed and chained at the waist, and white hair slicked back in a wet slab. In her prime, Tokuda could stop a conversation with a raised eyebrow or start a riot with a look. Today, her face was like a collapsed star. Still powerful, but drawing everything else inward.

She sat down; the guards removed her shackles when she was locked under the table. She didn't flinch, didn't blink.

"Well," said Tokuda, surveying Leilani's face. "I suppose you're here to gloat."

Leilani clicked on the recorder and slid it between them. "I'm here for information."

"Of course you are. That's what you island cops always want. To know what the big bad wolf did with the little pigs." Tokuda's voice was raspy, almost amusing. "But I'm not in the storytelling mood today."

Leilani studied her. "It's better than solitary. Or did you get used to that in LA?"

A flash of irritation. Tokuda had lasted all of four weeks in Los Angeles before a multi-agency SWAT team plucked her from a Koreatown walk-up. The extradition paperwork had run three inches thick, but the U.S. Marshals liked nothing more than bringing down a dirty cop. Especially one from Hawaii.

Tokuda let out a sound halfway between a laugh and a cough. "They eat their own in LA. But the food is better."

"So, you confess the California charges?"

Tokuda looked at the ceiling. "I confess to being a woman with poor taste in business partners."

"You should've stuck to surfing," said Leilani. She let the silence work, counting out the beats until Tokuda spoke again.

"You're not here to bust my balls, Detective." The old command voice surfaced. "You need to know about the spiral. About the Mastermind."

Leilani inclined her head. "That, and why you ran. You had to know it would end like this."

Tokuda's expression softened. "I ran because I didn't want to give the Host the satisfaction. You know what it's like, watching the game unfold, knowing you're another piece on the board?"

"I'd prefer to be the player," Leilani said.

"Ha. That's what they all think. But here's the thing." Tokuda leaned forward, voice lowering, and Leilani saw a trace of the old cop in her, the one who'd once cleaned up an entire district with nothing but sarcasm and a baton. "You're outmatched. You and Torres and whoever's running the show back in the Governor's office. You think this is about armored cars, or some tatted-up street crew? No. It's about legacy. The Mastermind is the face."

Leilani tapped her knuckles on the table. "Tell me about the Host. Who are they?"

Tokuda gave a slow, sideways smile. "You ever notice how, when a snake sheds its skin, the new one is always shinier?"

"I'm allergic to metaphors," said Leilani. "Names, please."

Tokuda considered this and shrugged with her cuffs. "He was the Chief of Detectives before I became the Chief of Police. He retired five years ago and lives in a condo in Kahala. But that's just the mailing address. You want him, you'll have to dig deeper. His name is Roland Kapua. He's the Host. He always was. He's likely not on the island anymore."

Leilani sensed a sick ripple in her stomach. Kapua's name had been on department walls for decades, a local hero, the kind who gave speeches at high schools about choices and consequences.

"Why would he back the Mastermind?" Leilani asked.

Tokuda lowered her gaze. "You think it's about

the money. It never is, not with people like him. It's about control. He made the network, piece by piece. He kept the old-timers in line and imported the muscle from the mainland. The Mastermind is his invention—a mask. Have you ever seen him in person?"

Leilani thought about it. "No one has."

"Exactly. It's all email, burner phones, encrypted messages. But the real moves?" Tokuda's eyes glinted. "That's Kapua. He arranges the targets, sets up the timing, and lines up the random tips to Internal Affairs when he needs to burn a pawn."

Leilani looked at Tokuda hard. "Why are you telling me this? Loyalty doesn't evaporate in a holding cell."

Tokuda's jaw flexed. "He burned me. He burns everyone eventually. He doesn't want partners. He wants foot soldiers and fall guys. I was the latter." She looked down at her hands. "You think the Feds will cut a deal if I testify?"

Leilani considered it. "I think they'd like to see Kapua in here more than you."

Tokuda let out a ragged breath. "You'd better get him quick. He's got a passport and a bug-out bag under every floorboard in Kahala. Once he knows you're onto him, he'll vanish. And the spiral won't stop."

Leilani switched off the recorder. "Anything else?"

Tokuda smiled, a last flicker of pride. "Yeah. Tell him I said aloha."

The guard knocked, signaling time was up. Tokuda stood, wrists clicking as they reset the cuffs. She hovered, as if she might try to shake Leilani's hand, but thought better of it.

As the guards led her away, Tokuda looked over her shoulder. "You're not like the others, Detective Kealoha. But be careful. The island doesn't always forgive."

The door slammed. Leilani sat, letting the cold air chew at her skin. She pressed her hands flat, noticing the tremor, a mix of victory and dread.

Kapua. She repeated the name, letting it echo inside her skull.

She stood, collected the recorder and her badge, and walked to the sally port. The hallway outside was empty except for the guard, who raised an eyebrow.

"Get what you needed?" he asked.

Leilani nodded. "Enough to make the next arrest."

The guard laughed, a dry bark. "They said you were tough."

"Tough doesn't mean stupid," she said,

stepping into the corridor, her footsteps sharp and certain against the floor. "It means you don't stop."

For most people, the walk out of a prison is lighter than the walk in, but Detective Kealoha felt the pressure grow with every step. Halawa's cinderblock corridors funneled her into a holding area lined with portraits of retired wardens, some stern, some smug, and all ghosts in cheap frames. She asked the desk sergeant for a glass of water and sat on a plastic chair, mind buzzing with the name Tokuda had offered and the thousand things she hadn't.

Ten minutes later, a guard beckoned her with a nod. "Tokuda is asking for you again."

Leilani blinked, checked her watch, and followed.

This time, they put her in a smaller room, windowless except for a fat square of one-way glass. Tokuda was already inside, cuffed to a new table. The old Chief looked less combative now, more human, as if the walls had siphoned off her bravado. Her lips were cracked, but her eyes still measured Leilani with predatory care.

"I thought you might have more to say," Leilani offered, sitting down across the table. "Or is this where you pretend to recant?"

Tokuda made a deep sound, almost a sigh. "You know how it is. Once you start talking, it's hard to stop." She tugged at her cuffs, an old cop's fidget. "I owe you all of it."

Leilani reached for the recorder again, but Tokuda waved a hand.

"Off the record."

The detective hesitated, but let the recorder sit, the light off.

Tokuda leaned forward, voice a half-whisper. "You asked where Kapua is? I'll tell you—he's still here on Oahu. Never left. Keeps a yacht in Kewalo Basin, slips out whenever he needs to meet with people the old-fashioned way. It's a forty-eight-foot Beneteau, registered as the Koa Legacy. Fancy, but not flashy enough to get the Feds' attention."

Leilani pictured the yacht, the white hull gleaming in the sunset, a ghost ship for secrets and backroom deals. "You said he's got a plan to leave?"

Tokuda nodded, jaw tight. "He's not stupid. He's always got three exit plans. Right now, he's waiting for the last big payout, and poof he's gone. Mainland or Asia. Wherever extradition doesn't stick."

"And you? Where do you fit in?" asked Leilani.

Tokuda smirked. "I was his shield. My job was to keep the local heat off, to play the part of the bitter old cop who didn't know which way was up. I was his deniability, you see? No one wants to believe a Chief of Detectives is the kingpin."

Leilani watched Tokuda's hands, still steady. "What about the spiral? Every time there's a hit, that symbol pops up. Who's painting it?"

The older woman hesitated, lips thinning. "No idea. It could be one of the street crews, or it's a joke. Or it could be that someone wants to get into your head."

"That's not good enough," said Leilani, voice rising. "If you want a deal, you give me the name."

Tokuda's smile was sharp and tired. "If I did, you'd be dead in a week. There are things you don't understand about this place. Some of the old blood—well, it doesn't want to go away. Kapua can't control all of it. There's always someone higher up calling the shots. The spiral is older than you think."

She leaned back; the chain rattling a slow rhythm. "I'll tell you what I will say. If you are looking for the Host, stake out the yacht. But don't go alone. And don't bring your FBI friend. He's already on somebody's list."

Leilani ignored the tremor of dread. "Why warn me?"

Tokuda's laugh was empty, like a chalkboard dragged over asphalt. "I told you. I got burned. I'd rather see you last a little longer."

The detective pressed: "Give me the crew. The people who pull the jobs."

"They rotate," said Tokuda. "Never the same three twice. Sometimes it's professionals; sometimes it's desperate kids. Kapua picks them, trains them, burns them if they screw up. The only one who's stuck around is the girl with the hands. She's been in every crew but changes her look like a gecko. Calls herself Momi, but that's not her real name."

"Momi. You got a last name?"

Tokuda shrugged. "Doubt it's the real one, but try Lau. Good with computers, better with lock picks. If Kapua trusts anyone, it's her."

The air in the little room was stale, and Leilani fought the need to pace. "Why tell me this now?"

A slow, pained smile creased Tokuda's face. "Because nobody else will listen. And because if you're going to blow up a snake pit, you ought to know what's crawling around down there."

They sat in silence, two old boxers waiting for the final bell.

"Anything else?" asked Leilani, at last.

Tokuda's voice softened, all the hard edges worn down. "Some ghosts don't stay buried in the lava rocks, Detective Kealoha. Watch your back. That's all."

The guard returned, his face as blank as before. Tokuda stood, her hands cuffed in front, and allowed herself to be led away. At the door, she paused, glancing back at Leilani with a flicker of something almost warm.

"Your husband always spoke highly of you," Tokuda said, voice echoing off the concrete. "Said you could see the whole board, when you pretended you couldn't."

The words hung there after she was gone. Leilani let them sink deep, a slow spiral of memory and regret. She didn't know what Tokuda knew about David, or why she would bring it up now. But it changed the color of the day, tilted the ground under her feet.

She waited until her pulse slowed, checked the hall and left the prison. The world outside was a riot of color and heat—green palms, red tile roofs and the bright flinch of sunlight on windshields. It looked clean, but the ghosts Tokuda warned about pressed at the edges of everything.

She fished out her phone, thumbs shaking. She opened a blank note and wrote, Koa Legacy —Kewalo Basin. Kapua. Momi Lau. Watch the spiral. She let her eyes close, letting the salty air settle her nerves. Some ghosts don't stay buried. And some detectives don't quit. She smiled almost despite herself and started planning her next move.

Outside, the world had turned up the volume. Tropical birds mobbed the fence line, shrieking at each other from the security lamps. The road glittered under the slap of sunlight, white hot and slick with oil. Detective Kealoha stood in the shadow of Halawa's intake port, letting the ultraviolet burn away the chill of Tokuda's last words.

Her car waited in the visitor lot, the windows too dark to see into, the roof already hot enough to fry an egg. She walked slowly, savoring the shift from prison bleach and old sweat to the jungle of real air. But every step seemed like it came with a ghost attached and Kapua's name echoing, Momi Lau tucked in her mental notebook, and the old wound of David's name, fresh again after years in the dark.

She fished her key from her pocket, fingered the edges, and looked back once, to be sure she was alone. She wasn't. Across the lot, under the lattice of a spindly banyan tree, a man waited. He wore a clean white shirt, jeans and old surf shoes, the kind David always preferred on off days. He leaned against the trunk, arms crossed, watching her with a stillness that made the sunlight seem brighter, the birds louder, and the heat meaner.

At first, she thought it was a hallucination, a trick of the migraine that had been trailing her since last week. But as she stepped closer, the resemblance sharpened. The same posture. The same square jaw, the same narrow, restless eyes. It couldn't be. David was dead. She'd seen the report and identified the tattoos.

The man shifted, as if sensing her scrutiny. Their eyes met, a snap of recognition so sudden that Leilani's knees nearly buckled. The man's mouth turned up, into the half-grin she'd memorized on the beaches of Waialua. He pushed off the tree and turned his back, vanishing behind the banyan with the practiced ease of someone who'd been trained never to be caught.

Leilani moved before she thought, almost dropping her keys. She cut across the asphalt, ignoring the blast of heat and the hornet-buzz of a scooter zipping past. The lot blurred, details smeared, and time dilated the way it did when she was close to something important.

Behind the banyan, there was emptiness. A scuffed path, a fresh sweat-stain on the trunk, and a single, jagged spiral carved in the outer bark. Still oozing sap. Still sticky. She touched it. The resin clung to her thumb, sweet and acrid. She wiped her hand on her jeans, but the feeling didn't leave. Whoever it was, he'd wanted her to see.

She stood there, letting the silence pile up around her. The spiral in the bark. How the man had looked at her, as if measuring her for a story he already knew the ending to. She shook herself back into motion, double-timed to the car, yanked the door open and slid in. The interior was an oven, the steering wheel nearly melting under her fingers.

She pressed her forehead to the cool patch of glass and steadied her breath. After a minute, she pulled out her phone and dialed Isaac Torres.

He answered on the first ring. "Kealoha. You alive?"

She meant to sound calm, but the words came out weirdly thin. "We have a name. Kapua. Former Chief of Detectives. Still on the island. He's running out of Kewalo. He's the Host. Everything points there."

There was a pause on the line, the faint hum of a busy office behind him. "You sure?"

"Certain as I'll ever be." She started the engine, let the AC crank, though it spat out more hot air. "Meet me at Ala Moana, near the marina entrance. I don't want to be alone."

Another silence. Isaac, always the chess player, heard what she didn't say. "On my way."

She almost told him about the man by the banyan, the David echo, and how the universe seemed to fold old wounds into new crimes. But the words snagged on her tongue and wouldn't come out. Instead, she put the car in reverse and watched the rearview mirror as if she expected the dead to follow her home.

She drove slowly, sweat running under her shirt, hands trembling just enough to make her hate herself. But the sap on her thumb stayed sticky all the way to the coast, and by the time she hit the marina, she'd let it harden, a small badge of unfinished business. Tomorrow, she'll hunt again. But tonight, she kept her ghosts buckled into the passenger seat and allowed the city's aftershocks to guide her home.

CHAPTER FIVE

Kai's Discovery

Most kids sprinted out to the playground at the first bell, but Kai Kealoha lingered in the hallway, a notebook pressed to his chest and a phone bulging forbidden in his shorts. He timed his steps so the last stragglers from Mrs. Kawano's math class wouldn't see him double back. Kai didn't particularly fear being caught; getting sent to the principal was almost expected in his family, so long as you didn't snitch or cry. But he preferred shadows. The air conditioner's chemical breath made his nose itch as he shuffled past the locked music room, the flagging banner for Respect Week still taped above the trophy case.

Past the water fountain, something new caught him. In the main corridor, a vinyl banner stretched across the ceiling, tied off with thick zip ties like a caution tape for grown-ups: PROUD TO BE SAFE—SPIRAL SECURITY SOLUTIONS. The logo was a black swirl, sharp and clean, with a red dot at the center. Kai stood there, pretending to tie his shoe, but his pulse jumped.

He remembered what his mom had told him last week over takeout poke, a rare night when she'd let her cop voice drop to human. "There's a pattern," she'd said. "Always a spiral, always a message." She'd meant it as a warning, but Kai heard it as a challenge. A puzzle left unsolved was a sin.

The halls weren't empty; a cluster of fourth graders squealed and shoved each other past the janitor's closet, and the library doors banged as the reading group migrated out. But nobody paid attention to the banner except him. Kai let the world drift into blurry edges. He kneeled, thumbed the lock on his phone, and raised it at hip-level. Click. The lens caught the spiral, and he snapped three more angles before stuffing the phone back inside the elastic waistband of his PE shorts.

He almost didn't see the security guard until she was right there. She wore a crisp navy blue uniform, sleeves ironed sharp, and walked with a kind of straight-backed authority Kai recognized from a hundred cop shows and a lifetime of family parties. The guard's hair was in a bun so tight it looked painful. On her shirt, above the heart, the same spiral was stitched in white. She paused by the drinking fountain, her gaze scanning the hall like an airport baggage carousel.

Kai dipped his head and edged against the lockers. He knew from experience that adults notice you if you look guilty. He made his face blank and let his feet slide in the gummy pink trail left by someone's juice box spill. The guard's eyes caught him. He nodded politely, the way his mother always told him to do. She nodded back, but her eyes seemed to keep counting, keep checking, as if tallying up all the secrets in the world and marking Kai as a likely source of trouble.

Once she rounded the corner, Kai shot down the side hall, skipping every other tile for luck. He aimed for the library, not because he liked the quiet, but because it was the one room where phones could be used for educational purposes. And what was more educational than solving a real crime?

The library was cool and overlit, with blue carpet and low shelves. A couple of girls in hijabs whispered by the picture books. The librarian was on her computer, face blue-lit and slack, probably deep in Wordle. Kai ducked into the nonfiction section, behind a shelf of battered war biographies. He slid down into a cross-legged squat and opened his notebook, not letting the phone fall out.

He flipped the phone out and checked the

photos. The spiral looked more sinister up close, the way it bulged at the midpoint, and how the lines closed in, hungry. He pulled up a Google Images search of crime scene spiral symbol Hawaii, and sure enough, the same shape flashed back at him from news clips and blurry cop reports.

Kai grinned. He knew it. He'd told his mom, but she'd said to leave it to the grown ups, which was code for don't do anything, Kai. That had never stopped him before. If the school had hired Spiral Security, and they had the symbol, then the people behind the robberies were watching the school, possibly controlling it. The spiral wasn't a clue; it was a warning.

Kai made a quick comparison collage, placing the school spiral next to one from a robbery photo. He circled the matching parts with his finger, zoomed and enhanced until the pixels bled together. He couldn't believe nobody else had spotted it, unless they didn't want to.

His phone buzzed. For a split second, Kai panicked, thinking it might be the school's cyber narc, but it was a calendar reminder. Hula practice after school. He dismissed it, eyes locked on the spirals.

He tapped out a message:

Agent Torres, Isaac, you've got to see this! The security company at my school has the SAME spiral as Mom's robbery cases! I think they're the bad guys, or they're spying on everyone? Let me know what I should do next. I can get closer to their office after class. I can try to get passwords. Kai.

He felt a warm bubble of pride. He could almost see the look on Torres's face, that mix of good job, kid and please don't get yourself murdered. Adults underestimated how much you could learn by paying attention and not getting distracted by Fortnite or gym class drama.

Kai hid the phone in his notebook and drifted deeper into the stacks; in case anyone came looking. He listened for the click of the guard's shoes, but all he heard was the soft, steady hush of the air vent and the distant echo of a math teacher shouting about denominators.

He flipped through his notebook, updating the map he'd drawn of the school. He added a red dot for the spiral banner and a blue line for the path of the guard. He copied down the numbers printed on the security flyer, the emergency hotline, and a PO Box address. If Torres replied, he'd be ready to follow up.

Kai knew the dangers of getting too involved. His mother's job was proof enough of that. But the mystery had its own gravity. He sensed it pulling at him, tightening its hold every time he saw the symbol, and every time he heard an adult mutter. "Not our problem." He wasn't a hero, but he liked the idea of being the first to solve the case, even if nobody gave him a medal or a parade.

He checked the clock. Seven minutes until the next bell. He crammed the notebook into his backpack and scurried back toward the cafeteria, keeping his head low. He ate lunch outside, under the monkeypod tree, where he could watch the front gate and see if the security people did anything suspicious.

He passed the banner again on the way. The spiral looked bigger this time, like it had grown to remind him who was in charge. He stuck his tongue out at it.

Outside, the wind tugged at the flags, and the shade under the tree was cool. He ate his PB&J slowly, scanning the lot. The security guard from earlier came out, this time with a walkie-talkie. She stood by the bike racks, not doing anything special, but Kai made a note anyway. Sometimes it was the small stuff that mattered most.

When the bell rang, he gathered his things and walked inside. He thought about the message he'd sent to Torres and let himself believe that he'd made a difference. He was part of something bigger than lunch and homework and after school hula. He'd found the clue that would crack the spiral open.

He whistled under his breath as he walked to class, already plotting his next move. If the security company really was the link, he'd find out. He was a Kealoha, after all. It was practically a curse.

The best part of Isaac Torres's hotel was the view of the canal. The worst was everything else. The walls were off-white, the carpets a gritty gray, and the furniture all mismatched from the last three government moves. He liked it because he could spill coffee on the rug, pin evidence to the wall, and nobody cared. Right now, every inch of the dining table was buried under case files, mugshots, printouts of emails and half-drained coffee cups, the ink bleeding into little brown Rorschach tests of guilt.

Isaac studied the whiteboard leaning against the kitchen counter. The spiral lingered, drawn in black marker, perfectly mirrored from the crime scene photos and bracketed with a dozen Post-its. He'd been working on the pattern for hours, tracing it through the robberies, the money laundering, the brief flashes of the Mastermind that everyone else dismissed as urban legend. It was supposed to be his night off, but in his line of work, sleep was for people who didn't have deadlines.

His phone buzzed. It wasn't the FBI's encrypted app or a text from Leilani. It was Kai. The subject line was all caps urgent: "SEE THIS!!!" Isaac didn't have to open the message to feel his gut tighten.

He clicked it anyway. The photos came first —a hallway, a banner and a close-up of the spiral logo, as crisp and precise as anything from a professional forger. Kai's message underneath was breathless: *Agent Torres, Isaac, you've got to see this! The security company at my school has the SAME spiral as Mom's robbery cases! I think they're the bad guys, or they're spying on everyone? Let me know what I should do next. I can get closer to their office after class. I can try to get passwords. Kai.*

Isaac let out a long breath and pressed his fist to his mouth, thinking. The smart thing, the agent thing, would be to call Leilani right now, let her handle it, pass the risk to the Honolulu PD. But the smarter thing, the thing he would want if it were his own kid, was to play it cool. Not scare Kai, not tip off anyone watching his emails, and not get the boy into more danger than he was already in.

He thumbed a reply: *Saw the pics. Good work, but DON'T go near their office. Stay away from them. No investigating. Keep your head down and act normal. Can you do that?*

He waited for the dots to appear. They did.

Kai: *I could check it out, you know. I'm not scared.*

Isaac: *That's an order. For real. If your mom finds out, she'll ground us both.*

The dots again.

Kai: *Fine. But you owe me shave ice. I'll send more pics if I get them. Do you think it's them???*

Isaac grinned despite himself. *Not sure yet. Could be nothing. But I'll look into it. Don't talk about this with anyone else.*

He hit send. The desire to call Leilani was strong, but he knew her. She was probably working a lead right now, running down a dead end with her usual determination. If he called, she'd worry, or worse, she'd storm the school and scare Kai into never confiding again. He'd keep this close for now.

He set the phone on the counter and turned his attention to the photos. This spiral was wrong. Or it was right, which was worse. Every criminal signature he'd ever tracked evolved, but this one stayed the same, bold, almost arrogant in its simplicity. It was a mark, a brand, a way to say we're here and you can't touch us. If it had found its way into the school system, it meant one of two things. The people behind the robberies were expanding, or someone wanted Leilani to see it, to recognize it. Either way, it wasn't good.

Isaac pulled his laptop over, fingers typing before his brain finished the thought. Spiral Security Solutions. The website was new, barely three months old. It looked expensive, with lots of stock photos and empty promises about community partnership. But when he dug through the business filings, there was barely anything. No history, no physical office, a virtual suite number in a downtown building. The CEO was a ghost; the address was a mail drop. The one employee listed was Ms. Jade Okimoto, Operations Manager, and her LinkedIn profile had all the warmth and authenticity of a Wikipedia page.

He clicked through the hiring announcements. In the past week, Spiral Security had picked up contracts at three schools and two medical offices. The press releases made it sound like they'd been around for years, but there was nothing prior to the last quarter. Every school that hired them had a major donor or board member linked to the city government, or to a person under investigation for corruption. The connections weren't smoke; they were flares.

He poured the last of his coffee and leaned back, thinking. He felt an impulse to smoke creep up on him, despite not having touched a cigarette in six years. He chewed the inside of his cheek instead.

Kai had stumbled onto something big. Not by accident, but because he paid attention. The kid had his mother's stubbornness, but none of her fear. Isaac knew he'd have to lock it down, keep him safe without pushing him away. He picked up the phone again, scrolled to Kai's number, and hit call.

It rang twice before Kai answered, voice a loud whisper. "Agent Torres?"

"Yeah, it's me. I saw your email," said Isaac, keeping his tone light.

"Is it important? Like, should I tell Mom? Or the police? Or should I keep watching?" There was a rustle, and a muted crunch of what sounded like chips.

"Hang back, okay? Don't mention it at home. I'll handle the investigation," said Isaac, fighting the impulse to parent the boy outright.

"But if they're bad guys—" Kai's voice was eager, almost proud.

"If they're bad guys, that's my job," said Isaac. "You stay away from their office, and don't go looking for passwords. No more investigating on your own. Understand?"

A disappointed sigh. "Yeah. Sure."

"Promise me, Kai."

A longer silence. "Okay. I promise. But you have to tell me if you find out anything."

"Deal," said Isaac. "And hey, nice work spotting the pattern. You're a natural."

There was a second of pure, electric happiness in the silence. "Thanks, Agent Torres."

Isaac grinned. "Now go do your homework. And delete this call from your phone."

Kai laughed, and hung up.

Isaac sat at the table for a while, not moving. The canal outside was blue and calm, with a few paddleboarders drifting under the footbridge, their shadows trailing like lazy fish. He wondered how so much could go so wrong in a place that looked so peaceful.

He opened his laptop again, this time cross-referencing the school district's security contracts with known entities from the Mastermind's old crew. Nothing on the surface, but the pattern was clear. Every place Spiral Security took over was within five miles of one of the old case sites. If it was a coincidence, it was the meanest one he'd ever seen.

He scrolled further, letting the code and data flow past his eyes, trying to see the gaps and the places where the story moved sideways. That was his job. Find the loose thread and pull until it unraveled. But now there were two threats, the one on the outside, and the one that could touch Kai and Leilani directly. He let the pressure settle in, being both a good agent and a good friend. He was good at one, but rarely both.

His phone buzzed again, this time with a message from an unknown number. It was a spiral emoji, nothing else. The timestamp was one minute after he'd called Kai. His scalp prickled, and he quickly scanned the room for any open windows, any odd shadows. He was used to being watched, but this seemed different, closer.

Isaac shut his laptop and leaned back, watching the spiral on his whiteboard. He thought of Leilani, chasing her own ghosts, and of Kai, too smart and too restless for his own good. The spiral seemed smaller, with the circles closing in. He'd have to be quick and careful. He wondered which would run out first, his luck or his time.

He glanced out the window before looking back at his notes. There were still patterns to find, and the night was young.

Evening in the Kealoha house was a symphony of comfort. Jasmine from the front hedge, a line of warm porch light on the worn steps, and the low, steady hum of a single oscillating fan turning the room into a tropical cathedral. In the heart of it, Naalei Kealoha moved with slow grace, arranging the day's plumeria and torch ginger in a tall blue vase. She hummed as she worked, the same ancient mele her mother had sung while weaving lei or scolding children. The kitchen clock ticked along with her, unhurried.

She loved this hour best. The sky beyond the screen door was the color of an overripe papaya, and for once, the house was nearly silent. Kai was doing homework, which probably meant plotting world domination or texting friends from the fortress of his bedroom. Leilani hadn't called, so she was working late or, Naalei frowned, trying not to worry her family with whatever fresh evil the Honolulu PD had dredged from the news cycle.

She placed the flowers on the side table and admired them. In another life, she might have run a floral shop, in Waimea or Hanalei, somewhere quiet, somewhere that didn't always bleed with old stories. But this was the house her husband had built, and after he died, she had poured all the softness she could muster into making it a true home.

Her phone beeped. She wiped her hands on her muumuu, and reached for it, already assuming it was another hula parent or a grocery sale alert. Instead, the number was unknown, the text a single symbol, black and cold.

A spiral. Centered on the screen, as if drawn by the tip of a bone needle, followed a message in perfect, unaccented English:

The Kealoha legacy of cultural preservation is

built on lies. Your daughter digs too deep. Remember your oath.

Naalei's hands stilled. She reread it, hoping it would change. It didn't.

She looked over her shoulder, as if the spiral might grow on the walls. The living room was unchanged, with sunlight on the lauhala mats, the old glass fishing float in the window, and the bowl of dried kukui nuts for good luck. She remembered every moment of making this space safe, and how little it mattered in the face of what the spiral promised.

Her knees threatened to give out. She caught herself, straightened, and reached for the pendant at her throat, a tiny kō leaf, carved from ancient wood, and soft from years of fingers worrying it. She held it like a rosary, breathing through her nose, and let the panic flatten into purpose.

First, the doors. She checked the front, and the side, clicking deadbolts with hands that shook. Windows next, followed by curtains. She did it all fast, methodically, the way her late husband had taught her.

"Never let them see you afraid. But always make sure they can't see you at all."

Back in the kitchen, she moved to the pantry, slipping her hand behind a row of stacked cookbooks. There, pressed flat behind a chipped copy of Island Cooking for the Soul, was the box. She brought it to the table, listening for any change in the hum of the house. The one sound was the echo of her own heartbeat, an old drum tuned by decades of fear and responsibility.

The box was koa, darker than any she'd seen in the souvenir shops, polished until it drank in the light. It was her mother's, and her mother's before her. It unlocked with a single click. Inside, the treasures of family survival: a bundle of photographs, some brittle and yellowing at the corners, and a folded packet of paper tied with red string.

Naalei untied the knot. The document inside was old, the ink feathered by time. But the spiral was there, and beside it, a list of names. Her own among them, as well as her daughter's. In faded pencil were the words: **Custodians of the Hidden —Do Not Forget.**

She flipped through the photos. There was her grandmother, a stern woman in starched white, standing at a school ceremony, her eyes narrowed not at the children but at the shadows behind them. There was Naalei herself, age twenty, shaking hands with a city councilman she now recognized as one of the men implicated in the old spiral cases. Every picture was a memory, and every name on the page a web that bound them.

She put the photos aside and read the document three times. It was not a will. It was not a warning. It was a contract, or a confession, that her family had always been the spiral's witness, sometimes its shield, and sometimes its sacrifice.

Naalei braced her elbows. She let herself mourn all the generations who had tried and failed to protect their children from other people's greed and other people's nightmares.

She stood steady in her resolve. She had been threatened before, but it was the first time since her husband's death that the threat had appeared like it might take everything left.

She considered calling Leilani, but her hand hovered over the phone, uncertain. The spiral never moved against the family unless it had to. If she called, if she panicked, it would tighten the knot around her daughter and grandson. No. She would call someone who knew the spiral better than any cop.

She scrolled through her old contacts, found the number, and dialed. The ring sounded twice, a gruff voice answered.

"Makani," said Naalei, fighting to keep the tremor from her words.

"Long time," he replied, suspicious but curious.

"It's happening again," she said, voice small but fierce. "The spiral has returned."

A long silence.

"Do you want me to come tonight?" Makani asked, voice softer.

"Yes," said Naalei, clutching the pendant. "Come before the moon rises. Bring what you have. I think we're being watched."

She ended the call and moved to the bedroom to gather Kai's things for school, as if it were another Tuesday night, as if she weren't already waging a silent war for everything she loved.

Outside, the evening slipped darker, and the spiral on her phone screen glared up at her, a challenge older than any mele she could remember. She whispered a promise to the ghosts in the hallway. Not again. Not my family. Not this time. She finished arranging the flowers, because nothing defied the darkness like beauty and stubbornness, and she had plenty of both to spare.

CHAPTER SIX

The Host Cornered

Kewalo Basin's marina in the off hours felt haunted, as if the ordinary world had let ghosts make their last phone calls before sunrise. Rows of yachts floated under the syrupy spill of twilight, their hulls casting bent shadows on oil-slick water, each motionless but poised for flight. The salt wind gathered the day's last heat from the concrete piers and mixed it with undertones of diesel and old fish. The nearby high rises seemed to hold their breath, windows catching the last pink and silver like a field of dying stars.

Detective Leilani Kealoha stood with her team outside the gate, the air prickling at her skin through the thin sleeves of her HPD windbreaker. She checked her gear, counting the slow, methodical rhythm in her head the way her late father had taught her. Holster. Radio. Flashlight. Backup cuffs. She let her eyes roam the docks, cataloguing every movement and every stillness. She didn't want to miss the signal when it came.

Next to her, Torres fidgeted with his earpiece, his suit swapped out for department tactical gear, still sharp, but nothing like the West Coast version of himself from nine months back. He glanced at her, the smile all tension and teeth, before scanning the slip numbers and the bobbing silhouettes of the yachts. They both knew the Koa Legacy was docked at B-12, and that Roland Kapua wouldn't be stupid enough to run tonight, not with the heat still licking his neck. But it was always better to expect the escape and to assume the worst.

A soft, measured voice crackled through Leilani's radio. "Units in position. Awaiting green."

She keyed the mic. "Hold at red. Eyes on target. Repeat, do not engage." She glanced over her shoulder. Three HPD officers crouched by a line of decorative planters, shifting nervously and pretending to be less visible than they were. Leilani tapped her foot, hating the nervous energy. She wanted the old crew, the ones who knew how to wait.

She turned to Torres. "Do you get seasick?"

He grinned, exhaling tension. "When someone else is at the wheel."

Leilani nodded, pretending to check her

phone. Through the gap in the slatted fence, she could make out the white hull of the Koa Legacy. It gleamed in the dusk, all polished teak and chromed steel rails, a forty-eight foot monument to the myth of honest living. The vessel's running lights threw neat cones of blue and green onto the water, making a flag for anyone who knew which boat to target.

She pulled Tokuda's notes from her jacket pocket, holding them up to the dying light. Kapua always slept aboard when the heat was on. Maintained a discreet crew of two, a deckhand with a record for amphetamines, and a second who rotated from the local dock union. He never hired security, never trusted outsiders, but always kept an exit open. The notes ended with a simple line, circled twice in red. He will fight to the finish if cornered. Known to carry.

Leilani pocketed the sheet and slung binoculars around her neck, the glass still smudged from Kai's last wildlife binge. She steadied herself against the fencepost, noting the solid ache in her hands, and trained the lens on the yacht.

The first thing she saw was a figure on deck, where Tokuda said he'd be. Roland Kapua, ex-Chief of Detectives, was a study in faded menace. He wore a dark aloha shirt, buttons done to the throat, and ironed khakis that almost hid the heavy-muscled calves. His hair was white now, clipped close at the sides, but he still carried himself like the king of the island's meanest streets. He moved methodically, his hands folded behind his back, head tilted to the far slips, pacing in the way of men who'd never learned to be idle.

Torres ducked next to her, eyes narrowing as he took in the scene. "Is it me, or does he look like he's expecting company?"

"Expecting, but not sure from where," Leilani muttered. She adjusted the focus, catching the glint of a ring on Kapua's right hand, one of the old department signets. She wondered if he still wore it as a point of pride, or as a bitter reminder.

Torres keyed his own radio. "Eagle to teams. Visual on target. Confirm no secondary movement below deck."

A different voice, the lead SWAT officer, answered, "Confirmed, no movement. All hatches closed except starboard."

Leilani swept the binoculars over the boat. The deck was immaculate, with every line coiled, and every surface gleaming. But there were two things that didn't fit. One, the main hatch to the cabin was open enough to suggest a watcher on the inside. Two, a duffel bag, black and heavy, sat zipped at the foot of the ladder to the main deck.

She handed the binoculars back to Torres. "He's about to go, or about to bunker in."

He didn't ask which was worse.

She straightened, scanned the horizon for last-minute complications. The night was calm, a jogger passing by on the bike path, a couple fighting quietly over a picnic basket, and, at the far side of the lot, an elderly man stringing bait onto a makeshift fishing pole. No extra heat. No spiral crew waiting in the wings. She allowed herself one slow breath.

Leilani keyed the radio. "On my go. Team One to main dock, Team Two flank at the water. Minimum sound. Do not light him up until I give the word." Her own voice was calm, but she heard the tremor hiding under the syllables.

Torres nodded, hand resting lightly on his holstered Taser. "He won't come easily."

"He never did," said Leilani. She walked to the gangway, tracing each step with care, the boards creaking with familiar complaint. In her left hand she held a copy of the arrest warrant; the right held her pistol at her side.

When she reached the boat, she stopped. Kapua didn't look up, not at first. He was watching something distant on the horizon, a freighter or nothing. But as she shifted her stance, he finally turned. His face was a geometry of age and purpose, creased with old sun and older frowns. His eyes, once coal-black, were shot through with veins but still sharp.

He spoke first, voice deep as a baritone bell. "Detective Kealoha. You traded up."

Leilani didn't flinch. "It's over, Roland."

He laughed, a noise without softness. "That's the thing about islands, Kealoha. The tide always brings it back." He nodded toward the warrant. "Is that for me, or for show?"

She kept her tone level. "You know why we're here. Don't make this ugly."

He watched her, and the slow movement of SWAT officers as they moved down the pier. His mouth twisted, half in contempt, half in admiration. "You learned after all."

She stepped closer, boots planted wide on the floating dock. "Roland Kapua, you're under arrest for conspiracy, obstruction, and aiding a criminal enterprise. Surrender now, or we'll come aboard."

He put both hands up, palms out. But the left curled slightly, like it was ready to drop and reach for something. "I've got nothing left worth taking. Except stories, Detective. And you've never liked those."

Leilani was close enough now to see the twitch at his jaw, the old trigger warning. She raised her voice, clear for the radios. "Don't do anything stupid, Roland. You won't get another chance."

He let the words hang between them. With

careful deliberation, he backed toward the open hatch. "You tell your mother hello," he said. "And remind her what happens to families that forget their history."

Leilani felt the words bite, but she didn't let them stick. She caught Torres's signal from the shadows. She made the call.

"Teams, board now!"

The strike team moved as a single, silent animal, years of muscle memory pushing them along the water like ghosts in blue. They hit the floating dock in a scatter formation, each member already calculating angles, escape vectors and the risk of crossfire. Torres was on point, a blur of black fabric and bottled nerves. Leilani caught the first rung of the yacht's boarding ladder, boots slipping on the condensation but her grip unbreakable. She took the climb in three pulls, drawing herself up and over the slick railing with the calm skill of a rock climber.

Her team fanned out, boots thudding on the rubberized walkways, weapons leveled at every hatch and vent. On deck, the Koa Legacy was more beautiful up close, the wood inlays still warm from the afternoon sun, the scent of salt and citrus clinging to every surface. The polished rails threw off enough light to dazzle, and Leilani saw herself mirrored, her hair wild, her face set, and her badge glinting from her belt like a dare.

Roland Kapua was already moving. The moment Leilani crested the rail, he pivoted away, his years of street-fighting surfacing in the way he kept one shoulder forward, eyes never leaving the threat. He feinted left, lunging for the open cabin hatch.

She anticipated his move, stepping inside the swing and driving her shoulder low. He hit harder than any sixty-year-old had a right to, but she absorbed the blow, using his momentum to drive them both into a pile of braided line. They landed with a heavy thud, and the only sounds were their ragged breaths and the creak of the hull beneath them.

Kapua rolled, but she stayed glued, legs scissoring around his torso as she reached for his wrist. He grunted and twisted, sending a sharp elbow up into her ribs. The pain exploded through her side, sharp, hot, dizzying, but she didn't let go. Instead, she used the motion to pull him further off balance, rolling them both toward the edge.

From the corner of her eye, she saw two officers surge up the ladder, weapons raised. They shouted warnings, but Kapua didn't blink. He braced his feet against the deck and heaved upward, tossing Leilani clear with brute force. She landed hard, breath knocked out, but spun to her feet instantly, training kicking in.

He charged again, this time with a length of coiled rope held like a garrote. She ducked, let it pass over her head, and slammed her palm into his solar plexus. He staggered, dropped, grabbing for her ankle. They tumbled once more, a tangle of limbs and curses, sweat, blood and old secrets.

Suddenly, the rigging line above them went taut, from the force of their struggle, or because fate wanted a say. A metal fitting exploded loose with a noise like a gunshot. It whirled past Leilani's face, missing her by an inch, and buried itself in the hull with a splintery crunch. The line snaked around Kapua's arm, pinning him to the deck.

She didn't hesitate. She fell on him, forcing his face to the slick boards, knee hard in his spine. Her hands found his wrist, twisted it until she heard the satisfying snap of resistance breaking, and ratcheted on the cuffs before the line stopped swinging.

"Roland Kapua," she said, breath ragged. "You have the right to remain silent, so shut the fuck up."

He turned his head enough to meet her gaze, the weight of decades in his voice. "You don't know what you're starting, Kealoha. You think this ends with me? It started before you were born."

She ignored the bitterness, the way it tried to stick. "Yeah. But it ends here for you."

The other officers moved in, helping her pull Kapua to his feet. He stood, dignity somehow intact despite the blood on his cheek and the rope burn around his arm. The badge on his belt buckle, old, dented, and full of ghosts, glistened as they marched him down the ladder.

On the deck, Leilani straightened, fighting to get her breathing under control. Her ribs throbbed with every inhale, and the taste of copper hung in her mouth. Torres joined her at the rail, looking her over for broken bones.

"You good?" he asked.

She nodded but couldn't quite hide the wince. "Never better."

Torres looked down the dock, watching as the team loaded Kapua into the waiting squad car. "You made that look easy."

"Wasn't," she said, grinning through the ache. "But I had a feeling he'd fight to the finish."

Torres clapped her on the shoulder, careful to avoid her bruised side. "One for the books, yeah?"

"Yeah," she said, thinking about Kapua's last words, the promise of deeper shadows waiting. "Let's hope the paperwork is easier."

He grinned, and together they climbed down, their bodies aching but spirits weirdly buoyant.

They'd cut off the head, or at least one head, of the spiral. Whether it would stop spinning was a problem for tomorrow.

For tonight, the one spiral that mattered was the slow eddy of water as it drifted around the empty hull, washing away the day's last light.

The blue strobes of the forensic van threw erratic shadows across the Koa Legacy's decks, mixing with the white glare of dock lights to render everything either harsh or half-invisible. Team members milled on the floating pier, swapping theories about what Kapua had planned next. Every so often, the faint snap of an evidence bag or the whine of a battery-powered camera cut through the quiet.

Leilani perched at the starboard rail, one arm braced for support, letting her battered lungs sip at the briny air. Her ribs ached where Kapua's elbow had landed, but she kept her hands from hovering over the wound, unwilling to show weakness with half the department now gawking from the dock.

She tracked the team as they led Kapua, now marginally less dignified in cuffed hands and a torn aloha shirt, down the gangway and into the back seat of a squad car. He didn't resist. If anything, the old cop gave the performance of a man already writing the press release in his head. His silver hair caught every scrap of light, each glint a reminder of all the times the island had bent to his will. Leilani felt a flicker of something almost like sympathy. Not for the man, but for the fall.

She exhaled through her teeth. Behind her, the forensic techs swept the cabin, dusting for prints and cataloguing the personal effects. An expensive pen, a pack of clove cigarettes, and a yellow photograph of Kapua and his two children from decades back. A junior officer emerged, hands shaking as he bagged a heavy envelope full of foreign currency. The lead tech held up a battered laptop and a satellite phone, both dusted with recent use.

Torres clambered up to the deck and dropped beside her, trying for nonchalance but wincing as he bent his knees. He offered a can of Coke from the cooler near the bow.

She cracked it and took a long drink. "You think they'll let us keep the yacht?" she joked, though her voice came out gravelly.

"If we're lucky, they'll let us keep our pensions," Torres shot back, but his voice softened. "Nice job. I was worried he'd get away."

"He never would have left," she replied, eyes on the horizon. "People like him always come back. It's the ego. The island won't let them forget."

Torres shrugged. "What about the spiral?"

She faced him, her jaw set. "He's one spoke. Someone else is spinning the wheel."

He grunted and looked down at the dock where Kapua sat in the back seat, backlit by the white and blue flashing lights. "He'll talk. They always do."

Leilani wasn't so sure. "He'll stall. He'll drag the story out, wait for the next twist."

Torres nodded, slipped away, probably to make his own after-action call. She was left at the rail, watching the forensic team finish their sweep. One officer, a long timer who'd once worked under Kapua, approached her with the awkwardness of a son returning home after being away.

"Detective Kealoha," he said, voice careful. "We found some stuff in the navigation locker. It looks like offshore bank documents and a detailed escape plan. He was booked on a private charter out of Maui for Thursday. Looks like he was getting ready to set sail."

She smirked. "He was always an optimist."

The officer hesitated, offering a small ledger, its cover cracked and faded. "You'll want this. It's got initials and numbers. Some kind of code."

She took the ledger and thumbed through it. The entries ran back years, each line a little darker and a little more frantic. At the very back, in unmistakable handwriting, was the spiral. Centered on the page, black and perfect.

She closed the book, heart thrumming with a new, raw energy. "Thanks. Anything else?"

"Yeah," the officer said, face flickering between respect and embarrassment. "My old man always said you'd be the one to clean up the department."

Leilani almost laughed. Instead, she nodded, tucking the ledger into her jacket. "Tell your old man I'm still trying."

He saluted with two fingers and vanished down the ladder.

Alone on the deck, she let the night settle. The city sparkled beyond the marina, neon and sodium lamps bleeding together in a long, wavering band. The spiral was still out there, possibly watching from one of those distant condos, waiting for her next move. She felt the gravity, the certainty that with Kapua behind bars, the wheel was beginning another turn.

Her ribs ached, but she didn't mind. Pain meant she'd survived, and survival meant she could fight again tomorrow.

She texted Torres. *Ledger looks good, more to come*. She dialed home, and Kai answered on the first ring.

"You get him?" he asked, breathless.

"Yeah," she said. "He put up a fight."

"Did you get hurt?" There was fear in his voice, the kind she never wanted him to carry.

She let the silence hang. "A little. But I'm tougher than he is."

A proud pause. "Nana says you always were."

She let herself smile. "Go to bed, detective junior. I'll be home soon."

She hung up before he could ask for details, pocketed her phone, and straightened to full height. In the distance, the waves lapped softly at the hull, indifferent to the drama of men and women. The spiral on the ledger still burned in her mind, but she was done running in circles. Next time, she'd go right to the center.

She took one last look at the city before turning from the rail, the echo of her footfalls solid on the deck, each one a small promise to herself and her family. Not again, not this time. And beneath the sodium glare, with the night closed tight around her, Detective Leilani Kealoha let herself believe she could outlast the oldest ghosts of the island.

CHAPTER SEVEN

Isaac's Dilemma

At 8:15 AM sharp, the Honolulu FBI field office was lit up like a hospital, overhead fluorescents bouncing off every hard surface, multiplying shadows beneath the eyes of anyone unlucky enough to report this early. Isaac Torres stood in the empty elevator, his breath clouding the stainless walls as if the building itself was exhaling nerves. He straightened his tie with two fingers, more habit than respect, and tried to imagine what kind of future started with a summons to an urgent policy review. The elevator doors parted with a hiss that was almost theatrical.

The conference room was colder than the elevator. That took effort. The walls were painted beige, and the window blinds were drawn tight. A single horizontal beam of morning light slicing the table into enemy and friendly territory. Supervisory Agent Morgan sat at the head of the table, notepad already open, pen capping and uncapping in a staccato rhythm. Flanking her were the two section chiefs, one ex-military, crisp in his posture and contempt, the other a civilian lifer with a cough and a talent for sarcasm. There was a carafe of coffee but no cups.

Isaac chose the seat directly across from Morgan, ignoring the power play and focusing on the light, which glinted off her glasses and turned her stare into a private solar event. He set his notepad down, neat and ready, but kept his hands off it. The ex-military chief nodded, as if checking a box.

Morgan cleared her throat. "Agent Torres. I assume you know why you're here."

He tried a faint smile. "I can guess. The Kewalo Basin operation didn't end the way some people wanted."

She didn't smile back. "Let's skip the small talk. We'll be direct. You have a pattern of exceeding protocol in joint task force settings, particularly regarding HPD Detective Kealoha. We have concerns."

The other agent cut in, voice reedy but sharp. "It's not about the arrests, Agent. It's about how you choose to communicate. Off-book meetings. Use of personal devices for case discussions. Selective sharing of files. Does any of that sound familiar?"

Isaac didn't flinch. "With respect, isn't that

how you get things done on this island? The usual channels are dead ends. I checked."

Morgan's pen snapped down. "That's the justification every rogue agent gives, Torres."

He watched the pen, not her face. "I wouldn't call what I do rogue. I call it effective."

She slid a folder across the table, the thick brown kind usually reserved for grand juries or internal affairs. "We'd like your response to this."

Isaac opened it. Inside was a spread of photographs, some from security cams, others clearly shot by Bureau assets in the field. He recognized his face twice. Once meeting Leilani at the old shrimp truck in Ala Moana Park, hunched over coffee, his expression unguarded. The second was in the HPD records room, with Leilani passing him a manila envelope, both laughing at something not visible in the frame.

He closed the file. "You had someone tailing us?"

The military section chief didn't blink. "We have someone tailing everyone, Torres. You're not special."

The civilian section chief leaned in, his breath fogging the table. "What's special is the way you keep skirting the line. We let it go during the Kaka'ako bust. We looked the other way during the Lim wiretap. But the Kapua sting. You did not disclose advance plans to command. You left a Bureau asset in the wind for six hours. Your own words in the log: Detective Kealoha had the better play, so I backed her call. That's not protocol."

Isaac stayed still, his right foot tapping under the table. "Detective Kealoha is the best cop the HPD has. She's the reason we have the Host in custody at all. So, yes. I trusted her call. Besides, with all due respect, That was an HPD operation. It was Kealoha's lead and her arrest. I was there as a courtesy."

Morgan waited until the silence built, at which point she pounced. "Which brings us to the real point. Your personal relationship with the detective. Is it impeding your objectivity?"

The word personal stretched for a beat too long. Isaac straightened his tie again, buying a second.

"With respect," he said again, "First, I don't have a personal relationship with Detective Kealoha and second, I don't see how grabbing a cup of coffee during work hours is material. Every exchange of information was relevant to the case."

The military chief was ready. "Why not report those contacts?"

He held the chief's gaze, noting the graying buzz cut, the hairline that looked like it had been measured with a ruler. "Because she's not a source or a partner. She's a peer. You want to close these cases, you treat local law as a peer."

Morgan scribbled something down and looked up. "If that's your argument, I hope it's in your own handwriting. Because this is about loyalty, Torres. Who are you loyal to? The Bureau, or a detective with a reputation for insubordination?"

That hit a little closer than the others. He considered that and leaned forward.

"I'm loyal to the mission," he said, voice flat. "If you want a memo in writing, I'll send it to the whole division. But you called me here for a reason, and it's not because I'm socializing with local PD. What's the real issue?"

The civilian chief looked at Morgan, who offered a practiced smile. "The real issue is command and control. It's the chain of custody for evidence. It's making sure you don't hand off sensitive materials to someone with no security clearance. The rules exist for a reason, Agent Torres. You will abide by them, or you'll be transferred to the mainland before the close of the month. Effective immediately, you're on written warning."

She slid a form across, already signed and dated.

He stared at it, reading the fine print. "You

want me to transfer?"

Morgan shrugged. "I want you to act like a Bureau agent. Not a tourist."

He grinned. "You ever try to get evidence out of a Honolulu witness? Or a confession out of a city councilman who owns half the judges in the territory? Following Bureau protocol gets you nothing. Detective Kealoha is well respected, and she gets results because she understands the people and the culture. Something the FBI might want to expand upon."

"Spare us the cultural lesson," barked the military chief. "You either work with us or you're gone."

Isaac watched the sunlight tick higher on the wall, bright enough now to slice through the shade lines and put a Morse code message across the table. He signed the warning, his handwriting smooth and practiced.

"Is there anything else?" he asked.

Morgan capped her pen, satisfied. "That will be all, Agent Torres. You may return to your detail."

He nodded, stood up, and gathered his things. As he reached the door, the civilian chief called after him, his voice casual.

"Oh, and Agent? If you're planning to see Detective Kealoha again, do it by the book. Her methods might play in the HPD, but they're poison in the Bureau."

Isaac nodded once, smiled politely, and closed the door with a satisfying thud.

In the hallway, he stopped, letting his pulse slow. The warning form was heavy in his hand, the ink already bleeding from his palm sweat. He rolled his shoulders, took a long breath, and started towards the parking garage.

The Bureau was a machine, and today he'd been reminded of his place in it. But machines could be hacked, and sometimes, they needed someone to run a parallel process to get the job done.

As he walked, Isaac fished his phone from his pocket, checking for missed calls. Three from Leilani. A fourth from a restricted number. He thought about returning the calls but drove instead. Let the day burn a little before he let the Bureau back in.

The underground parking garage below the field office hummed like a bunker for a war that never ended. The ramps echoed with the tinny rattle of tires and the hum of industrial lights. Isaac's shoes sounded weirdly loud as he crossed the oil-stained concrete, his shadow lagging as if it, too, resented the summons. He found his car, a black Toyota sedan, Bureau issue but already personalized with beach sand in the floor mats and two empty water bottles rattling in the passenger footwell.

He got in and closed the door with a hard slam, letting the outside world become nothing but a hush. The silence was so complete it amplified his own pulse, ticking behind his eyes. He buckled the seatbelt but didn't start the engine. Instead, he sat with both hands on the wheel, gripping it so tight his fingers faded to the color of parchment.

A minute passed. Then another. He ran a thumb over the fake leather steering wheel and stared at his reflection in the darkened screen of the infotainment system. He looked tired, older than his years, and faintly ridiculous with the tie still knotted around his neck. He yanked it loose, breathing hard as the knot gave way. His shirt collar wilted, a minor rebellion in the vacuum-packed air.

He thought about the meeting, letting it spool through his mind in reverse, detail by detail. Morgan's laser beam stare, the photos and the signed warning. He hated it when she asked if he was loyal to the Bureau, or to her? If it weren't for her, the Bureau would have nothing to show for almost a year of work.

He wanted to stay with the Bureau, of course. He wanted to be the man who never looked back and never decided for the wrong reasons. But the question echoed, the emphasis shifting with every pass until he was no longer sure what answer made sense.

He let out a sharp breath and slapped the dash, hard enough to sting. It didn't help.

He checked his phone. Three missed calls from Leilani, each spaced about fifteen minutes apart. Her message tone was a soft ukulele riff, almost mocking him. He dialed her back, but stopped. What was he supposed to say? "Hey, I got threatened with transfer for not ratting you out?" Not a conversation for the phone.

He scrolled to her last text instead. It was simple. "Kewalo Basin was a win. We did good. Call me?"

He set the phone in the cupholder and started the car, letting the engine rattle through his seat. The radio kicked on, playing Hawaiian oldies, all steel guitar, and heartbreak. He turned it off.

He drove without thinking, letting his body handle the mechanics. Out of the garage, right onto Ala Moana, then a left at the first intersection. Honolulu moved at its own speed, cars too slow in the right lane, too fast in the left, and tourists hovering in crosswalks as if the world would pause for their photo op. He merged, he signaled, he rolled the windows down so he could taste the salt and shake off the Bureau's air conditioning.

Each red light was a checkpoint, a forced

interval for his brain to relive the conversation, the threat, the implication. Sometimes he sped up a little too fast when it turned green, so he could feel the control. Sometimes he coasted, letting other cars push ahead while he drifted in their slipstream.

He checked the rearview mirror obsessively. It wasn't paranoia if they'd already tailed you once, but each time he looked, it was the same flow of rental minivans and battered Tacomas. He told himself he was being careful, not nervous.

He let the car take him to the water, past the hotels and the sunburned clusters of tourists on Waikiki, down towards Diamond Head where the road thinned and the city got quieter. On the left, a family was lined up at a sidewalk shave ice stand, the kids already blue-lipped and grinning. The dad wore board shorts and a polo; the mom had a flower in her hair. Isaac slowed almost to a stop to watch the pure, unfiltered joy of it. The little girl pointed at the rainbow syrup and jumped in place. The dad laughed, and the sound traveled through the car window like a warm breeze.

Isaac sensed something tighten in his chest. He pulled through the intersection, heading into the neighborhoods where nobody cared about the Bureau or its warnings.

At a four-way stop, he let his foot hover over

the brake, indecisive. He could turn left and go to the field office, pretend nothing had changed, grind through another day of paperwork and chain-of-command and silence. Or he could go right, back into the city, towards his hotel suite, and a plan he hadn't yet allowed himself to imagine.

He turned right. The car surged forward, the engine's hum almost enthusiastic.

He made a dozen more turns, never quite taking the direct route. Sometimes he sped up, threading through traffic with aggressive precision. Other times he eased off, letting the city dictate his next move. Each time he checked the mirror, he saw himself, tired, rumpled, but clear-eyed.

By the time he pulled into the lot behind his hotel, the day had shifted. The tension was still there, but it was less like a trap and more like a challenge. He shut off the car and sat for another minute, letting the silence soak in. He picked up his phone, thumbed through the missed calls again, and set it aside. He had a plan. It was risky and stupid, but it was his. He let that settle, felt the rightness of it. He got out of the car and headed inside, ready to start his own investigation, even if the Bureau didn't know it yet.

Isaac Torres's hotel suite was a one-bedroom

in a 1970s walk-up a block from the canal. The rent was more than he'd paid in D.C., but it came with a breeze if you opened the right windows. The first thing you saw when you entered was a print of Waimea Bay during storm season. Fifty-foot waves, and surfers looking like ants. There were three more canvases in the hall, all ocean scenes, all done by local artists. The kitchen magnet set was themed. Painted flip-flops, a hula dancer with a missing hand, and the inevitable pineapple.

He dumped his keys into a cracked wooden bowl by the door and pulled off his shoes. The carpet in the hall was thin, patched in two places where he'd spilled coffee last month in a fit of frustration. He ignored the faint smell of fried garlic from the neighbors and made a beeline for the spare bedroom, which doubled as his personal war room.

The room was windowless except for a single slit, where the city's sodium glare filtered in like swamp gas. The air was already warm; the desk fan working overtime. Against one wall, he'd cleared space for a whiteboard and three cork panels, bought at the office supply store. The first corkboard was already dotted with thumbtacks; the second, still in its shrink wrap. He flicked on the desk lamp and booted up his laptop, which glowed to life in a cascade of login screens and blue-white light.

He started with the pile of printouts. Every page was a duplicate, quietly run through the HPD copier after hours, or photographed in the field and uploaded to a cloud nobody else could access. Case files for the armored car hits, transaction reports flagged by the Feds but never followed up on. Photos of the spiral symbol at three different crime scenes. Red string, two spools of it, lay in the desk drawer, next to a roll of blue masking tape.

He worked by routine. First, arrange the files by date. Next, by location. Finally, by type of hit; direct action, diversion, or inside job. For each, he wrote a summary on a sticky note and placed it on the board. He drew lines between matching elements. The same model of getaway car, the same brand of smoke canister, and the bizarrely brief window between alarms tripped and authorities on site.

Next came the witness statements. Some were useless; others gold. He highlighted mentions of the masked figures, always silent. He compared those with spiral signatures and drew more string. By the end of the hour, the board was already looking like a disaster zone, but the patterns were emerging, ugly and insistent.

He made coffee, an entire pot, and drank it black from a chipped mug with the words **Federal Agent, Don't Even Think About It.** The caffeine hit like a wave, bouncing off the headache that had been building since the Bureau meeting.

When he came back, he added the new data. Printouts from the cultural preservation grant database, which he'd hacked into using the old backdoor password from his Quantico mentor. The grants had been awarded to foundations with vaguely Hawaiian names, but the listed directors were all ghosts. No social media, no LinkedIn, no DMV photos. He made a list of the shell companies, tacked it to the lower right, and started cross-referencing names from the armored car jobs.

Halfway through, the doorbell buzzed. Takeout. He'd ordered Vietnamese, something fast and filling. He answered the door, exchanged brief pleasantries with the delivery guy, set the bag on the kitchen table and forgot about it.

He was deep in an email dump from the first armored car company when he caught a flicker of movement on the wall. It was the breeze nudging the corner of a photo. He pinned it back with a tack and stepped back to look at the overall map.

The spiral wasn't merely a symbol. It was a literal movement, each heist circling back to a new target, never revisiting old territory but always overlapping the jurisdiction of someone about to be deposed or indicted. It was surgical, brutal, and, he admitted, elegant.

He remembered what Leilani had said once at a department barbecue, after two beers and a failed attempt to teach him slack-key guitar. "Everything here comes back around. If you're smart, you watch the circle. If you're not, you get swallowed by it." He'd laughed, but the words stuck.

On the wall next to the whiteboard, he'd hung the photo of him and Leilani outside of a work context. It was from the same barbecue. She was holding a plastic plate piled with kalbi ribs, looking at him with an eyebrow raised, daring him to challenge her on something. He couldn't remember what. His own face looked surprised and slightly sunburned, caught mid-sentence. He paused by the photo for a long moment, fingers grazing the side of the frame.

The night deepened. The lamp cast long, weird shadows onto the wall, making the red strings look alive. He made another pot of coffee. At one point he called up Leilani's number, thumb hovering over the call button, but let the phone time out. He wanted to have something real before he pulled her into this.

He set up the financial spreadsheet, lining up grant dispersals with the dates of the biggest hits. Every time, the same pattern. Money moved, an armored car was hit, and another cultural foundation got its funding. He drew the lines on the board, and the spiral grew denser.

The interruptions were the wind battering the building and the steady tick of the kitchen clock. Once, a neighbor slammed their door and shouted in Tagalog. The world outside his room faded to white noise.

He muttered out loud, something he never did on the job. "This isn't organized crime. This is organized history." He scribbled a note. Check old land rights cases to see if any spiral companies have claims.

He sipped the next cup of coffee and realized he hadn't eaten since lunch. He wandered out to the kitchen, opened the takeout, and ate two cold spring rolls while reading through a printout of offshore bank wire receipts. The food was flavorless, but the numbers tasted real. He saw half a dozen names repeat, none of them familiar, but one, David Kekoa, jumped out. A former HPD detective who died in a surfing accident, his body mutilated by sharks. There was a time, according to the notes, when Kekoa had been a rising star, a straight shooter with zero tolerance for corruption.

He made a new page, pinned it next to the Leilani photo, and wrote: Kekoa: middleman? He wiped his hands on a napkin, and it left a faint orange smudge on the financial report. He liked the evidence of work, the way it dirtied up the sterile perfection of the Bureau.

Back at the board, he reviewed every link, every highlighted name. The spiral wasn't a mark of arrogance or a calling card. It was an admission, a dare to the system to catch up. And the more he mapped, the more it became clear. Someone was engineering the crimes and the aftermath. Witnesses always failed to appear. Judges rotated off cases right before trial. Prosecutors recused themselves with paper-thin excuses.

He typed up a summary, formatted in the style of the official Bureau reports, but with a few lines he'd never risk in a real document. The suspect is leveraging local cultural organizations to mask money movement. He uses spirals to signify order, not chaos. One step ahead of us, but always one.

He attached the summary to the board, and stepped back, arms folded. The room looked like a bomb had gone off, but to him, it was almost beautiful.

He checked the time, nearly 3 a.m.. His eyes were gritty, but he didn't feel tired. He sat on the spare bed, letting the patterns swim in his vision, the board becoming a living thing, breathing the same stale air as he did.

He thought about calling Leilani again, but held off. One more day, he promised himself. One more link, and he'd have enough to go to her with. He shut off the lamp, leaving the room lit by the cold glow of the laptop screen. The spiral appeared to be everywhere, looping in the dark. Tomorrow, he'd find the center.

He was at the field office before sunrise, the streets empty except for garbage trucks and the occasional scooter. The sky was a thin gray band over the city, and the air already clung to the skin, hinting at a day that would end in sweat. The lobby fluorescents had been on all night, but inside the security guard blinked in a slow motion daze, running Isaac's badge through the scanner twice before waving him toward the elevators.

The records room was four floors up, locked behind two keypads and a battered magnetic strip reader. The hallway leading there was painted the same color as old milk and lined with a decade's worth of out-of-date Most Wanted posters, some curling at the edges, but all faded to the point of irrelevance. The place was like a time capsule of the world's least interesting secrets.

He signed in at the records desk, scribbling a fake case number from memory. The admin didn't look up. She nodded and punched a code into the logbook. "Third terminal on the left, Torres," she said, not bothering to ask what brought him in so early. Nobody ever did.

Inside, the records room was chill and dry, humming with the combined effort of three air conditioners and a wall of servers in a glass-fronted closet. The light was so bright it seemed clinical. There were rows of rolling file shelves, each loaded with banker's boxes and thick legal folders, and at the far end, a row of computer terminals, their screensavers looping through a slideshow of Bureau training quotes ("Do the right thing, even if nobody is watching.")

Isaac took his seat at terminal three. His hands hovered over the keyboard, already slick. He wiped them on his pants, typed in his credentials, and his heart rate spiked when the first screen prompted for a second-factor code. He used the old one, from the task force lead who'd never changed his password, and got right in.

He started with the preservation grant files, cross-indexing the list of shell companies he'd mapped the night before. Each hit was a small shot of adrenaline. He found four new matches, two of which had been greenlit for additional funds last month. He wrote the account numbers down in a small spiral notebook, his handwriting trembling slightly. He set the tempo. Every ten entries, look up, scan the room, take a deep breath and go back to work.

Next came the offshore accounts. He keyed in the routing numbers, each keystroke like a tick of a metronome. It wasn't about money; these accounts tied into a web of consultants, legal trusts and donations that all led to the same two or three IP addresses. Each one carried a faint scent of risk. He copied what he needed onto a secure thumb drive, checked the drive for errors, and erased the browser history out of reflex.

Halfway through, the door banged open. A man in a cheap suit and with the hairline of a much older bureaucrat walked in, clutching a box of stale doughnuts. Isaac didn't turn, but shifted windows to an unrelated background investigation, something about a missing laptop at the airport. He clicked through two screens slowly, letting the man pass without comment.

After the man left, Isaac ran the access report for the spiral cases, to be safe. Nobody had noticed the files being touched. No red flags in the system. He kept going.

His palms were wet again, the tremor in his left hand more obvious now, so he switched to copying physical files. He found two envelopes marked CONFIDENTIAL—JUDICIAL and thumbed through them, looking for mention of the spiral or Kapua. Inside, photocopies of signed testimony, chain of custody reports, and half-legible notes from agents who'd left the Bureau before Isaac joined. He scanned the important bits before stuffing the envelopes back exactly as he'd found them, down to the angle of the paper clip.

It was almost eight when he checked his watch. The first wave of agents trickled in, their conversations echoing in the hall. Isaac capped the drive and pocketed it. His head was pounding, but his mind was crystal clear. He signed out at the desk, smiling at the admin, who was now mainlining coffee and crossword puzzles in equal measure.

"Find what you needed, Torres?" she asked, barely glancing up.

"Always do," he said, the Bureau version of small talk.

The lobby was busier, the security guard replaced by a younger guy with earbuds in. Isaac nodded, flashed his badge, and walked out. The sunlight, so cold in the records room, now baked the glass doors, and squinted, unsure which world was the real one.

He took the stairs to the parking lot, not the elevator, sensing every step as a thump in his pulse. He pulled out the thumb drive to check it was real and shoved it deep into his pocket, clenching his fist around it until his knuckles ached.

He'd done it. He had everything he needed to go to the next level. He let the car door slam behind him, shut out the Bureau and its endless humming, and breathed. Let the game begin.

The air in Isaac's suite was thick, humid from a day spent shut against the city. He didn't bother with lights; the laptop's screen filled the room with enough cold blue to see by. The board was still up, red strings crisscrossing like veins, but his focus was on the spreadsheet, every cell a small bomb.

He'd poured a mug of coffee the moment he got in, but it had gone cold before the login screens finished blinking to life. He sipped it anyway; the bitterness working as a small, necessary punishment.

He started with the account numbers, plugging each into the digital equivalent of a meat grinder, cross-referencing them with the grant distributions and wire transfer dates. For a while, it felt like any other audit, tedious, predictable, and soothing in its own way.

A name jumped out.

First, he saw it in a minor foundation, three grants over three years. Next, it was attached to an event funding form for a cultural dance festival. It kept repeating, like a glitch. Naalei Kealoha. Sometimes as a signatory, sometimes as a listed reference, but always spelled perfectly, even in places where other names were initials or generic "Admin."

He frowned, highlighted all instances, and filtered for duplicates. He double-checked the data. Each transfer to a cultural foundation on Oahu came within seventy-two hours of a heist. Most were small, but three, each right after a major job, were five figures or more. Each one listed the preservation of heritage in the memo. And all the email notifications for those grants CC'd the same office.

He ran a quick background check to be sure it wasn't a coincidence. The details lined up. Naalei Kealoha, kumu hula, founder of a nonprofit that hosted dozens of cultural events every year, lauded by the city council. A regular feature in the local papers. Also, Leilani's mother.

He froze, hand locked on the trackpad. He wasn't sure what he was looking at. The numbers didn't lie, but the implications turned his stomach. He moved through the folders again, more frantic now, tracing the money from offshore accounts to intermediary banks in LA, and to the foundations. Every time, the path ended within a block of Naalei's home.

He attempted to rationalize it. It's possible she was a pawn or a passive recipient; the funds laundered through her orgs without her knowledge. He pulled up the grant paperwork, the board rosters, the sign-off sheets.

Her name was everywhere. She'd received the money. She'd signed for the events. She was a recipient of the cultural preservation grants. Some of the cash had gone directly to public festivals where Leilani sometimes volunteered.

He gazed at the screen until the letters blurred. The room was still except for the whirr of the desk fan and the soft click of the clock. He pushed away from the laptop and stood, the movement so fast he knocked over the cold mug. Coffee spread across the carpet, leaving a dark, ugly stain.

He paced, one hand massaging his scalp, the other clenched around nothing. He muttered to himself to keep from yelling. "No way. No fucking way."

He looked at the photo of him and Leilani, the one from the barbecue. He remembered the way she'd talked about her mother, always in the past tense, like she was already worried about how the old stories might surface. He returned to the spreadsheet, desperate for a loophole. There had to be a simple explanation, a mistake in the data. But the more he looked, the tighter the spiral wound.

He clicked open the task force database, and ran a check on every witness, every person questioned in relation to the heists. Naalei's name was never mentioned. Not once. But in the court records for the preservation grants, she'd testified half a dozen times about the integrity and security of her organization's funding. Each statement coincided with the heists, each public donation an echo of the crimes themselves.

He slumped back into the chair; the world narrowing to a single point. The evidence was clear. Naalei Kealoha had been laundering money for the spiral. And Leilani, how could she not know? Or worse, what if she did?

He let his head drop to the desk, pressing his palms into his eyes until everything turned red. He could hear his own heart, and under it, the faintest trace of the ocean outside, breaking on the reef. He stayed that way. Slowly, he straightened and reached for the phone. He stared at Leilani's number, finger hovering. He was about to hit call, but the words caught in his throat.

What do you say when you find out the person you trust most might be the reason the spiral kept spinning?

He let the phone fall, unanswered. The coffee seeped deeper into the carpet, the stain growing, impossible to clean.

Night closed around the room like a blackout curtain. The city's energy retreated to a few distant sirens and the occasional low growl of a motorcycle running alongside the canal. Inside, the single light was the laptop, its blue glow sharpening the lines of Isaac's face and making the world seem far away, an aquarium viewed from the bottom.

He sat at the kitchen table, back straight, hands folded. The folder of printouts lay before him, a slab of unavoidable truth. The names on the top page, Naalei Kealoha, the grant foundations, the heist dates, stared back, each one refusing to blink. For ten minutes he didn't move. He stared, letting his mind try every detour before circling back to the same sick realization.

The air in the suite was warm, the desk fan having given up after midnight. Isaac shrugged off his suit jacket, draped it over a chair, and unknotted his tie. His shirt was wrinkled, sweat-stained under the arms, and when he rubbed his eyes, he felt the sandpaper grit of exhaustion behind the lids.

He got up, walked to the shelf, and poured himself a whiskey. The bottle shook in his grip, and the glass clattered on the countertop. Liquid splashed over the rim, soaking the bottom corner of the folder, darkening the paper. He looked at the mess and drank it in three swallows.

He sat again, picked up a pen, and began

sorting the papers. The routine helped. Email headers on the left, wire receipts in the middle, witness statements on the right. Every page brought a wave of clarity, and with it, a new dread.

On the side of the laptop, someone had left a photo from a community event, probably an intern, months ago. It showed Leilani and her mother, side by side, arms slung around each other's shoulders, both smiling the same smile. There was a crowd behind them, a riot of leis and bright shirts, with the ocean in the background. Isaac reached for it. He pulled it closer and set it atop the pile of evidence. He picked up his phone. Viewed the screen. Put it down and did it again.

It would be simple to call Leilani, to warn her, to beg her for an explanation. But what would he say? "Your mother is involved in the spiral?" Or, "I think the Bureau is about to blow up your family, and I have the matches." Every script seemed both impossible and false.

He opened a new email window, addressed it to his supervisor, and wrote two sentences and deleted them. He tried again, this time making the case as clinical as possible, no emotion, merely the facts. When he read it back, it sounded like a death sentence.

He poured another whiskey, slower this time, and took the glass to the table. His hands shook so badly he had to grip it with both. In the dark, the hum of the refrigerator and the laptop fan were the only company. He thought about every rule he'd ever broken for the Bureau, every line he'd ever blurred because it served the greater good. Was this different? Was he trying to protect Leilani, or himself?

He picked up the folder and turned the pages again, as if the facts might rearrange themselves under the right pressure. They didn't. If anything, the narrative grew sharper. He closed the folder, rested his chin on it, and gazed at the photo. He remembered Leilani saying, "You can't fight the circle. You have to outlast it." He wondered if she'd known, deep down, that she'd been running in place all along.

He tried her number once more. This time, he let it ring all the way through. No answer. He didn't leave a message. He opened his eyes wide, fighting the need to close them. The exhaustion now was more than physical; it had worked its way into his bones, his sense of who he was. He imagined sending the evidence, imagined Leilani's face as she read the official report, and imagined the way her world would fracture so she couldn't joke her way through.

He finished the whiskey and set the glass down with a clink. The echo was soft, but final. He took the folder and placed it on the table, aligned with the laptop. He found a clean sheet of paper and wrote: For Official Record—Eyes Only. He laid the photo on the bottom, so it was the last thing anyone would see.

He turned off the laptop, let the room go dark, and sat with his hands pressed against his forehead, elbows braced, body shaking. He thought of the spiral, of the way every turn brought you closer to the same inescapable center. He wondered if he'd ever really left the circle, or if all this time, he'd been spiraling in the dark, heading toward this moment.

He let his eyes close, and in the silence, finally allowed himself to be tired. In the morning, he would have to choose.

CHAPTER EIGHT

Naalei's Secret

T he house was dark except for a band of yellow slanting through the kitchen doorway, cutting across the rug and pooling near the worn rocker. Leilani entered through the back, shoes quiet against the steps, muscles buzzing with a tiredness she couldn't shake off in the car. She paused inside the door, letting her eyes adjust, taking in the scent of steamed rice and flowers, jasmine tonight, a little plumeria wilting from the vase in the entry. The AC was off, and the air seemed slow and warm, wrapping her in memories so thick they almost suffocated.

Naalei sat, knees locked together, hands clamped white around her phone as if she'd been holding her breath for hours and needed something solid to anchor her down. She wore her favorite lavender muumuu, but the color didn't suit her tonight. Her skin was gray under the table lamp, eyes wide as if she'd spotted a car swerving into her lane.

Leilani said nothing at first. The house was too quiet, the quiet that swallowed up words and spit them back in the wrong order. There was a half-finished lei draped over the arm of the sofa. The needle still stuck through wilted orchid petals, three hula implements, a pair of 'uli'uli rattles and a carved ipu, lined up on the shelf behind the TV. The familiar mess was all there, but the energy was off. A tremor ran through the space that Leilani couldn't pin to any one thing.

She dropped her backpack at the foot of the stairs and moved toward her mother, making extra noise so she wouldn't startle her. "Mom?" she said, voice soft. "You're up late."

Naalei didn't look up. Instead, she held out the phone, screen illuminated, thumb shaking at the message. The spiral filled the screen, black and perfect, burned into the text thread like a hole burned through paper. Beneath it, the words.

The Kealoha legacy of cultural preservation is built on lies. Your daughter digs too deep. Remember your oath.

Leilani felt the air thin. She was seven again, standing outside a neighbor's house as the roof caught fire, knowing she was supposed to run for help but too transfixed by the colors licking up the night.

She took the phone, scrolled through the

message, and scrolled back, flipping through the string of threats that had preceded it. The spiral appeared in every one. Sometimes alone, or punctuated with the words: legacy, oath, protect, and silence. She read them all, mind already sprinting through the protocols. The best way to get the texts on record was to secure the phone, and trace the number if it wasn't already spoofed. But none of that mattered with her mother sitting like an abandoned doll on the couch, her feet bare, one slipper missing.

"You okay?" Leilani asked, though the answer was obvious.

Naalei's first response was a small nod, as if she could will herself into calm, but her body betrayed her. Shoulders hunched in on themselves, hands fidgeting, all the while her gaze locked not on Leilani but somewhere above her head. "It's nothing," she managed. "Some people with too much time. Happens every time there's a big case in the news."

Leilani tried to keep her voice steady. "Mom, this isn't the usual stuff. This." She tapped the screen. "Is targeted. They know you. They know me."

Another silence, broken by the slow tick of the kitchen clock and the faint rattle of a gecko from behind the baseboards. Naalei twisted her hands, pulling them apart with visible effort.

"You remember when you were small, you asked why I had to go to so many meetings for the hālau?" Her voice was thin, stretched out over the bones of memory. "Why I had to talk to all the politicians and sponsors? Why I always came home with one more box of documents and one less smile?"

Leilani nodded. She remembered, though she'd assumed her mother was another adult doing adult things. "You always said you were keeping the culture alive."

"I tried," Naalei said. She stared at her hands now, as if reading her own future in the creases of her palms. "But I also kept other things alive. Things I never meant to, and things I never knew were crawling under the surface. We all did. Anyone who was anybody in the culture circles, we had to take money from where we could get it. There was never enough. For grants, for festivals, for the kids who couldn't afford costumes or music or bus fare to the competitions."

Leilani sat next to her on the couch, careful to keep a hand's width between them. Her mother's voice was cracking open in a way she'd never heard, after her father died, and after the worst fights. "What are you saying?"

"I'm saying," Naalei said, and now her hands moved in her lap, wringing a knotted edge of her muumuu, "I took the money. From them. From the spiral, I guess, that's what they're calling themselves now. I thought it was a foundation, some mainland philanthropist trying to make his name with a legacy project, but every year the donation got bigger and the questions got smaller. I signed the papers, I signed the grant receipts, I wrote the thank-you letters and smiled for the pictures." Her fingers clenched, and she looked up, eyes rimmed with red. "I told myself I was doing it for you. For your father, for all the kids who'd never see their language in a schoolbook or hear their song on a stage."

Leilani pressed her lips together, fighting to keep her face from betraying the storm in her head. The room pressed in on her from all sides. The trophy wall, with its decades of plaques and black and white photos of Naalei in her glory years. The side table topped with a lava rock bowl and a pyramid of coconut candies. The stairs, still painted the same garish blue as when her dad did it on a dare. All of it was foundation, all of it was story. And now all of it was under threat, not from the outside, but from inside the house, from blood and bone.

She reached out, took her mother's hand, thought better of it and set her hands in her lap. "How long?" she asked. "How long have you known?"

Naalei exhaled. "Long enough." Her jaw

quivered. "First it was little things. Unusual signatures. Letters coming from PO boxes, not offices. I tried to pull back once, but the next week we got a visit from a nice young man in a suit who brought us more funding than I'd ever seen. Told me my work was important to the island's true culture." The way she said true made it sound like a curse. "I wanted to believe it, so I did."

"But you knew," Leilani said. It wasn't a question, but Naalei flinched anyway.

"I knew when the spiral started showing up," her mother whispered. "At first, on emails. Later, on envelopes. Someone painted it on the gate at the hālau. I knew it was a message, but I convinced myself it was a prank." She laughed, a small, mean noise that didn't belong in her throat. "We always want to believe the best story. It's a family curse."

The air tasted damp, like a rainstorm waiting on the other side of the mountains. Leilani stood and paced the width of the rug, arms crossed, heart thudding with the fury of a thousand silent arguments. "Did anyone else know? Anyone from the board or the community?"

"Everyone who's anyone has taken money from the spiral at some point," Naalei said. "But not everyone knew what it meant. Some thought it was an odd sponsor. Others... well, they liked not asking questions."

Leilani turned, eyes stinging. "Did you ever think to tell me?" she asked, voice spiking higher than she meant.

Naalei lifted her chin, but the effect was more child than parent. "No mother wants her daughter to think she's a coward or a fool," she said. "Especially not when her daughter is a cop."

Neither one moved. The silence grew and twisted, heavy with years of unsaid things. The kitchen clock ticked over to the next hour, and somewhere in the distance, a dog barked twice and stopped.

Finally, Leilani asked, "Why now?"

Naalei's hands folded around the phone, squeezing it tight. "Because I think the spiral wants me to. Or I think I want to, before they take the chance away from me."

She blinked and wiped her eyes with her hand. "I saw a man today. I thought it was your father, the way he used to stand under the mango tree when he thought no one was looking. But it wasn't. He had a spiral tattoo on his wrist. Like the one from the old news photos."

Leilani, eyes closed, counted to four, and opened them. "They're watching us."

Her mother nodded. "They've always been watching. I finally noticed."

Outside, the wind picked up, rattling the screen door. The old peace returned, the peace that came from knowing exactly where every threat lived and how to stare it down.

Leilani saw the frailty in her mother's spine, the defeat in the droop of her shoulders. She saw not a survivor, but a victim, too.

"We'll fix this," Leilani said. She didn't know whether it was a promise or a dare.

Naalei wiped her hands on her dress, and her composure returned. "I hope you can," she said. "Because I don't think I can anymore."

They sat together on the couch, not touching, but not moving away. The phone's screen darkened, but the spiral stayed, a ghost imprint on the glass. It would be there in the morning, and the morning after, and every morning until someone had the guts to erase it for good.

For now, they watched the wind shift the curtains and listened to the old house creak, each sound a memory, each moment a step deeper into a spiral of their own making.

Leilani woke before dawn, unsure if she'd slept or drifted in a low orbit above her pillow. She checked on Kai, who was sound asleep, splayed out on the bed, blanket twisted around his lower body, looking like a butterfly crawling out of a cocoon. The house held a hush she'd heard after storms, a vacuum that suggested nothing good waited in the daylight. She found herself in the kitchen, feet bare on cold tile, a mug of coffee warming her hands more from ritual than from temperature. The living room was still dark. Her mother's silhouette sat at the kitchen table, arms folded, the phone now face down beside her, as if out of sight meant out of mind.

Naalei turned as Leilani entered, chin tilted as if bracing for more questions. She wore a different dress, white with scattered green fern prints, and her hair was twisted up with a clip that looked ready to snap.

"Want to see it?" Naalei's voice was quieter than usual, a thin wire stretched over a pit.

Leilani set her coffee on the counter more forcefully than necessary. "See what?"

"The paperwork. All of it." She glanced at the kitchen clock, barely five. "Might as well get it over with."

She rose, knees creaking, and padded down the hall to her room. Leilani waited at the threshold, resisting the need to follow, to play cop and daughter and executioner all at once. The sound of dragging furniture echoed, then a clunk, followed by wood splintering. A minute later, Naalei returned, a battered accordion folder hugged to her chest.

She set it down with a finality that reminded Leilani of old family funerals, the kind where nobody cried but everyone left feeling hollowed out. The folder bulged at the seams, kept together with a strip of faded duct tape and a sticker of an 'iwa bird mid-flight.

"Go ahead," Naalei said, gesturing as if welcoming an audit.

Leilani opened the folder, eyes flicking from page to page. At first, it was what she expected, letters from small grant agencies, printouts from obscure state offices, and a handful of glossy pamphlets for past festivals. Each grant had a cover sheet, typed in dry bureaucratic English, with a signature page. But halfway through the stack, the pattern shifted. The sponsors got more exotic, the money bigger, and the names more cryptic. Instead of clear grant administrators, it was always "Foundation for Local Heritage" or "Preservation Initiatives," with a first initial and last name attached.

Leilani slowed, fingers tapping each page in rhythm. The names on the bottom of the forms itched at her memory, Akana, Souza, Vierra. Not unusual names for the islands, but she saw the next. R. Kapua. The handwriting was blocky, not unlike the all caps scrawl from the emails the task force had flagged last week. She flipped to the next. M. Lau signed with an exaggerated flourish. She'd seen that signature in the evidence locker, scribbled across a shipping manifest from one of the heist runs.

She glanced up at her mother, searching for any sign that this was a sick joke. There was none. If anything, Naalei looked older in the pale kitchen light, her lips pursed so tight they nearly vanished.

Leilani kept reading. Each letter from the Island Heritage Foundation came with precise dollar amounts, none ever round. $2,493 for the spring hula festival. $17,001 for the cultural exchange to Hilo. $10,610 for the repairs to the hālau roof. Every grant was accompanied by a typed thank you from Naalei, with a CC to three different addresses, one downtown, one in LA, and one in Hong Kong.

The coffee soured in Leilani's mouth. She paged through a stack of event photos, her mother shaking hands with a series of local politicians, posing beside banners with the spiral logo in the lower corner. In one, a man with a blurring of gray hair and a suit stood off to the side, looking directly at the camera. She recognized the face instantly. Kapua, the supposed Host, now in federal holding and denying every charge.

"You kept all this?" Leilani's voice was smaller than she wanted, almost a whisper.

"I thought it would keep me safe," Naalei said. "Or that's what I told myself."

Leilani flipped to the earliest letter, from ten years ago. The same pattern, a grant, a thank you, a signature from an untraceable foundation officer. Each year the numbers grew, the events scaled up, and the spiral crept closer to the middle of every document.

"You see this, right?" Leilani said, spreading the papers across the table. "These are fronts. Every one. The money is being laundered through you, and through the festivals. Did you ever check the addresses?"

Naalei's lips moved, but nothing came out. She gripped the table instead, fingers whitening. "At first, yes. But when I started asking, the grants got held up. The paperwork doubled. The following week, three of my friends lost their funding. A month later, someone left a dead bird on my car. After that, I stopped."

Leilani steadied her breath. "You let them use you."

Naalei's jaw locked, then relaxed. "I let them help me. I thought I was getting something out of it. I thought we all were. There are kids dancing right now, kids who found their voice, who never would have made it to competition if not for that money."

"But that's not all that matters!" Leilani slammed the folder closed, instantly regretting the outburst. "You know how many cases we have in the city right now, all tied back to these accounts? How many witnesses are dead, or vanished, because somebody like Kapua bought their silence with dirty money?"

Naalei flinched, but didn't look away. "And you think I don't know that? You think I don't see every news story, every time another family buries a child?" She swallowed, eyes going shiny. "What was I supposed to do, Leilani? Shut it all down and allow the hālau to die, let the traditions go back into the lava rock with the bones? You don't know what it's like, watching your whole life shrink to a budget line, one that no one in the city cares about unless you beg, or steal, or make a deal."

The words lingered in the space between them, as heavy as humidity. The kitchen clock ticked, the minute hand edging past the hour.

Leilani paced, not trusting herself to sit. She ran a hand through her hair, backtracked to the table and rifled through the folder again, eyes searching for anything she'd missed. Every piece of evidence lined up. Every signature matched what she'd seen on the forensic boards. There were a few notes clipped to the side, handwritten in a language mix of Hawaiian and English, all in a spiky hand she recognized from a crime scene note months earlier.

She found the page and shoved it towards her mother. "This one. You got a thank-you card from R. Kapua. You know what this really is?"

Naalei nodded, voice so soft it almost didn't register. "A marker. So, I'd remember who to call if I ever needed more."

Leilani leaned over the table, hands spread. "You never called? Not once?"

Naalei's eyes met hers, and the answer was written there. Leilani pushed away, the kitchen chair scraping on the tile.

"You don't get it, do you?" she said, pacing now, unable to stay still. "This isn't merely money; it's a pipeline for every bad thing the spiral crew ever did. Every armored car they hit, every dirty judge, every bribe, it all comes back here. To this house. To you."

"I know," Naalei said, letting her head fall into her hands. "I know."

Leilani stopped at the window, staring out at the faint edge of sunrise. The city was blinking to life, but the house stayed cloaked in its own darkness.

Neither spoke. The lone sound was the clock, marking the seconds as if waiting for them to fill the space with something better.

Finally, Naalei said, "I thought I was protecting our culture." Her voice quivered, and Leilani saw her as a person caught in the rip current, not strong enough to swim free. "Instead, I may have helped destroy it."

Leilani couldn't trust her own voice, so she nodded. She stared at her mother, at the pile of evidence that now implicated them both in something bigger and dirtier than either could have imagined. She felt the need to scream, to throw the whole folder out the window and watch the wind scatter it across the city. But she stood there, still as stone, letting the weight press down.

"We're going to the U.S. attorney first thing," Leilani said at last. "You'll give a statement. All of it. Every name, every payment, every time they called or wrote or showed up in person."

Naalei nodded, eyes closed. "Okay."

"You're going to need a lawyer," Leilani added, though she had no idea if she meant it as a warning or comfort.

Her mother didn't reply.

They stood there; the day brightening outside, the paperwork still splayed across the kitchen table, and Leilani had no idea how to put her family back together. She knew it wouldn't be enough, no matter how hard she tried, to keep the spiral from spinning one more time.

They didn't say a word for nearly an hour. Leilani gathered the folders, stacking them in the crook of her arm, and methodically sorted the debris of the night into a single, contained mess. Her mother watched, face hollowed out, hands folded in her lap like a student waiting for the principal's verdict. At some point, the light crept into the kitchen, pale and apologetic, and neither seemed to want to claim it.

When the last paper was tucked away, Leilani walked to the lanai door and slid it open. She expected her mother to resist, to want to stay inside with the walls and the locked doors. Instead, Naalei followed, silent and barefoot, her steps careful on the old planks.

The outside air was rich with the scent of flowers. Even this early, the world was awake. Frogs croaking from the canal, a night shift myna yelling from the phone wires, and somewhere the neighbor's sprinkler ticking through the hour. The lanai was lined with planters of ti, monstera and a tired papaya tree with one stubborn fruit still clinging to it. They sat on the steps, knees barely touching, and listened to the island cycle through its next breath.

Leilani spoke first. Her voice was dry, almost

clinical. "You said something last night about calling Makani. Why?"

Her mother's hands worked against each other, the sign she was still awake. "I called him last night. At first I thought it was to gossip, you know how he is. But he asked me if someone was sniffing around the grant money. He said a lady from the mainland was sniffing around, asking where it all was. He said he'd never seen a spiral logo before, not until last month, but now it was all over his mail. He sounded scared, though he attempted to make a joke of it."

Leilani pressed for more. "Did you tell him about your own threats?"

"I tried," Naalei said. "But he changed the subject. He said not to worry, that he could take care of himself. But he's not that kind of tough, Leilani. He's soft inside, like your father was. I think he's in over his head."

The air thickened, holding the weight of all the years Naalei had kept her own troubles out of sight. Leilani picked at the step, thumb digging into the wood until it splintered.

"You need to call him back," Leilani said. "Today. Tell him not to meet anyone alone, not to open the door if he doesn't know them. I can send a car by his place, keep eyes on him until this shakes out."

Her mother looked up, startled. "You really

think it's that bad?"

Leilani nodded. "I know it is." She turned, her features sharpened by the rising sun. "Who else, Mom? Who else got the same money, the same threats?"

A slow exhale, like wind off the mountain. "Three or four kumu that I know of. All from the island. All the people I've worked with, or against, at some point. Some of them are proud, they'd never admit to taking a cent, but I know they did. We all did."

Leilani didn't look away. "I'll need names. Numbers if you have them. You'll write it all down right now."

The old pride flared on Naalei's face, a last flash of resistance. "I'll write it."

They let the words settle, crowded out by the sounds of the neighborhood waking up. Two dogs barked at each other across the street, and the faint beep of a delivery van reversing through the block. At that moment, the world seemed stubbornly ordinary.

Naalei rested her head in her hands, elbows digging into her knees. "I ruined everything," she whispered.

"No," Leilani said, voice gentler than she'd meant it to be. "But you made it a lot harder to fix."

The phrase hung between them, neither comfort nor rebuke. A fresh gust brought the smell of distant rain and the bittersweet tang of cooked ginger from a neighbor's stove. The sky was cut by the first jet leaving for the mainland, the contrail a white knife dividing yesterday from now.

"Can I ask you something?" Naalei's voice was soft, careful.

Leilani nodded, looking out over the yard.

"When this is over." Her mother's hands trembled, folding and unfolding. "Do you think you'll be able to forgive me?"

Leilani didn't answer right away. She stared down the line of the street, thinking of every lie she'd heard from every criminal, every excuse that was a way of ducking the truth. She tried to picture herself as a daughter, not a detective, but the role never quite fit.

"I don't know," she said finally, her voice level. "But I'm not going anywhere. We finish this together."

A silence stretched between them, but it wasn't empty. It was packed with the weight of everything they'd survived, and the new dread of what would happen next.

The two of them sat there, mother and daughter, on the lanai steps as the sun cracked through the clouds and the street filled with light. They didn't touch, didn't look at each other, but they shared the same silence.

From somewhere, a line of hula music drifted over the fences, faint but sure. The spiral was still out there, somewhere in the city, waiting for its next move. But there was the small promise of the new day, and the two of them breathing it in together, as if it could somehow make up for all the darkness before.

The ti leaves rattled. The world kept spinning. And on the lanai, the Kealoha women braced for the next wave, side by side.

Leilani didn't wait for the second ring. She needed Isaac to answer now. He did, with a low, groggy "What's wrong?" that sounded like he'd torn himself out of a dream.

"I've got something to tell you," she said. The words came out in a single exhale, tight and flat. "My mom's connected to the money. All of it. Direct lines from the Mastermind's crew, through shell foundations and fake grants. She's been taking it for years, without knowing who was really running the show."

On the other end, Isaac made a sharp exhale that meant he already knew or at least suspected. He grew silent for a heartbeat. "I know."

Leilani froze, staring at the phone as if the pause might explain itself. "You know?" Her voice snapped up an octave. "What do you mean, you know?"

Isaac's voice, when it came, was steadier. "I saw the same pattern in the grant ledgers and the shell company filings. I recognized a few names from other cases, but I couldn't be sure. I was still putting it together. I didn't want to say anything until—" He hesitated, fumbling for a word that wouldn't sound like a lie. "Until I had proof."

It stung more than Leilani expected. The two of them, despite all their different habits and histories, had always shared everything that mattered. No secrets. That was supposed to be the deal, the way to survive in their line of work. She sensed the betrayal bloom, hot and immediate.

"You could have come out and told me," she said, voice rising. "We're supposed to be partners, Isaac. You don't keep this shit back. Not from me. Not now."

It seemed like she was shouting into the empty kitchen, but she didn't stop. The words tumbled over each other, harsh and ragged. "You think this is about protecting my feelings? You think I'm too fragile to hear the truth? That's not your call."

Isaac let the tirade slide off him, as if he'd known it was coming. "I didn't want to hurt you," he said. "But this isn't about that. I. Look,

I figured it was a coincidence. That your mom got looped in as a front, or she thought it was all legit. I was waiting to see which way it broke. I didn't want to point fingers until I had something solid."

Leilani pinched the bridge of her nose. The rationale made sense, but it didn't help. If anything, it made it worse. "You know how this works," she said, quieter now. "You know how fast a reputation burns. Once this is out, there's no putting it back."

"I know," he replied. "I'm sorry, Lei. I really am."

She paced the length of the lanai, and back again, the phone pressed hard to her cheek. "There's more. It's not only her. There are three or four other kumu on the island. All of them tied up in this web, all of them bought off with charity grants and hush money. If we don't handle this right, it'll torch the entire leadership of the hula community."

Isaac whistled low. "Jesus. That's...bigger than I thought."

"It's always bigger," Leilani muttered. She could visualize the dominoes lined up, ready to fall. "We have to get ahead of this. Control the story before the press does. If we don't, everything goes up in smoke."

He didn't argue. He'd seen it happen too many

times, the slow-motion detonation of public trust, the way a single headline could turn a city against itself in a day.

"So, what's the move?" he asked.

Leilani had already decided. She'd spent the last half hour on the porch, watching the sky lighten and darken again, running through every path. Most of them ended with someone she loved in handcuffs, or worse. "We go to the U.S. Attorney first thing. We give a statement, full, clean, without filters or spin. We lay out every payment, every name, every threat. We do it as a team. If there's a chance that some of the kumu were coerced, or tricked, we get that on the record before anyone else does."

She heard the hesitation in Isaac's next breath. "That's risky, Lei. Your mom could end up on the front page. Or in a cell."

She pressed her lips together, jaw set. "She knows. She's ready to do what's right. She doesn't want to run anymore."

Isaac let that sink in. "And you?"

"I'm more worried about the community," Leilani said. "If this comes out the wrong way, it destroys everything. The schools, the festivals, and the apprenticeships. Years of work gone overnight. But if we tell the truth, if we tell it first, it's enough for people to see the difference between being a victim and being a villain."

He was quiet, and she could almost hear him turning it over in his head, weighing the angles, the risks, the fallout. "Okay," he said finally. "I'll be there. Tell me when and where."

"Tomorrow morning, first thing. At the federal building right after I drop Kai off at school."

There was a pause, softer now, as if the fight had been drained out of them. "Hey," Isaac said softly. "We're going to get through this. You know that, right?"

She didn't answer right away. She stared out over the yard, watching as the neighbor's cat picked its way through the ti plants, unbothered by the mess of human drama. She needed to believe him; to believe anything.

"I hope so," she said, and hung up.

She spent the next hour at her mother's side, helping her piece together the names and numbers that would soon become evidence. When the list was finished, Leilani read it again, making sure there were no mistakes. She locked it in her bag and sat with her mother, side by side, until the sun was high enough to draw a new set of shadows across the kitchen floor.

When she left, Naalei didn't say goodbye. She squeezed Leilani's hand and let her go, as if that alone would be enough to carry them both through whatever happened next.

Leilani drove downtown with the windows open, letting the ocean air cut through the rising panic. She parked in the shadow of the state building and tried to convince herself she was ready. Isaac was waiting for her at the curb, a coffee in each hand and his tie already loose. He gave her a thin, tired smile as she approached.

"You sleep?" he asked.

"Did you?" she countered.

They both shook their heads, and Leilani almost smiled. "Let's get this done," she said, and together they walked into the building, ready to burn the old secrets down and start again with whatever was left.

In the marble lobby, they paused by the elevator banks. Isaac touched her arm, a quick, gentle squeeze.

"I've got your back," he said, and this time, she believed him.

They rode the elevator in silence, the city unfolding below like a map of every choice they'd ever made. When the doors opened, they stepped out together, partners again, and faced the day with what seemed like hope.

CHAPTER NINE

The Mastermind Revealed

T he conference room was a bunker, double glass, reinforced door with keypad, no outside windows. Overhead, a dull circle of LED panels simulated daylight without heat. There were three chairs at the table, but two were in use. The third, the one for a hypothetical supervisor or legal rep, had been pushed into the corner, facing the wall as if exiled for bad behavior.

Leilani sat closest to the door. Her arms were folded so tightly across her chest that the biceps pinched white against her blouse. Her badge, still clipped to the front, reflected the false sun in a stutter of light as she moved. She didn't take her eyes off the man across from her.

Isaac Torres wore his Bureau face today, clean shave, crisp suit, and the Bureau-issued tie in ocean blue. He had a laptop open; the screen angled, so that she saw everything but could touch nothing. On the desk, a battered legal pad, a flash drive on a lanyard, and a manila envelope bristling with colored tabs. There was also a glass of water, untouched.

Neither spoke for a full minute. The only sounds were the HVAC's gentle hiss, the steady tick from a cheap wall clock, and the soft buzz of Isaac's phone as texts accumulated out of sight. He finally broke the silence.

"I appreciate you coming in early." The tone was neutral, all business, but a muscle twitched at his jaw.

"I didn't have a choice." Leilani's voice was a scraped-out version of itself, dry and salt-stung. "You said this was urgent. So, let's get it over with."

Isaac nodded and turned the laptop around. The first image was a photo, high school yearbook vintage, staged and a little embarrassing. David Kekoa, mid-twenties, slightly softer at the jaw, hair cut almost military, lips pressed in a careful line. It was the sort of photo you'd use to reassure a parent, or a judge, that you were going places.

Leilani flinched. "What is this?" she said. "You could've emailed it."

He clicked again. A time jump, David in a surf contest, grinning and battered, hair wild, an arm raised in exhausted victory. The right bicep was marked by a bold black tattoo, a spearhead, its barbs curling at the ends. He looked alive.

Isaac spoke gently. "You told me once that Kekoa's body was identified by that tattoo."

"Yeah, because it was the one thing left that wasn't chewed to hell. Is this a trip down trauma lane, or are you getting to the point?"

He clicked again, and this time the screen was a frame from grainy security footage, dated four weeks ago. The subject wore a baseball cap and sunglasses, but the jawline was visible, as was the posture, slightly hunched, left shoulder forward, as if bracing for a blow. The man walked with a limp, favoring his left leg.

"Surveillance pull from the Makiki armored car hit," Isaac said. "Now look here." He drew a line on the screen with the cursor, hovering it above the man's hand. "Pause at two seconds, frame twenty-four."

He let the image freeze. In a blur of pixels, the man glanced over his shoulder, and the sleeve of his shirt shifted. On his bicep, a segment of the spearhead tattoo was visible, with the same curl at the tip. The angle was imperfect, but the curve and size matched the earlier photos.

Leilani didn't move, but her nails bit hard into her own forearms. "That's not possible," she said. "I identified David. Myself. You know that."

Isaac kept his eyes on her. "I know. But you also

know what facial recognition can do with grainy footage."

"Software can be gamed. If you don't have DNA, you have nothing."

He exhaled, slow and deliberate. "I was hoping you'd say that." He reached for the envelope, removed a clear plastic sleeve with a lab printout inside.

"After the hit, HPD recovered a blood sample from the car door handle. Not enough for a full genome, but enough for mitochondrial comparison. The sample came back ninety-eight percent match to the remains you identified as Kekoa."

She barked a laugh, loud and sharp. "You're telling me my husband staged his own death and reappeared eight years later to knock over an armored car?"

"I'm not telling you anything. I'm giving you the data." He slid the sleeve across the table. "It's not this one hit, Leilani. He's shown up at four other crime scenes. A shadow, always masked. The DNA doesn't always match, but the tattoos do. There's a voice match to one call to the station; the analysts say the cadence is identical. They ran it twice."

She reached for the sleeve, but stopped, as if touching it would make the lie real. Her whole body seemed to shrink, the breath leaking out like a slow puncture. "No. No way. It's a copycat. A cousin, or someone hacked the database. You saw what happened to the last officer who tried to go public with a whistleblower tip. You know what HPD's internal affairs is capable of. And I know." Her voice broke, and returned, steelier. "That if my husband were alive, he'd never do this."

Isaac's voice dropped to a hush. "I wanted to believe that. I really did. But you need to see the rest."

He clicked on another file. This time it was raw audio, played through the laptop's tinny speakers. The first sound was static, then a voice, distorted, but clear.

"Leave the spiral alone. If you push further, we won't only take your money. We'll take your future."

Leilani's head snapped up. Her eyes met Isaac's, and the panic there was raw enough to shatter the glass between them.

"That's not," she started.

But he clicked again, running an analysis overlay, spectral lines, voice waveforms and cross-comparison graphs. "I sent this to three labs. All of them agreed. The odds of it being your husband's voice are better than ninety percent. Nobody else in the family matches."

Leilani shoved the table hard enough to rattle the laptop. "I was there when the body was found. I saw the sharks. I saw the tattoo. That was what was left of my husband in that bag, Isaac. You're telling me this because you want me off the case. You need to undermine my credibility, so when I find the real spiral, nobody will believe me."

Isaac shook his head. "It's not like that."

"What is it? You want me to chase a ghost while you clean up the mess?"

"I want you safe," he said, and it was the first thing he'd said that sounded like the truth.

She made a sound, a low animal noise, and pushed her chair back. It skittered, legs scraping against the concrete. "Don't patronize me. If this is a setup, I'll find the angle. If it's not, somebody has gone to a hell of a lot of trouble to bring him back from the dead."

Isaac reached across, put his hand palm-up, not quite touching. "Leilani. Look at the evidence. I'm not your enemy."

She stared at his hand as if it were a scorpion. Her lips curled back. "You're the sole person in this room who still thinks so."

She stood, and in doing so, caught the chair. It toppled, clattering to the floor, a sudden violence that echoed off the glass. She didn't bother to pick it up. Instead, she gathered her bag, her badge, and, after a brief hesitation, the manila folder.

At the door, she paused, back rigid. "If you're right, you'd better hope he's merciful. Because if he's not, this city is screwed."

She was gone before Isaac could respond, the heavy door slamming shut with a mechanical certainty. The only movement in the room was the lazy spin of the chair she'd knocked over, making a slow, unsteady spiral on the polished floor.

Isaac gathered the evidence back into its envelope as if the act of order could calm the storm that had passed through. He considered calling after her, or following, but in the end he sat alone, and listened to the fan hum overhead, trying to imagine a future in which he hadn't detonated the best friendship he'd ever had.

The single honest thing about the Kalanianaole Highway at night was that the air pretended not to care. Salt wind, old asphalt, a slick shimmer of sea mist that didn't so much cool as coat the skin in permanent gooseflesh. At this hour, the city's drunks and after shift stragglers had been pushed to the safe lights, leaving the coastal stretch bare but for the shifting shadow of a traffic cone and the hunchbacked outline of an abandoned food truck at mile marker 22. Leilani Kealoha's Explorer sat at the shoulder, lights off, a single blue LED painting the dash in regret.

She'd been there two hours already, windows cracked enough to catch the whiff of brine and deep-sea rot. It helped keep her awake. So did the Sig resting on her thigh, and the stack of granola wrappers growing like urban lichen in the cupholder. She had not, despite her best efforts, stopped replaying the conversation in the conference room.

A click, a frozen video frame. David, alive, his body stuttered into being by a handful of digital ghosts. The cursor circling the tattoo, the jawline, the glint of old sunlight on his neck. She kept blinking, half expecting to find him next to her in the passenger seat, in the process of rolling his own cigarette, or peeling the label off a Gatorade bottle, or working a crossword with that lazy, annoying confidence that drove her up the wall and down again. But the other thing in the car was the radio, tuned to a quiet band of dispatch chatter, where no one used first names and every word was one inch away from violence.

She thumbed her phone, checked the time. 11:33. The target window, if you trusted the

Bureau's math, was between midnight and 2 a.m.. After that, the only things liable to rob the armored car were a sleep-deprived nene or some local joyriders. She rested the phone on the dash, face down.

Outside, the ocean ran black to the horizon, cut by a ragged silver line where the wind torqued the swell. The other lights came from the one flickering streetlamp by the old marina gate and, every so often, the sweep of passing headlights on the upper road, too distant to matter.

She checked the rearview more out of habit than hope. No movement, nothing but the hunched silhouette of the food truck and, on the far side mirror, the slow pulse of her own brake lights. She leaned back, let her head tip against the rest, and watched the condensation bead and race on the windshield, each drop a new trail with its own logic and destination.

She wasn't a crier, but if she were, this would've been the time. Instead, she ground her jaw until she tasted metal, and let her foot tap a nervous code into the mat.

The radio broke in with static and a flat voice: "Unit two-oh-nine, status check."

She pressed the mic. "Two-oh-nine, holding at highway east. All clear."

"Roger. Next status in twenty."

She released the button and let her hand fall. The weapon was already growing warm against her skin. The inside of the car seemed smaller, more personal. She'd once driven this same stretch with David at two in the morning, back when the world was slightly out of focus and the most dangerous thing was a loose dog in the middle of the lane. She tried not to think of that, but her mind circled back, a stubborn terrier.

She rubbed her temple, kneaded at the knot between her eyes. There was no escape. The evidence played back in a relentless, acid loop. The DNA swab, the tattoo and the voice on the tape. Isaac's face, a perfect mixture of regret and certainty, as he held out the folder like a judge reading a sentence.

"It's not possible. I saw him. I saw the tattoo."

And yet. She ran through the timeline again, trying to find the gap, the trick, the sleight of hand. If someone had faked David's death, it would've required time, planning and a cruelty she wasn't sure anyone on the island could muster. But the spiral had always been more than rumor, and rumor, she'd learned, was the skeleton key to every locked door in this city.

She fingered the radio again. There was nothing to say that wouldn't make her sound as unhinged as she felt.

A minute passed. At 11:49, a shape moved on

the opposite side of the street, briefly caught in the spill of the streetlamp. Leilani tensed, every muscle shrinking to a single point of focus. She slid the weapon off her thigh and let it rest, barrel down, between her knees.

The shape resolved into a person, average height, trim, moving in the easy shuffle of someone who'd spent a lifetime in flip-flops. The head was covered by a hoodie, but the hands were bare, tanned, knuckles darkened by old scars. The figure didn't hurry. Instead, it paused at the curb, stooped to pick up a stray can, and lobbed it expertly into the trash bin by the marina gate.

Her heart thump, three beats too fast.

The man, or the ghost, or whatever he was, turned and looked straight at her car. She ducked, but not fast enough. In that second, the figure lifted a hand and made a slow, spiraling motion. He faded into the darkness, as if the street itself had swallowed him.

Leilani stayed still, barely breathing, her fingers locked white around the weapon. Sweat broke on her neck and across the backs of her knees. She counted to twenty before she trusted herself to move.

She popped the door, letting in a blast of cold, marine air. Her feet hit the gravel, steady and silent. She kept her body low as she moved to the rear of the car, crouching behind the fender. She watched, waited, every sense straining for a trick or a tell or a second sighting.

Nothing.

She walked to the shoulder and looked both ways. Still nothing. She edged toward the marina, stepping as quietly as a bare foot would allow. The trash bin was empty; the sidewalk freshly swept. No sign that anyone had been there, save for the faintest wet print on the curb. It was almost gone by the time she saw it, erased by the humid air.

She checked the upper road, the bike path and the perimeter of the food truck. No movement, no sound but the distant roar of a wave breaking hard on the reef. She holstered the Sig, stopped and drew it again, not trusting the calm.

Back in the car, she slammed the door a little too loudly. The glass rattled. She sat with her hands gripping the wheel, the knuckles pulsing with every beat of her heart. If it was David, or someone wearing David's skin, he was better at hiding than she was at seeing. She sat there for a while, the blue dash light slowly dimming, the world outside turning darker and stranger by the minute.

At midnight exactly, the radio chirped again. "Two-oh-nine, status?"

She pressed the mic, voice steady as steel. "All

quiet."

She thumbed off the radio, and leaned back, eyes wide and unblinking, as if she could will the next ghost into showing itself. She didn't let herself cry. She sat, and stared, and waited for the world to come apart in the way only the truly impossible could manage.

CHAPTER TEN

Kai in Danger

Kai didn't walk home from school often, but when he did, he always took the long way home. He said it was for exercise, or to avoid the kids who liked to throw musubi at each other near the bus stop, but mostly he liked how the neighborhoods changed block by block. Big houses with barking dogs and wall-to-wall security cameras gave way to yards patched with old tires, a chunk of jungle overtaken by sleeping cats, and a run of cinderblock apartments with cars jammed nose-to-tail. He liked how the breeze felt different in each microclimate. The way light bent gold and blue through the monkey pod branches when it was almost evening.

Today he noticed the shift as a cold spot in his belly.

It was still light, but the sun was behind the ridge and the shadows in the cross streets looked thick as ocean water. Kai tried to act like he wasn't glancing back every three steps. He counted telephone poles instead, like his mom told him to do when he got nervous. Sometimes he'd talk out loud, pretend to do math homework, anything to chase off the tickle at the base of his scalp.

At the corner of Wilder and Keeaumoku, he heard the footsteps. Not the shuffle of some auntie walking home or the slap of slippers from other kids, but the rhythm of actual shoes, careful ones, keeping pace far enough behind to sound casual. He stopped to tie his shoe; the laces were triple knotted. The footsteps stopped, too.

The craving to sprint home warred with the small, stubborn part of him that refused to give anyone the satisfaction of seeing him run. He looked up at the sky, checked for birds (three, all pigeons), and hunched his backpack higher and crossed the street.

Half a block later, the footsteps were back.

Kai ducked into the old service station parking lot, the one with a cracked mural of King Kamehameha and an abandoned vending machine full of sun-baked soda. He hid behind the pay phone (broken for as long as he could remember) and waited. His heart had the weird, jumpy thud it got before big tests or after he ate too much li hing candy.

He held his breath. In the reflection of the

vending machine glass, he saw them. Two men, not old but not high school either, both in dark shirts and pants that didn't fit right, walking side by side but with a military way of staying spaced. They didn't look at him, but when he bolted down the cut through behind the gas station, they did too.

Kai's hands were slick on the straps of his backpack. He told himself it was probably some lost dads or undercover security, but he didn't believe it. He thought about texting his mom, but that would make it real, and she'd already had the worst week ever.

He speed-walked down to the creek, taking the shortcut nobody else liked because it smelled like dead frogs and had one entire section of the sidewalk collapsed into the water. The men followed, silent except for the scrape of one's heel on concrete, which made a rhythm that stuck in Kai's head. Left, right, pause. Left, right, pause. They never closed the distance, but floated behind.

He wanted to scream at them, or laugh, or throw his algebra book and make a joke of it. But he kept walking until his calves burned, and the sidewalk ran out, and he was forced to cut through the empty church parking lot.

He risked a look back, but the street was empty. The two men appeared, still walking, but with a new confidence, like they knew he had nowhere left to go.

Kai ducked behind a dumpster, pressed himself against the sticky vinyl, and waited. He counted to twenty and risked a peek. The men had stopped, conferring in low voices. The shorter one pointed at the church and at the houses beyond. The other one nodded, checked his phone, and looked directly at Kai.

He ducked back, heart hammering. He fumbled with his own phone, hands shaking so hard he nearly dropped it. Mom would kill him if she knew he was in trouble. She'd kill him harder if he didn't tell her. He typed out a text and deleted it. He didn't want to get her fired or something worse. Instead, he ran.

He hopped over the low wall into the community garden, barely clearing the wire fence. He crashed through rows of taro and papaya, sprinting until he hit the alley behind the animal hospital. His breath was coming in ragged puffs, lungs burning, sweat cold on his arms. He risked another look. The men were there, two rows over, moving parallel but not closing in. One of them stooped to pick up a fallen flower, then dropped it, still watching.

Kai doubled back, zigzagging through the maze of garden beds, losing sight of them for a few precious seconds. He popped out the far side and made for the main road, cutting between the houses with the blue Christmas lights still up, even though it was April. He felt a surge of hope; thinking he'd finally lost them. The relief made his knees weak, but he kept moving, up the last stretch of his own street, almost home. That's when he saw them again, waiting at the end of his block, standing in the shadow of a parked van.

He nearly tripped, recovered, and slowed to a walk, trying not to look like a total maniac. He could see his house, the porch light already on, and the hint of movement behind the curtain. He didn't turn around. He didn't have to. The men were still there, watching, not in any hurry.

He reached the steps, forced himself to breathe, and unlocked the door with the code only his family knew. He looked back one last time before going inside. The men hadn't moved.

He shut the door quietly, hoping nobody inside would see his hands shaking or his shirt stuck to his back with sweat. The desire to tell someone was almost overwhelming, but he headed to the kitchen, poured himself a glass of water, and drank it all in one go.

His grandmother was watching the news, but not really watching it. She hummed to herself, braiding a new lei. He would have liked to collapse into her arms, but that wasn't how things worked in their house. He retreated to his room, shut the door, and let the adrenaline shake through him. He went online to distract himself with games or memes, but every noise from the street sent his stomach into free fall.

The day was winding down in the department, all the detectives gone or holed up behind thick office doors, so when Leilani's phone rang she almost ignored it. The caller ID showed Kapule, Mrs. Kapule, the queen of the neighborhood watch and the sworn enemy of lost packages and stray cats. She thumbed accept, expecting some complaint about teens or fireworks.

"Detective Kealoha," said the voice, thin and wavering but urgent. "There are men watching your boy. I saw them from my window. Two men, dark shirts. I don't like the way they move. I called 911."

For half a second, the words bounced harmlessly off the shell of her police-brain, categorized as gossip, but the air in the room changed. Her body shifted into cold, precise action.

"Where?" she said. "Are they on my street?"

"They follow him every corner. He runs, they run." A pause, the rattle of breath. "Your mother is at your house, but he is almost there. I think they mean something bad."

Leilani hung up mid-sentence. Files scattered from her lap as she stood. She left her desk, her office and the polite pretense of order behind. She ran flat out, past the captain's glass cube (a quick flash of her mom's porch, Kai's face lit in porch light), to the stairwell and down, barely touching the steps. The parking lot was a field of dirty light and old gum wrappers. She fumbled the car key, dropped it, cursed, and got it in on the second try.

She called home with one hand and jammed the car into reverse with the other. Two rings. No answer. She called again, and again, voice each time a little closer to screaming. The engine howled as she hit the main street. A red light caught her, and she ran it. Someone honked. She didn't care. She flipped on the blue and white flashers and hit the siren.

She kept one eye on the mirror and one on the phone, which she switched to speaker. No answer from the house. Her mind filled in the worst, two men at the door, Kai not fast enough, her mother fumbling for the phone. The car was too small, too slow. She cut the corner at the Safeway, clipped a parking curb and bottomed out, cursing as she heard the scrape. Her hands were wet on the wheel.

She pulled her rover radio from the charger under the dash.

"Dispatch, Kealoha, badge 1068. I received a call that two men were following my ten-year-old son home from school. Is there a patrol unit in the area?"

"Detective, we have a unit en route. ETA two minutes."

She dropped the radio onto the seat and focused on the road. The streets blurred, but the memory was sharp. A week ago, she'd told Kai he was safe, that the spiral was a threat to people who played in the shadows. But now she pictured the blue house at the end of their block, Kai on the steps, two men watching from down the street, their faces blank, hungry for whatever made the city bleed.

She made the turn onto her own street, tires squealing, and saw the patrol unit parked in front. Kai stood in the doorway, talking with the patrol officer, a grizzled veteran, who she knew would pay attention to whatever Kai said. He was pale but unhurt, a glass of water in one hand and his phone in the other. Her mother hovered in the entryway, moumouu trailing, one arm around Kai's shoulders.

There were no signs of the men. Leilani left the car in the street, not bothering with the brake, and sprinted up the steps.

Kai's face twisted with relief and embarrassment as she hugged him so tight he dropped the water. "Mom, I'm fine! Grandma made me tea."

"Tell me what happened," she said, still breathless.

Kai talked, words tumbling over each other. "I saw them after school at the old gas station. They followed, but never came close. When I got to the church, I ducked them, but they were waiting down our street. I think they wanted me to see them."

Leilani was already cataloguing. "Did they say anything? Try to stop you?"

"No," said Kai. "All they did was watch."

Leilani pulled the officer aside. "Anything since you arrived?"

"No," said the officer. "Kai gave me a good description of the men, so I'm gonna cruise the neighborhood and see if I can find anything. I'll let you know what I find."

She grabbed him on the upper arm. "Thanks," she said. The officer returned to his patrol car and pulled away from the curb.

Her mother spoke next, her voice soft but fierce. "He's smart, this one. Didn't come straight home. I watched when he got to your block.

When he ran, they slowed down. As if they wanted to look harmless. But I saw their eyes."

Leilani exhaled, some of the panic bleeding out, replaced by anger. "They're sending a message."

Kai's hand shot up. "I got a photo of one! I pretended to be texting, but I got him." He pulled up the gallery, showed her a blurry image of a man in a baseball cap, mouth hard, eyes like dead coral.

"Good," she said. "Send it to me and delete it from your phone." She took a deep breath. "No more solo walks. From now on, you go straight home with a friend, or I pick you up. You hear me?"

He scowled. "That's not fair. I didn't do anything."

Her anger spiked. "You got yourself tailed by professional muscle. That's what you did."

He looked away, and she saw the old, stubborn shame in the set of his jaw. She softened. "Come here," she said. She put a hand on his head. He didn't flinch.

Naalei cleared her throat. "Let the boy talk, Leilani. He's been shaking since he walked in the door."

Kai tried again. "It's not about me. I found something the other day at school. The security company they hired has a spiral logo. Not on their badges, but on everything. Their papers, the laptops, the guard car. It's like the spiral is hiding in plain sight."

Leilani's mind raced through every case file, every offhand tip from the Bureau, every time the pattern repeated in the last four months. She was going to tell him he was imagining it. That it was nothing. But she knew better.

"Show me," she said.

Kai pulled a wrinkled flyer from his backpack and handed it over. At the bottom, in faint gray ink, was the spiral. It was tighter, more stylized, but still the same mark that had been burned onto their mailbox last summer. "They're everywhere now," he said.

Leilani had a sudden urge to call the station, to escalate, to order patrol cars for every block between here and his school. But that would make them targets in a new way. She put the flyer on the table, sat down hard, and stared at her son.

"You know what this means?" she asked.

He shrugged, trying to be casual. "It means they're scared of us. Right? Otherwise, why bother?"

Her mother made a noise, halfway between a laugh and a sob. "You see? He thinks he's invincible."

Leilani pinched the bridge of her nose. The pain was sharp, and it helped. "It means you're leaving. Tomorrow. You and Grandma are going to Maui with Uncle Kimo."

Kai's face broke, disbelief and betrayal in equal measure. "No way! You can't. What about the investigation?"

"I'll handle the investigation," she said. "You handle not dying before the eighth grade."

He argued, but the words fell apart. He looked to Naalei for backup, but the old woman simply nodded.

"It's for the best," she said, gathering Kai into a side-hug. "Your uncle will keep us busy, and we'll all sleep better."

Leilani leaned back, trying to swallow the guilt. She spotted the clock and saw it was past five, the sun still edging over the eaves. There would be hours of phone calls, logistics, paperwork. She would need to check in with the Bureau, alert Isaac, and reach out to the marshals if things got worse.

But for now, she let herself sit with her son and mother, and the tension drained from her bones. The house was quiet except for the old wall fan and Kai's heavy, sullen breathing.

She closed her eyes, long enough to imagine

a world without threats or spirals or men in the dark. The three of them, safe, baking a pie or watching dumb game shows. But when she opened her eyes, the spiral flyer was still there, and her son was already plotting to beat her at her own game.

"Go pack," she told him, but this time her voice was soft.

Kai stomped down the hallway, slamming the bedroom door for good measure.

Her mother turned to her, eyes bright and hard. "You're doing the right thing."

Leilani didn't believe it, but she nodded anyway. The worst part about being a detective was knowing how the story ended before it started. The worst part about being a mother was trying to rewrite it every day.

She looked out the window, saw the street empty, and tried to memorize the light cutting through the plumeria branches. She spotted a patrol unit cruise by. She moved to the kitchen table, opened her laptop and pulled up the schedule for the next flight between Oahu and Maui. She booked two tickets and closed her laptop. She pulled her phone and sent Kimo a text with their arrival time. She sat back and wondered what was going to happen next to ruin her day.

CHAPTER ELEVEN

David's Return

The documents and laptop recovered from Kapua's boat cracked open a world of rot that neither Isaac nor Leilani had suspected ran so deep. Every night for three straight nights, they hunched over the battered conference table at the temporary task force HQ, devouring gigabytes of files, printouts, and cross-referenced lists that sprawled across every surface, held down by cold coffee mugs and sweating cans of Diet Coke. The air in the cramped office grew thick with sweat and the sour tang of institutional disinfectant, as if the room itself wanted to be sterilized of whatever they were about to uncover.

For Isaac, it was a return to the comfort of digital trench warfare, scripts running in the background, names lighting up like warning buoys as his algorithms picked out connections between police officials, business addresses and shadowy wire transfers. Leilani, more analog, moved sticky notes and colored flags on a massive whiteboard, slowly constructing a web that at first seemed improbable, then indisputable. They pieced together the bribery chain, the laundering fronts, the shell companies used by politicians who'd smiled on TV with leis around their necks. With every new discovery, Leilani noticed an unfamiliar tightness, pride at their progress, but also fear. If the Mastermind could subvert this many powerful people, what else was he willing to do?

At the close of the third night, Isaac's eyes itched with fatigue, but a stubborn piece of the puzzle nagged at him. He scrolled through another directory of property transactions, almost on autopilot. Buried among generic holding companies and routine deeds, a single document in the Mastermind folder caught his eye. It was a recent purchase of a defunct warehouse above the old plantation flats, signed over in a hurry by an LLC in the Caymans. The place was registered under an unremarkable name, but the signature line read Roland Kapua in a hand that Isaac, by now, could recognize in his sleep.

He poured another cup of coffee, the pot now mostly sludge, and began to dig. He pulled up the county's public utility dashboard on a hunch, running queries against the warehouse's address. That's when he saw it. The place was now drawing ten times its historical power average, all of it at night. It was as though the warehouse were alive, pulsing in the darkness while the mountain slept. And yet, there were no lights visible on any satellite pass, no vehicle registrations tied to the property, and not a repair permit on file.

Isaac's pulse kicked up a notch. He flagged the site and fired off a summary to the full squad, but immediately called Leilani over to his screen. "Check this out," he said in a low voice, not waking the exhausted detectives snoring in the next cubicle over.

Leilani, running on pure adrenaline and half of a banana from six hours ago, glanced at the spreadsheet, at the map, and back at Isaac. "That's up by the old Hamakua sugar line," she said, her brow furrowing. "There's nothing out there except feral pigs and busted irrigation pipes."

"Exactly. But someone's running a ton of juice through the place. More than the whole subdivision down the hill."

She studied the energy graph, the address and the deed. "You think it's a server farm? Or what? Crypto mining?"

Isaac shook his head. "The Mastermind's not in this for Bitcoin. This is something else, like a data dump or a comms hub. Or it's a red herring.

But it seems... wrong."

Leilani stood up and paced in a tight circle, her hands on her hips. "We need eyes on it. If Mastermind is using it, we can't roll up with blues and sirens. He'll know before we get out of the car. We do this quietly."

Isaac nodded, already pulling up floor plans and historical permits to sketch the building's likely layout. "We'll need night-vision. Thermal if you can get it. And someone from the surveillance team who doesn't spook easily."

Leilani gave a half-smile, the kind that meant she was already planning two steps ahead. "I'll ping Kawika. He's got the best low-light gear on the island, and he owes me a favor."

They spent the next hour prepping, Isaac assembling a digital toolkit of secure comms and remote access exploits, Leilani methodically checking her sidearm and pulling faded outdoor gear from her locker. By midnight, the plan was set. Recon the warehouse from the tree line, sweep for cameras, and log any activity. No contact unless absolutely necessary.

The drive up the old mountain road was slow and silent, the only sound the grind of loose gravel under the battered department Explorer. Leilani cut the headlights well before they reached the turnoff and coasted the last hundred yards in darkness, pulling off behind a stand of wild guava that masked the lot from the main road. The warehouse itself was invisible from below, but as they crept up the embankment, Isaac could see the faintest pulse of blue-white light bleeding out through the cracks in the warped metal siding.

They set up the surveillance kit inside the shelter of overgrown ironwood trees, Kawika deploying a directional mic and two night-vision monoculars. After double-checking the perimeter for motion sensors, and finding none, and finding a single weather-beaten security camera pointed at the front gate, Leilani took the lead, inching closer to the building's side wall. The hum of machinery was louder now, rising and falling along with muffled voices.

At three a.m., the first movement, a shadow slipped from a side door and skirted the lot, scanning the ridge with a flashlight that never quite pointed toward the tree line. The figure was tall, broad-shouldered, and moved with the deliberate confidence of someone who was afraid of very little. Isaac zoomed in with the monocular, heart hammering as he glimpsed the face in the reflected light.

He handed the monocular to Leilani. "Is that who I think it is?" he asked.

Leilani peered through the monocular. "Fuck," she said. "That's Michael Kahananui, my former boss."

Kahananui, the former Chief of Detectives after Kapua, had disappeared with the former police chief during the shootout at police headquarters and hadn't been seen since he tried to shoot Leilani while making his escape. They had an active arrest warrant out for him.

They watched as he unlocked a battered shipping container, pulled out a heavy duffel bag, and returned inside, locking everything behind him. No one else moved, but the electrical hum grew louder, more frantic, as the night wore on.

By dawn, the blue-white pulse had faded, and the previous night's footprints were already half obscured by blown leaves. Kawika packed up the gear while Isaac and Leilani headed to the Explorer, careful to leave no trace.

In the post-stakeout haze, they reconvened at the station, debriefing their findings to the task force. The consensus was clear. Whatever was happening in that warehouse, it was Mastermind's current base of operations. Isaac thought It was too soon to storm the place, but they would keep it under twenty-four-hour watch until they had enough to justify a full-scale raid.

It was Leilani who voiced what they were all thinking. "If Mastermind's running this operation out of the mountains, he's not hiding evidence. He's building something. Or planning something. And we don't have much time to figure it out. Besides, we have a warrant for Kahananui, and we know he's on the property. That's all the probable cause we need."

The mountainside warehouse looked dead until you stood close enough to hear it breathe. The corrugated metal roof, scorched and sun-pitted, listed at the ridge like a bad haircut. Half the windows were nothing but dark rectangles, jagged glass at the bottom, and old birds' nests at the top. The rest were blotted with vines or sheets of warped plywood, curling up at the edges to reveal slivers of inside, rows of industrial racks, the suggestion of barrels, along with a gutted forklift. The whole thing hunkered in a drainage cut above the sugarcane flats, as if bracing for the next hurricane.

It was almost midnight when Leilani and the HPD tactical unit staged their arrival. The trucks drove in with lights out, crawling the final three hundred yards on gravel and pitted asphalt. Night pressed around them, thick with rain and a kind of unfinished sweetness that belonged to cane country after dark. The air had weight, sticky and sweet, like the tension before a street fight.

Leilani sat in the van, kitted out in a Kevlar vest over her T-shirt and her old jeans. The vest pinched at her bruised ribs, Kapua's last gift, and every breath reminded her that she was held together by more will than bone. She ran a fingertip down the barrel of her service pistol, checked the safety again, and forced herself to keep her hands still.

Torres, pressed into the corner beside her, looked up from his comm headset. "You good?" he asked, his voice pitched low for the small space.

She hoped to say never better, but it came out closer to "Yeah, let's do this." Her teeth ached from clenching.

On the opposite bench, two SWAT officers were rehearsing the entry, fingers flicking through imaginary door frames, breathing slow through their noses like pro athletes. One had a shotgun across his knees, taped at the grip; the other a subgun with a tiny strip of neon tape on the buttstock. In the semi-dark, they kept their eyes on her, waiting for the cue.

The driver slowed, rolling past the shredded fence line, and killed the engine. The world was so quiet it was as if the entire block of jungle was holding its breath. A wind gust slapped the side of the van and made the whole chassis shiver. Rain beaded on the windshield.

Torres keyed his mic. "Units two and three, in position?"

Static followed by a clipped reply: "Unit two, east door."

"Unit three, north, ready."

Leilani flexed her hands. The need to rub her side was overwhelming, but she didn't want to show it.

The plan they had agreed on was simple, if such things ever were. The task force had tracked spiral money and comms to this warehouse three days running, each night past midnight, always the same encrypted ping, always the same dirty route through a relay in Ka'a'awa. Whatever was inside, it was big, and it was going to move tonight or vanish for good.

Torres leaned in close, voice so soft it barely registered. "Last chance to call an audible."

Leilani looked through the van's tiny porthole at the warehouse, at the fog rolling over the cane and at the wet gleam of the steel doors. She pictured her son and mother, sleeping twenty miles away, and almost against her will, she pictured the face from the photo Isaac had shown her. The impossible one. David.

"No audibles," she said. "We end this."

The team spilled from the van in practiced silence, boots splashing in the shallow puddles, guns held tight against the body. Leilani followed the wall around the east corner, breathing hard, teeth chattering a little from adrenaline rather than cold. Torres moved point, flashlight off, counting each step by muscle memory. At the service door, they stopped, crouched low, and listened.

Inside, nothing. No generators, no laughter, and no buzz of a guard shift. If there was anyone on the other side, they were playing statue.

Leilani nodded once. Torres gave the hand signal, and the first SWAT officer hit the door with a charge so tight the hinges popped clean, slamming it inward with a hard metallic shriek. The second was already in, covering right, followed by Leilani, who rolled in low, gun up.

The smell was the first shock, a mix of bleach, old sweat and something vaguely sweet, like spilled soda fermenting on hot metal. The first room was a cage of mesh and wire, crates stacked to shoulder height, every surface dusted with a powdery gray film. Past the cages, an aisle ran fifty feet to a set of inner doors, thick plywood over ancient security glass.

She edged around the cages, checking each corner. There were three doors out of this section, all painted the same sickly yellow, all closed. She could hear the north team banging two rooms over, shouts followed by the scatter of something heavy falling.

Torres held at the inner door and shot her a look. "Ready?"

She swallowed, nodded, and braced herself against the frame. At three, Torres kicked the door. A split second later, the world exploded in noise.

Flashbangs, three of them, exploded in a chain, flooding the next room in migraine white and a sound like the ocean ripping in half. Shouts, staccato and high-pitched, cut through the thunder. She blinked and forced herself through the haze.

The main warehouse floor was four times the size of the lobby, lined with more racks and scattered with boxes, half unpacked computers, and a wall of monitors still running a flicker of digital readouts. There were at least six people scrambling for cover, some in cargo shorts and threadbare shirts, others in the dress uniform of local security. One had a pistol; the others grabbed for pipes or chunks of rebar, the way you'd grab for a lifeline before a flood.

She picked the one with the gun and dropped him with two shots to the vest. He folded, yelling but not out. To her right, Torres moved smoothly, covering the far side of the floor, his gun already barking in measured rhythm.

A woman in sweats screamed, ducked behind an upended file cabinet, and crawled for the next row. Two men in Hawaiian shirts, one ripped across the belly, the other with a sock cap pulled low, rushed Torres and hit the ground hard, but not before getting a wild punch in that rocked him back.

The air was choked with gunpowder and the bitter reek of chemical smoke. Someone turned on the alarm, an old burglar system, shrieking and warbling, but underneath it all, she heard the faint, electronic whine of a server farm kicking on. It was almost comical, if you didn't think too much about how many bullets were flying. Then the real shooting started.

From the catwalk above, two men in black rain slickers opened up with automatics, spraying the floor with a fan of red tracer. Leilani dove behind a crate, rolled, and came up behind a stack of printers. One round punched through, splitting her left sleeve and grazing her bicep. She hardly noticed it, the pain buried under all the other old hurts.

Torres yelled, "Top deck!" and fired back, emptying half a mag in three seconds. The first shooter spun, and sailed over the rail in a flail of arms and legs, landing on a pile of canvas tarps. The second ducked back, reloading, and tried to make the bridge across the next catwalk.

Leilani chased him, weaving between the racks, knees burning as she took the stairs two at a time. Her lungs ached. She'd lost her backup team somewhere behind the commotion, and it was only her, the pounding echo of boots, and the blur of a man scrambling for an exit.

She caught him as he reached for the fire door. He swung the rifle at her, but too slow, she slapped it down, punched him hard in the temple, and drove his face into the mesh fencing. His body slumped, but the fire door kept swinging open, and beyond it was a hallway thick with whiteboards, charts and the blue shimmer of LCDs.

She stopped. The pain in her side was so sharp she almost dropped to her knees. But the sight ahead cleared her mind. A wall covered with maps of Honolulu, each marked with small red spirals; printouts of armored car schedules; clippings from every major theft in the last year, each highlighted and annotated in a tidy, almost beautiful hand. There were files labeled with the names of local businesses and a table stacked with gold and bone and delicate shells, arranged with more care than the rest of the warehouse combined.

Cultural artifacts. Leilani stepped forward, unable to stop herself. There were wooden ki'i figures, hundreds of years old, wrapped in fresh ti leaves. A shark-tooth club, chipped and blackened with age, resting atop a coil of antique kapa cloth. A row of stone adzes, each tagged with a museum number. The objects radiated a quiet power that dwarfed the violence outside.

Next to the table, a computer bank ran its silent blue glow over a stack of ledgers and thumb drives. She caught the top page. Transfers to foundations in Samoa, grants to nonprofit orgs in Maui, bank movements as recent as last week. She recognized the handwriting. David's. She'd know it anywhere. Her jaw tightened until she felt a sharp pop in the bone.

She turned back toward the hallway, gun up, and there, at the far end, was the silhouette of a man. Not any man. David.

He stood still, as if by standing still he could turn invisible. His hair was longer than in the photos, but the posture was exactly as she remembered. Head tilted, left shoulder slightly forward, hands loose at his sides as if ready for either a fight or a dance. The shirt he wore was a bright Aloha number, blue and white, torn at the sleeve. On his bicep, clear as day, was the spearhead tattoo.

For a full second, the world collapsed to the two of them. The gun in her hand seemed like it belonged to someone else.

"David?" she said, her own voice strange in her ears.

He didn't answer. Instead, he took one slow step towards her, eyes never leaving hers. The shock that passed through his face was brief, a flicker of guilt, a shadow of pain. Like that, it was gone, replaced by a familiar calm, the kind he always wore before he did something reckless.

"You shouldn't be here," he said, almost in a whisper.

She felt her mouth go dry. "You're alive. All this time—"

He cut her off, not with words but with the look in his eyes. There was no welcome there, but a hardness she had never seen before.

Behind her, a fresh gunfight erupted on the warehouse floor. Shouts and a chorus of suppressed weapons, the thud of boots coming closer. David's eyes flicked once to the melee, then back to her.

"I'm sorry," he said, and that was measured, clinical, like a physician breaking bad news. He raised a black pistol and aimed it at her.

She leveled the gun at him, hands steady for once. "Don't move."

He did not.

"You're under arrest. Drop the gun," she said, the words feeling hollow.

He almost smiled, but it was gone as quickly as it came. He raised his hands, palms open, a gesture of surrender that was also, she realized, a dare.

"Do it," he said. "Finish it."

She stared at him, at the line of the tattoo, the angle of his jaw. For a heartbeat, she couldn't breathe.

He said, "You look tired, Lani."

He lowered the pistol and set it on the rail next to him.

The urge to scream was strong, to close the gap and throttle him, to do anything but stand there with her ribs screaming and her brain refusing to believe. Instead, she drew a deep, shaking breath, and said, "On your knees."

He hesitated and, giving in to gravity, he lowered himself to one knee, hands still up.

Down below, the fight was ending. The warehouse filled with the thunder of HPD boots and shouted orders, the language of men and women who had trained a lifetime for this single ugly hour. Leilani kept the gun on David and listened to the approach of her own personal storm.

"Don't move," she said again.

The night outside raged, but in the warehouse, time stood perfectly still.

The warehouse bled sound, footsteps, boots slapping the metal stairs, and a volley of distant shouts as the last pockets of resistance got swept up in the main floor sweep. But up here, in the dead blue glow of the server corridor, everything was blood and breath and the high-tension cable stretched between Leilani and David.

"On your knees," she repeated. She advanced; the pistol locked in both hands. Her ribs felt like they were splinting with each inhale, but she ignored it, focused on the slow motion scan of David's face for any hint of the old him, any sign that this was a nightmare, or a trick, or something other than the obvious.

He kneeled, hands up, and his palms turned out. He didn't flinch when she clicked off the safety. "I expected more SWAT," he said, as if it was a conversation between traffic stops.

"They're busy," she said. She stopped at ten feet, shifting her weight in a cop stance, shoulders back, core braced for anything. "You're under arrest. Don't move."

He smiled, the old offhand one, and she nearly lost her nerve. "Arrest me for what? Being a better fundraiser than you?"

She gritted her teeth. "Conspiracy. Murder. Armed robbery. Laundering money through my mother's—"

He laughed, low and sad. "If you think your

mother didn't know, you're dumber than they say."

She was tempted to break his nose with the butt of her gun for saying it, but she made herself hold still. She kept the barrel leveled at his forehead.

From the catwalk below, a fresh burst of gunfire rattled the metal. David used the noise to shift subtly, knees angling for leverage.

She saw it coming, but not in time. He was up and at her before she could step back. Her husband's body, muscle memory, and leverage and the old snap of bone on bone as he slammed her wrist into the rail. The gun skittered off the catwalk and clattered two stories down. Her hands were numb, a shockwave up to her shoulder, but she countered with a knee to his thigh, and a low uppercut that would've taken a regular man's chin off.

He dodged, grabbed the collar of her vest, and spun her into the wall. They were pressed together, chest to chest, and she could smell the sweat and fabric softener and salt of him, the mix that once meant home. Now it was a pure threat.

They broke, danced a half step before locking up again. She aimed for the eyes with her thumb, but he had her wrist and twisted. He was stronger than she remembered. It could have been the years, or the extra fifteen pounds of fanaticism. She gritted her teeth, bit his forearm hard enough to taste the skin tear, and he cursed and let go.

She staggered, caught herself on the steel column, and spat out blood.

"I don't want to hurt you, Lani," he said, hands open now, as if they'd been sparring at the Y, all those years ago.

"Stop running," she snapped. "Stop hiding behind your bullshit."

A thump behind her, a body rolling down the stairs, followed by a crash and more boots. She glanced for an instant, and David was on her, forearm to her throat, pinning her against the column. The pain in her ribs ignited. She clawed for his eyes, gouged, but he bled and took it.

"Let go," he said. "You don't understand."

"You killed people," she spat. "You committed more crimes than I can count. Tell me what I don't understand," she yelled.

He pressed harder. Her head filled with static, her vision narrowing to a single thread of color. "I'm trying to save this place," he said. "Everything you love, they're tearing it apart, piece by piece, until there's nothing left but condos and golf courses."

He let up. She pulled in half a breath.

"You're a murderer," she whispered.

He shook his head. "You're still playing by rules they wrote for you. I broke the rules so there'd be something left for our son."

She saw it on his face. He meant it. The clarity of his conviction was worse than hate, worse than madness.

She feinted left, twisted, and drove her forehead into his nose. He grunted, stunned, and she pulled free, whipped a baton from her vest and swung for his kneecap. He blocked, but not all the way. She heard the pop of cartilage, and his leg spasmed.

They circled, both panting. In the silence, she realized the fight on the warehouse floor was nearly over, with one set of footsteps still running, closer now.

David grinned and wiped a sleeve across his bleeding mouth. "You're the one person I ever respected," he said.

"Bullshit," she said, but her voice was weaker than she wanted.

David did something that broke her concentration. He reached into his pocket slowly, deliberately, and pulled out a thin obsidian blade, one of the old types, the kind that broke easily but cut anything. He ran it across his palm, a neat line of red, then made a motion with his hand, an old hula sign for protection, or at least that's what her mother used to say.

He held it up, bleeding, and smiled again. "For our family," he said.

She hesitated for half a second, but it was enough. He lunged, caught her bad wrist again, and in the same motion jammed the blade into the vest at her ribs. The armor took most of it, but the tip sliced under the seam. White fire spread through her side.

She screamed, elbowed him in the mouth, and with both hands, shoved him down the stairs. He tumbled, hit every tread, and landed in a pile, sprawled and bleeding.

She staggered to the railing, blinking through tears. "Stay down," she yelled. "It's over."

But it wasn't. David rolled, braced himself on the wall, and, dragging the bad leg, limped toward the artifacts table. She saw what he was after, a satchel by the base, stuffed with ledgers and, probably, a handful of the real treasures.

She half ran, half crawled down the steps. The pain in her side was a black hole, but she could still see, could still move.

He grabbed the satchel, turned, and pointed the knife at her. "You don't have to chase me, Lani. You could let it go."

She picked up a broken steel bar from the stair

landing. "Not my style."

He grinned, teeth red, and said, "That's why I loved you."

She hated him for saying it, but mostly she needed to survive.

They closed the distance. He swung fast, but she caught his arm with the bar, trapping it at the wrist, then kicked his bad leg out. He fell, the knife spinning free. She hit him once, twice, three times, across the back and shoulder, until he stopped struggling. She rolled him over, got her knee in his sternum, and fished a set of flex cuffs from her belt.

He stared up at her, pupils wide, face gone slack and old. "I hope you never figure out what this really means," he said, and his voice was soft again, almost kind. "It'll ruin you."

She got his hands behind his back and cinched the cuffs so tight they bit the skin. "Shut up," she said, but it came out a whisper.

She looked around. The warehouse floor was settling, officers collecting the wounded, paramedics darting between bodies. Torres limped toward her, one arm hanging loose, face smeared with blood.

"You got him?" he called, voice breaking.

She nodded, still straddling David. She couldn't feel her legs.

Torres reached her, then kneeled down, out of breath. "I'll call it in. You did it, Lei."

But she wasn't sure. She wasn't sure of anything, except that her husband was alive, and so was she, and nothing would ever be that simple again.

She stood, fighting for balance. Her side gushed heat and wet, but she let it bleed. She forced her body upright and stared at David, who lay perfectly still, eyes closed, lips turned in a ghost of a smile.

In the distance, she heard sirens. Not the urgent kind, but the weary, post-action kind that signaled an end, or at least an intermission.

She braced a hand on the stair rail, took a shaky breath, and looked down at her own hands. They trembled, not with adrenaline, but with something closer to grief. She retrieved her pistol and holstered it.

"Take him," she said to Torres. She didn't watch as they hauled David upright, didn't look at the faces of the SWAT officers or the medics as they passed. She stared instead at the artifacts table, at the careful way everything was arranged. In the middle, a simple wooden figure, nothing rare, nothing valuable except to those who remembered.

She reached out, touched it, and the world stilled again. The pain caught up, and the world resumed its spin.

Leilani stepped out of the corridor, into the riot of lights and bodies and noise, and knew that the spiral hadn't ended tonight. Not by half. But she felt the true shape, sharp, ancient, and capable of turning anyone in its path to dust.

She wiped her cheek, streaked with her own blood and tears, and limped to the exit. The storm outside had passed, leaving the hard blue glare of the morning to come.

Leilani made it three paces into the loading bay before the world detonated. Smoke grenade, fat canister, shrapnel-dinged, rolling under the row of steel carts where the paramedics had triaged the wounded. The hiss was instant, and suddenly everything was thick white cotton, air searing her nose and lungs. Her eyes watered so hard she couldn't see, couldn't breathe. She clawed at her vest for the gas mask she hadn't remembered to bring. Someone shouted, "Get down!" but it was already too late. The smoke bellowed up, thicker than midnight, and behind it she heard the clatter of a metal grate and the sudden echo of boots on concrete below.

She ducked low, hands over her head, but the flashbang came anyway, second canister, this one yellow-striped and rigged for noise not light. It rolled to her feet, bounced once, and blasted out a pressure wave so brutal it slapped her eardrums into silence. All around her, the warehouse split into chaos. Cops and suspects both scattered, tripping over bodies, the noise compressing every thought into a single hard line.

She blinked, and the next thing she saw was the shape of Torres, hunched over the wounded, eyes wild in the fog. "He's gone!" he yelled, though his voice sounded tinny, distant, as if through a TV behind a wall.

She spat out a mouthful of blood and forced her knees to move. The old pain in her ribs flared, and blood soaked her shirt from the knife prick. The pain was almost pleasant compared to the burn in her eyes and throat. She blinked again, and the world reassembled, smoke rolling in lazy, predatory sheets, the floor scattered with brass, a dozen blue and yellow jackets crawling over the fallen. In the swirl, a single spot of darker shadow, moving away, towards the back stairs, or the elevator, or nowhere at all.

She charged, boots hammering, ignored the twist in her ankle and the dizzy edge of hyperventilation. She reached the base of the stairs as the trapdoor slammed shut, the ring of steel on steel echoing up the risers.

She screamed, "He's under!"—no other words, no need.

Torres fumbled for his radio. "All units,

suspect has gone below, repeat, below! We need perimeter north and west! Leilani, wait for backup, I repeat." But she was already gone, slamming down the service ladder two rungs at a time, pulse so loud she couldn't hear the rest.

Below the warehouse was a subbasement, colder than outside, with wet air thick with oil and mold. The concrete was old, and lit by a single line of naked bulbs bolted to the ceiling. She barreled down the corridor, ricocheting off the cinderblock as she ran. Each breath hurt, but she kept the pace, tunnel vision narrowing to a simple goal. Forward, always.

The hallway bent left, then right, then dropped in a sharp slope. There were boot prints, faint but visible, David's, unless someone else wore size twelve hiking boots and dragged one leg like a sandbag. The prints smeared as she ran, fading into the next patch of shadow. Ahead, another burst of smoke, this time with the sharper tang of burning insulation and copper. Someone had shorted the lighting; bulbs popped in sequence as she got close, plunging the tunnel into darkness.

She flicked her flashlight, but the lens was already fogged from the upstairs blast. She wiped it on her pants, which smeared the grease. It didn't matter; she had seen enough to find the next door, a fire exit with a battered panic bar, wedged open with a crowbar.

She slammed into it and burst out into the open air.

The night was a hurricane. Rain ripped sideways, hitting so hard it left welts on exposed skin. The warehouse was set halfway up a hill, but the door led out to a steep cement ramp, overgrown with crabgrass and slick with moss. She slid down, lost her balance, hit the asphalt hard enough to crack her left kneecap, but used the momentum to roll up and run again.

The drainage ditch overflowed, water gushing so high it almost hid the next set of boot prints. She saw them anyway, heading west, into the black line of pine and ironwood trees that rimmed the property. The floodwater was up to her shins, then knees, icy cold in the heat of summer, but she waded through, teeth clenched, hand still clutching the useless flashlight like a club.

Above the roar of water, she heard him, first a cough, and a single word, "stop" or "go," impossible to tell.

She pressed harder, ignored the acid fire in her lungs, and broke free of the ditch. The ground changed here, no more cement. It was dirt and trash and the endless tangle of undergrowth. Her boots sank to the ankle, then to the shin. Each step was a fight, but she kept moving.

A shape darted ahead, tall, limping, both

hands out to clear the way. David. There was no question. His movement was burned into her bones, the cadence of his steps, the fraction of a second he paused on each foot. He was heading for the tree line, and beyond, the old aqueduct that ran parallel to the mountain road. She remembered the layout from a thousand Sunday hikes, back before the world shifted sideways.

"David!" she shouted, voice ripped to shreds by wind and rain.

He didn't look back.

The storm intensified, with rain coming so hard it was almost a wall. Her shirt clung to her skin, the Kevlar vest growing heavier with every step. She could barely see, even with the flashlight now cleaned on the inside of her arm. But she kept it pointed straight ahead, steady as a sniper rifle.

Every fifty yards, the terrain changed. First mud, gravel and the brittle crunch of fallen pine needles. The ground angled up, and every time she hit a patch of flat, she doubled the pace, gaining a little with every stride.

The trees closed in, and the air grew still. The canopy was so thick the rain sounded like static on a dead radio. She switched off the flashlight, relying on memory and the thin blue haze of lightning that filtered through the branches.

There, a break in the trunks, enough to show

another flash of movement. David, or what was left of him, hauling ass into the darkest patch of woods.

She followed, slower now. The ground was treacherous, slick with wet leaves and invisible roots. More than once she went down hard, hands and knees both cut open on sharp stone. She didn't stop to check the damage; the pain that mattered was the one that kept her moving.

It must have been fifteen minutes before the woods opened onto a small clearing. The aqueduct was a concrete trough big enough for two people to walk side by side, dry in summer but now raging with runoff. A rusted ladder climbed down into the spillway. There were fresh marks on the rails, slippery with blood.

She gripped the top rung, tested the ladder, and slid down, her boots skidding on the slime. The aqueduct was loud, so loud she couldn't hear herself breathe. She shone the light down the channel, and for one instant, caught him, a pale blur in the current, struggling for the far side.

She jumped in.

The water nearly knocked her over, but she steadied herself against the wall and waded as fast as she could. She saw him ahead, half submerged, gripping the far bank with both hands. He pulled up, body falling over the lip, and vanished into the brush.

She scrambled after, clawing up the mossy cement and onto a patch of grass so green it looked fake in the lightning. The sky above was alive, white sheets of energy flickering so fast it hurt to look. She scanned the horizon, blinking away the afterimages.

There he was. On the next ridge, silhouetted against the wild, electric sky. From here, she noticed the blood running down his calf, a line of red on the gray of his jeans. He turned to look at her. The distance made his features unreadable, but he stood, defiant.

She yelled, "I'll find you!" but the wind carried it away.

He disappeared over the crest, into the thick darkness beyond.

She hesitated, but this time it wasn't out of pain or fear. This time it was because she knew, as sure as her own heartbeat, that if she followed, she would either finish the job or be finished by it.

The rain came harder, if that was possible. She wiped her face, smeared with mud and blood and who knows what else, and started the climb.

The ground was worse here, slick with new runoff, each step a battle for traction. Her muscles trembled, the old wounds in her side and shoulder burning like fresh ones. She lost count of how many times she slipped, fell, and got up again.

On top of the ridge, the world grew silent, as if the storm had drained all the sound from the air. She shone the flashlight out. Nothing. No movement, no sign.

She crouched and listened. Under the drip of rain, under the hiss of wind, there was something else. The steady, rhythmic crunch of footsteps on gravel, farther up, deeper into the mountain. He wasn't running anymore, walking deliberately, pacing himself for the long haul.

She holstered the flashlight, looked at the city lights below, and set off after him. No backup, no radio, nothing but her own stubborn refusal to stop. The mountain was waiting. And somewhere ahead, so was David. She pressed forward, boots sinking into mud, rain washing the blood from her hands, each step a promise that this time, she wouldn't let him go.

CHAPTER TWELVE

Mountain Chase

The first thing to go numb was her right hand. Leilani noticed it when she reached out, parted a curtain of wild guava, and her fingers failed to register the usual knife-edges of leaf and thorn. They made a noise, though, a faint wet snap, not unlike the noise a rib makes when it gives, and that brought all the feeling back in a rush. The ache in her side, the slice along her left bicep, the fire at her kneecap that had started as a sharp ping and now bludgeoned her with every step. She stood there, one leg planted, hands fisted in the dark, and let her jaw hang open to catch a drag of wet air. The world tasted of iron, bark and the green electricity that preceded a real Hawaiian squall. She kept moving. There was no other option.

The mountain rose above her in stacked bands of color, blue to black to a yellow-brown visible on the highest ridge where the trees surrendered to naked stone. The path, if it could be called that, was little more than a suggestion, traced by the violence of old storms and the occasional pig hunter. Still, there was a logic to the wildness. Every ten meters, the ferns reset, the dead branches pointed toward the city as if haunted by their own gravity. The mud kept the memory, every slide and furrow an echo of something that had passed this way before.

She looked for the clues. Here, the ragged arc of a boot, deeper at the toe, dragging at the heel. There, a blunt divot in the moss, nothing at all unless you knew the difference between a falling nut and a man's size twelve boot coming down hard. David, always a touch heavier on his left. He used to joke about it, said his bones had a GPS, that he could cross Oahu blindfolded if you spun him in the right direction.

She pressed a palm to her ribs. The pain was real but not dangerous, she guessed; the vest had taken the worst of the blade, and adrenaline did the rest. The rain made the wound feel alive, and for that she was grateful. Dead nerves made mistakes.

A wind battered the canopy, loosing a patter of rain that, in a blink, became a torrent. The green tunnel ahead shivered, turning gray. She ducked her head and scrambled forward, the sudden downpour stinging her raw. Her boots squelched, slid, and found a grip on black roots woven tighter than anything in the city.

The higher she moved, the colder the world grew. It was a Hawaiian joke; cold on Oahu meant seventy, but not enough for a jacket. But here the mist condensed and clung to her skin, crawling down her neck, soaking the waistband of her jeans until she felt clammy and small. She continued to move, always up, always towards the pulse of a man ahead whose logic she understood better than any living cop. Each time she checked her six, she saw the rolling wall of clouds, and the bright bruise of her own flashlight painting the world in dull blue arcs.

Time ran out, lost all meaning. She tripped once, hard, on a buried root, and dropped to a knee in the thick mess of earth and rotted leaves. The jolt lanced through her ribs, and for an instant she nearly blacked out. She bit down on her tongue, tasted blood, and rode the spike until her vision came back. Then she noticed the print in the mud. Deep, fresh, the sole uneven on the outside, the tread worn smooth at the toe. David had been here less than a minute before.

She levered herself upright, exhaled a single curse, and limped forward. She made herself slow at the next fork; ears tuned for any sound but her own wild pulse. It was there, a faint rustle, a deliberate silence in the canopy above. He was close.

The path bent right, sharper than any trail should, and here the earth had dropped away entirely, eaten out by old runoff and a summer's worth of storms. She could have gone around, could have risked the gully and the sharp rocks below, but the quickest way was up and over. The face of the ridge was a mere ten feet, a mix of moss and slick red mud, the terrain that was made for losing shoes and skin. For half a second she considered the odds, dug her boots into the base and started up.

The world inverted. Her hands, blood-slick, found holds in the roots and kept her from pitching backward. Every muscle in her core screamed as she levered up, foot over foot, half climbing, half praying that the next grip would hold. She reached the top and flopped onto the new plane, breathing hard, cheek pressed to the carpet of needles. She let herself believe she was alone. The clouds parted, and in that white slot of mist she saw him.

Fifty meters ahead, silhouetted by the last blue of the city lights below. He was limping hard, his left leg dragging like a dead weight, but his hands were steady and he held himself upright, head scanning for every threat. He might have heard her, or it was the animal sixth sense that said he was being followed. His face turned fast, and he was gone again as he ducked behind the knot of ironwood.

Leilani's heart hammered against her ribs. She wanted to call out, to demand he stop, that this end now, before the world got any darker. She thought of her son, of every old promise that said she'd keep him safe. And she thought of the way David used to tuck Kai in, one arm a cradle, the other holding a paperback like a shield.

She forced herself up and into motion, following the break in the trees. The world narrowed to that one patch of ground ahead, each step a negotiation with her own pain. The ridge turned muddy again, the earth loose underfoot, but the prints stayed clear, proof that he was still ahead.

Another turn, and now the trail was gone. Raw lava rock polished to a shine by decades of wind and water. The path pitched toward the sky, a sixty-degree hell that dared you to fall. She found the old seams; the holds left by the ancient flows and climbed.

Halfway up, a stone gave out. She slipped, clawed for the next, nails tearing, and her body dangled above the drop. Below, the city lit the low clouds gold and orange, a reminder of all that would vanish if she let go now. She dug in, teeth bared, and made the next grip. Her side shrieked in protest, but her hands did not fail.

The world opened to a knife-edge of ridge, not two feet wide, wind lashing from both sides. She crawled, knees bleeding, and when she dragged herself to the highest rock she saw his silhouette, clear as sunrise, standing not fifteen meters away.

David, hands at his sides, head tilted. Through the rain, she could see the shine of water on his face, could read the intention in the set of his jaw.

She rose to her feet. "David!" she yelled, the sound lost almost instantly to the wind.

He flinched, a birdlike motion but did not turn. He stepped to the very edge of the ridge, one hand balancing in the thin air. Behind him, the world fell away into a tangle of clouds and mist, nothing but the promise of a long, clean drop.

"This doesn't have to end like this!" she tried again, but the answer was the thunder, closer now, rattling the very stone beneath her feet.

He turned and met her eyes across the void. The storm broke for real, and the rain came down like judgment.

She didn't blink. She took one step, her boots sliding on the wet rock, ribs screaming with every inhale. The gap between them closed, but never fast enough.

When she reached the last patch of ridge, she found it empty. The mist was curling and rising, and the evidence of a man's footprints vanishing over the far side, towards a line of boulders only locals would know. She steadied herself, wiped her mouth with her shaking hand, and started after him again, the trail now a memory and a promise, and her own voice drowned by the storm.

The storm was no longer a presence above; it was an organism, alive and starving, gnawing at the ridgeline with wind and rain and the occasional hammer blow of lightning that bleached the forest to the bone. Leilani should have been afraid of exposure, of a night spent frozen to the marrow or dashed against the rocks by a stray gust. Instead, she thought of the flicker ahead, the memory of a man weaving through the bamboo and never quite letting her close the gap.

She hit the ridgeline and nearly fell over, boots skidding on a slab of moss-glazed basalt. For a heartbeat, her world tilted. Rain slick rock. Void to her right, roots clawing the void to her left. Her arms pinwheeled, the useless one half contributing, and the momentum pitched her forward. She was flying, her stomach gone, the taste of adrenaline spiking like gun oil on her tongue. Her left foot caught on an exposed ohia root, and everything snapped back, bone against wood, a fresh jab of pain up her side as she slammed into the mud.

She lay there, face mashed against wet leaves, blinking as the storm shook the trees. From this close, the forest was all detailed. The bristled cilia of moss, the way each raindrop ricocheted off the waxy leaves, the black rivers of mud carving through the underlayer. She dragged in a breath, found her air shredded by the ache in her ribs, and let out a low, animal groan. Using the root as leverage, she hauled herself upright, palms scored and muddy.

She didn't have time to check for breaks. Every second lost here was another fifty feet for David. Up ahead, the path was barely a shelf, a bad joke, a thread along the ravine that must have gone a hundred feet down, the bottom concealed by a pulsing bank of fog. The trail was a slurry now, mud with the consistency of spoiled poi, and her boots gave little warning before each slip. She focused on the micro, the next step, the way her body shifted and held, the small wins of not falling. Each step bled more heat from her, but she kept the line.

Halfway across the shelf, the rain became blinding. Wind drove the drops sideways, raking her cheeks and ears, turning her vision to static. She ducked her head, pressed low to the slope, and when the wind slackened, she looked up to see him again.

This time, David was close. The mountain magnified sound; she could hear the slide of his boots, the thump as he pounded through the softer patches, and once, the hoarse, involuntary bark of pain as his bad leg betrayed him. He was using a stick snapped from the wild guava, and he jammed it into the ground with every second step, a rhythm so familiar she could have called the beat from memory.

The sight froze her, not from fear but from the way it cracked open a piece of the past. She was nineteen again, on this same ridge, except the world was green and gold and the water was the sweat on her brow. David had dragged her here, claiming it was the best path for learning the island on foot. "Don't be afraid of the edge, Lani," he'd said, laughing as she crept along the ledge. "The wind's not trying to kill you. It's trying to make you honest." He'd held her hand, and when she slipped, he caught her by the backpack and spun her, laughing, before setting her safe again on the path. It was a stupid, corny memory, and it came back now so bright it burned.

She watched him hobble ahead, and the contrast made her want to vomit. The ridge bent left and then up, steeper than before. She clung to the rock, nails black with dirt, and powered through the old hurt. Above, the trees thickened, and she could smell the shift as she entered a new belt, ohias this time, their flowers gone but their branches dense and low, perfect for concealment. She ducked under a limb, nearly caught her scalp on a hook of bark, and forced her way into the tunnel.

Inside, the rain quieted, but the wind became

a moan, vibrating every trunk in a chorus of sound. Light was a suggestion; mostly, it was shadow, broken by the phosphor of her own breath and the steady blue of the city below. Here, the earth held. Her boots found better purchase, and she sped up.

As she picked up speed, she could hear him. Not the noise of movement, but the grunted curses, the muttered expletives that always came when David was up against it. She felt a laugh bubble, but it came out raw, almost a sob. She swallowed it down and focused on the chase.

She burst through the last thicket of trees and onto a small shelf, barely the size of a parking spot. Here the wind had carved a space, and the rain battered it from three directions. In the clearing stood David, leaning on his stick, breathing hard, face turned toward her with a look that was impossible to parse.

She saw his face clearly now. Older, skin weathered by too many years outside, eyes so bloodshot it looked like he hadn't slept in a month. The beard partially concealed the scars, and she wondered when he'd gotten those. His mouth was twisted in that familiar half-smile, the one he used when the joke was how bad things had gotten.

They stood that way, the two of them, the storm flattening their hair to their skulls, every inch of them soaked through. The world shrank to this spot, this impossible place where the past and future met, neither sure which side would win. She thought he might say something. Instead, he nodded. A single, tired tilt of the head. He turned and limped toward the wall of rock at the far side of the shelf.

She knew this shortcut. A narrow gap between two boulders, half concealed by ferns, a fissure that led up and around to the old communications tower on the summit. It was the local way to shave twenty minutes off the climb, if you didn't mind spiders and the chance of breaking an ankle. She watched him disappear into the fissure. She bent double, hands on her knees, and sucked air through her teeth.

Her body felt spent, muscles jittering from cold and fatigue. She waited a heartbeat before starting after him, because that was what she'd promised, and she'd be damned if she let him have the last laugh this time.

She jammed her shoulder through the wet curtain of ferns, feet scraping for purchase, and forced her way into the dark. The wind and rain howled at her back, but the thing that mattered was the ghost ahead, and that she could bring him back alive.

Inside the boulder fissure, the world shrank to a crawlspace of rock and fog, no wider than

Leilani's own shoulders. The walls pressed in, slick and cold, and the air reeked of wet lichen and ozone from the static overhead. The light was the bright flicker of distant lightning, which painted the passage in flashes of negative, before plunging it back to a darkness so perfect she felt blindfolded.

She should have crept forward. Instead, she forced the pace, knuckles scraping on the stone, toes slipping for traction with every step. Up ahead, the path doglegged right, narrowed more, but the blood trail, now a real thing, fresh on the wall, meant David was still beyond the next turn. She ignored the spike of hope that meant; hope was a luxury for when you had a plan.

Her radio was useless, drowned out by the squall and the thousand feet of mountain overhead. Her phone was smashed somewhere in the mud below. All she had was the Sig, and the memory of every case that said cornered suspects made the worst kind of company.

At the end of the squeeze, the world opened in a hard-edged surprise, a ledge four feet wide, slick with moss, and pitched at a lunatic angle above the bowl of a raging waterfall. The drop was obscene, a sheer two hundred feet to the rocks below, all of it running wild with the runoff that now foamed and churned like a living thing. The rain came sideways. The wind howling up from the void to slap her face and freeze her in place.

David was halfway across the ledge. The stick was gone; now he used both hands, palms flat to the rock, inching sideways in a crab-walk that would have looked ridiculous on any other human. For him, it was the only way forward. He glanced back, saw her, and his face registered something like fear.

He shouted something, a word or a fragment, but the wind shredded it before it reached her. He pressed on, and Leilani followed, every sense stretched to the breaking point.

She hugged the wall, boots angled out, and started across. Each footfall was a negotiation, a test of mud and friction, her bad side begging for relief at every shift of weight. She refused to look down.

A bolt of lightning hit somewhere above, so bright it made her teeth buzz. In the afterglow, she saw David jerk, almost lose the line, steadying himself with a bare hand on the rim of rock above. Blood smeared down from his wrist, made a ribbon that the rain diluted and erased. He was close now, less than ten meters, the two of them alone on the spine of the world.

The ledge betrayed her. A fist-sized chunk gave under her right boot, the stone shearing away with a soft, almost forgiving sigh. Suddenly there was nothing beneath her, and she dropped, hip smashing into the wall, both arms scrambling for a hold.

She caught a knob of lava rock with her left hand. The force wrenched her shoulder, made her scream. The world tilted. Her toes dangled in space, boots skating uselessly for purchase. Every muscle spasmed, and she felt the old break in her side go from background ache to white-hot siren.

Above, David turned, staring back. Their eyes met, and in that infinite tick of time, she could have sworn she saw him consider coming back for her. He didn't.

She gritted her teeth, used every ounce of leverage, and heaved up, forearm scraping the rock until her skin burned. Inch by inch, she clawed towards the ledge, rolled flat, gasping, her heart hammering in her throat. The rain washed over her, cold and hard, but she barely noticed. All that mattered was the next breath, the next second not dead.

When she finally stood battered, she saw David had reached the far end. He was waiting at the culvert, the final approach to the summit, a knife-edge of dirt and roots with nothing on either side but cloud and the memory of what used to be a forest. He held himself tall, chest rising and falling, face unreadable in the storm. For a split second, he hesitated.

She forced herself upright, her hand pressed to her bleeding side, and stepped forward. The pain was now the whole of her, but she used it. Each stagger, each grind of bone on bone, reminded her what she was fighting for. She eyed him, and for once, he didn't look away.

Lightning lit the mountain, the universe gone blue and white. In that second, Leilani saw him as he once was. Young, alive, the old David who'd kissed her on this very ridge and dared her to jump the gap because she was scared. The vision snapped away, replaced by the man who stood before her, broken, cornered, older but still impossible.

She reached the far end, collapsed against the wall, and looked up. David stood thirty feet away. Nothing left ahead of him but sky.

"David," she said, voice ruined by wind and rain. "You have to stop."

He didn't answer but set his jaw and waited.

She witnessed the options play out in his eyes. The run. The jump. The surrender, if there was anything left of the man she once loved. She took another step, the mud slick under her feet, and nearly slipped again. He caught the motion, tensed, as if preparing to lunge or defend. But he didn't move. He was exhausted and losing blood.

He stood still and watched her. As if waiting to see which version of the story she'd choose.

The one where he was still worth saving, or the one where he was another body in the storm. She took another step, now a breath away.

For a heartbeat, everything stilled. The mountain, the wind, and the rain seemed to pause, the world holding its breath. The clouds above exploded in light, so loud it made her bones rattle. And just like that, the chase was over. They stood together and waited to see who would speak first.

CHAPTER THIRTEEN

Cliffside Showdown

F or a few seconds, neither spoke.

David was the first to move. He lifted his chin; the rain running in cold rivulets off his face, and with a slow, uneven shift of weight, straightened his posture. The spearhead tattoo, black and sharp, seemed to twitch with the vein beneath it. He looked older than she remembered, jaw set in the same stubborn line but gone tight with exhaustion and pain. The left leg, ruined by an old rugby injury, and then again tonight by her baton, dragged a little as he pivoted to face her, but his eyes didn't flinch, despite the wind scraping grit and water across the ledge.

Leilani planted both feet, using the bunched moss and a snarl of ferns for traction. The rocks here were slick, with the runoff pooling on every flat slab. She thumbed the safety on her Sig, leveled it at center mass, and shouted to be heard above the storm. "It's over, David! There's nowhere left to run!"

He barked a laugh, rough as gravel. "There's always somewhere," he said, but he made no move to close the distance.

A gust hit them both, flapping the edges of his torn shirt and plastering her hair in black, wet ropes to her jaw. The sky pulsed with the threat of more lightning; in the blue-white glow, his silhouette loomed impossibly close to the edge. The basalt was fractured there, a single misstep away from fifty feet of empty air.

"Don't do it," she said, softer now, almost a plea. Her voice shredded, each word forced through a throat scoured raw by cold air and adrenaline. "Don't make me pull the trigger."

She saw the David from a decade ago. The one who read her mind before she spoke, the one who never locked the front door because he trusted the universe to take care of its own.

But the moment collapsed. He gave her that smile, the one he wore when he was about to break her heart, and shifted his gaze to the rocks below. She no longer faced David, the missing husband and father, but David the master criminal.

"You don't understand what I'm trying to do," he said, voice barely audible but strong. "Everything I've done is to protect our culture, our heritage!"

A shock of lightning split the sky. For an instant, it carved him into a pure shadow, tattoo a stripe of darkness, eyes gone hollow and bright. The night fell back into its old tricks, wind and wet and the drumbeat of her own pulse in her ears.

"You're not protecting anything!" she yelled. "You're killing people, robbing, blackmailing. You turned the spiral into a weapon."

He shook his head. "It was already a weapon, Lani. I put it in the right hands for once."

She risked a step closer. Her boots skidded, but she caught herself, muscle memory and years of mountain rescues keeping her vertical. She was shaking now, not from fear, but from the animal logic that said every second this standoff lasted was a second closer to death, his or hers or both.

He grinned again, wiped the water and blood from his mouth, and let his arms go loose at his sides. "You still don't get it. The system was broken. Rigged from the start. I had to work outside it to save what matters."

"The ends don't justify shit," she spat.

He shrugged, as if the old argument was beyond him now. "What's the alternative? Trust the feds to sweep it up? Let the donors and haoles auction off what's left of us in some mainland gallery? I did this so our son wouldn't grow up to be a joke, or a number, or another fucking loss on the evening news."

The mention of Kai landed like a punch. She forced her left hand to steady, willing the gun barrel not to tremble.

"Surrender," she said. "We can fix it. Tell your side. At least face him before—" She stopped, couldn't finish the sentence.

He made a noise in his throat, half laugh, half choke. "You'd have me rot in a cell. You know what they do to guys like me?"

"I'd visit," she said, the words slipping out before she could kill them.

That finally got to him. His face flickered, something unguarded in the line of his eyes. "You'd still do that? After all this?"

A flash of the old smile. "Stubborn," he said. "You're like your mother."

"I'm my mother's daughter," she snapped.

He didn't answer. The entire world was them, the rain and the pitiless wind trying to sweep them both into the void.

She took another step, now within ten feet, the drop at her back, the barrel of the Sig still dead-on. She observed the seam of his scar above his right brow, the white against the tan, and wondered if it would still split the same way if she hit him now.

"Put your hands up, David. I'm not asking again."

He didn't move.

"I mean it," she said. Her voice flattened, cop voice, the one she used on jumpers and panicked kids. "Don't make me hurt you."

"Wouldn't be the first time," he said. The line stung more than the rain.

She scowled, eyes burning. The wind whipped a branch against her calf, nearly buckled her, but she recovered.

David's stance shifted, weight to the bad leg, left arm a hair forward, almost like he was preparing for a tackle on the rugby field. She felt the change and braced.

"I did it for you, too," he said. "You're the one who saw what mattered."

She tried to keep her face stone, but a crack ran through it, plain as day.

The next lightning bolt lit the world so brightly she lost her night vision. He must've timed it, or he knew her too well, because in the next second, he moved.

The blur of his arm, the kick of his boot, the sudden violence in a space too small for both of them. The Sig wrenched sideways, her trigger finger screaming. They grappled, and she felt the twist, the familiar flex of tendon and bone from every wrestling match they ever had in bed or out. His left hand caught her wrist hard, but her right elbow came up and split his lip wide.

He staggered, and she regained the gun, but didn't fire. Not yet.

"You can't save us," she said, breathless. "You're not a savior. You're a fugitive."

He spat a glob of blood, wiped it on his sleeve. "Better than being a ghost."

A sharp wind nearly toppled her. She dug in, heart a knotted fist, every muscle screaming for an end to this.

He lifted both hands in mock surrender. "Last chance, Lani."

She hesitated, but that was enough.

He lunged, not at her but at the side, arms wide, as if he could fly straight off the mountain and never look back. She tracked him, muscles tensed for the shot, but instead of firing she ran, boots slipping, arms outstretched, desperate to stop him from making the final leap.

She caught his arm as his foot caught on the lip. They tumbled, rolled, her ribs slamming against rock, his knee finding her thigh. They landed tangled in wet ferns, the void yawning a yard away.

He was on top, hand pressed to her chest, but this time there was no violence left. He breathed, staring down at her like he couldn't decide whether to kiss her or break her neck.

"I love you," he said, rain mixing with tears on his face.

She didn't answer. Her hands were pinned. The Sig was gone, somewhere in the mud, and now it was them, and the sky, and the storm.

Another flash lit the ledge, and in the harsh blue, she saw it, his face, ruined and beautiful, and the truth that after all of this, her love for him was gone.

They lay there, suspended in time, waiting to see who would move first.

She didn't know who shifted first. Perhaps it was him, arms trembling with restraint, or it was her, the battered instinct screaming at her to never let a threat sit so close for so long. Either way, when the storm dropped into a hiss instead of a howl, their bodies broke apart, rolling in a tangle of knees and elbows, boots churning through the mud and moss.

Leilani got one arm free, jammed a thumb toward his eye, but he batted it away with the speed of someone who'd lived this fight a dozen times in his nightmares. She twisted at the hips, trying to throw him off, but his hand found her wrist and pinned it to the stone. With the other, he dug at her shoulder, fingers pressing the wound that had been opened by the baton hours before. Her vision blurred, the nerves beneath the bruise lighting up the brain's panic lights, but she stayed present. She'd been hurt before. She'd been hurt by him before.

"I'm not letting you win this," she grunted, and for a split second, the line made them both snort a savage laugh, with teeth gritted and nails biting skin.

He pressed her down, the weight familiar and alien at once. "If you think this is about pride, you're missing the whole point," he growled. His breath was hot against her cheek, a blend of coffee, blood and the bitterness that had grown in him ever since he'd lost his badge. "This isn't about you or me. It's about not being erased. Don't you see that?"

She waited for a weak moment and jabbed her knee up, found his groin, and used the leverage to reverse their places, rolling so that her left hand could palm the side of his head and slam it twice into the mossy stone. The impact left blood on the green, a Rorschach that almost looked like a spiral if you squinted. He grunted, not out, and brought an elbow down into her ribs so hard she felt something give.

The pain was exquisite, sharp and clear, and it gave her a rush of clarity. She spat blood into his face, a splatter of copper on tan. "You murdered for this," she hissed. "You put bullets in men who never saw it coming. What does that buy you?"

He smiled, a red line across his teeth. "It buys us time. It buys us the chance for our son to grow up with a name that means something."

The wind hit then, gusting across the ledge and nearly taking them both with it. She used the moment to break free, crawling backwards toward the treeline, boots barely finding purchase on the rain-slick rock. He followed, limping, one arm cradling his head. Lightning backlit him, a shadow puppet strung up against the clouds, every scar on his neck and face laid bare.

She grabbed for the Sig, fingers closing around the butt as he advanced. He didn't slow, didn't dodge. He came at her with a low, stubborn charge. She raised the gun, meaning to fire, but his hand was already on her wrist, squeezing so tight her fingers spasmed and the weapon dropped into the mud with a heavy thud.

She punched him hard, using the heel of her palm like a hammer. It broke his nose. She saw the cartilage flatten, the blood fountain down his shirt, but he didn't go down. He caught her by the collar and yanked her forward, mashing their faces together so close she tasted her own iron on his lips.

"You left me!" he roared, spit and rain in her eyes.

"You were dead!" she screamed back, voice warbling with effort. "You vanished and left us to pick up the pieces."

He shoved her hard, and for a split second she lost balance and flailed for a hold, hand grabbing at a clump of ferns but getting nothing but air. He caught her again, this time by the harness of her vest, and it was almost tender, the grip that had once steadied her on a thousand dives or hikes now the one thing between her and the drop.

He set her down, then kneeled above her, both hands pressed to the ground. The rain made it hard to see his eyes, but when she blinked the water away, she saw them, wide, bright, and so full of the old hurt it nearly finished her.

"I had to disappear," he said, voice going small, almost a child's confession. "They would've eaten us alive. They would've taken Kai, you, everyone."

She panted, forcing herself upright, refusing to let the pain slow her. "You abandoned our son. You abandoned your entire family."

"I gave him a future," David said, shaking his head. "Not the one we wanted, but at least he gets a shot. That's more than we ever had."

The words hung between them, heavy as the low cloud scraping the summit.

She got her feet under her and came at him again, this time in a tackle that would've impressed her old HPD instructors. She rammed her shoulder into his gut, and they fell to the ground, rolling toward the edge, neither in control, grabbing at whatever might slow the slide.

A root, old and gnarled, caught her ankle. She wrapped around it, used it to anchor herself, and twisted so that he nearly rolled off the side. At the last moment, he grabbed her leg, and they both teetered on the rim, gravity arguing for a murder-suicide.

She looked down, saw the ocean gone blurry and rain-lit, the void below ready to swallow them both. She looked up, saw him, eyes bright, face wet with blood and water.

"We could both let go," he said, a calm in his voice that chilled her to the bone. "It would be easier."

"Coward," she spat, and, with a last jolt of adrenaline, yanked her leg up and brought her boot down on his wrist. The bone cracked, the grip loosened, and he slid back, collapsing onto the muddy ledge.

He moved to get up, but this time she was faster. She had the gun back in her right hand, and she leveled it, finger straight but close to the trigger.

"Stay down," she said. "Don't move. Not another inch."

He was breathing like a bellows, chest heaving. "You're going to bring me in? After all this?"

She nodded, tried to keep her arm from shaking. "You'll stand trial, like anyone else. You'll answer for every life you took."

He laughed, slow and hollow. "You think the city will let me live that long? You think the spiral dies with me?"

She blinked, the rain streaming down her face, eyes burning from the salt and the effort and the heartbreak. "I don't care," she said. "But I can't let you walk away. Not again."

He wiped at the blood on his face, leaving a smear on his cheek. "You'll never forgive me, will you?"

She hesitated, then said, "I loved you once. But I love our son more."

That got him. He closed his eyes, the old anger giving way to something softer, something like grief. When he spoke, it was almost a whisper.

"Make it quick, then. For his sake."

Her head hurt. She pressed the pain down, and advanced, gun still level, hand steady. "We go together. You in cuffs. Alive."

He nodded, the smallest, saddest gesture she'd

ever seen.

But as she stepped forward, a branch gave way under her boot, and in the split second it took for her balance to vanish, he surged up, grabbed the muzzle of the Sig, and yanked her forward. The gun fired wildly; the bullet was lost to the night, and they were both tumbling again, this time for real, with nothing to catch or slow them.

They hit the ledge hard, rolled, bounced, mud and blood and stone a blur. At the last instant, she caught the rough edge of a split boulder, arms burning, nails ripping down to the quick. He slid over, but his hand caught her ankle, and suddenly it was them and the drop and the old bond that refused to break.

He dangled there, hanging off her ankle with one hand, his feet kicking in space, and his weight nearly enough to pull her off after him. She screamed, from effort and pain and terror. The gun was gone, lost in the slide, so now it was a question of who could hold on longer.

He looked for a toehold on the face, but it was slick with water and old moss. He looked up at her, and all the anger and pride were gone. His hand slid off her ankle, and he grabbed a piece of lava rock with his fingers, dangling one-handed.

He sneered at her, and at that moment, as the lightning crashed overhead, she saw that if the situation were reversed, he would send her over the edge to escape.

She reached for him, her grip straining to hold on with one hand. Her side screamed, her knees and forearms bloody and raw. She looked down, saw his fingers slipping, and realized it would take everything she had to save him.

Their fingers touched for a moment, flesh on flesh, and for a heartbeat she remembered every gentle thing he'd ever done. How he cradled their son. The way he laughed, mouth wide, head thrown back, and how he once told her she was the one good thing left in the world.

Her other hand slid on the rain-slick rock. Her nails found a groove, but that wasn't enough. Her body shook from the effort.

"Let go," he said. "And we'll go together."

Tears flowed hot on her cheeks despite the rain. She would not leave her son the way his father had.

He swung his free arm up and grabbed for her wrist. She saw his fingers slip from her rock, and with tears in her eyes, she pulled back her hand. His hand missed her wrist by a whisper.

She watched him fall, body twisting, arms windmilling. He vanished into the twilight, swallowed by rain and wind and the silence that followed.

She hung there, arms numb, body quaking.

She thought she might let herself fall after him to end the pain. But in her mind, she saw Kai. She pulled herself back up, inch by inch, until she lay flat on the muddy ledge, chest heaving, lungs burning. The rain poured down, washing the blood and dirt from her face, from her hands, from the world.

She stayed that way, staring into the sky, until the storm died.

Rain hammered her spine, each drop a new needle against her skin. She was shaking so hard she barely noticed the pain anymore; everything from her ankle to her ribs to her face hurt, but nothing like the hollow that had opened in her chest.

She crawled to the edge, mud slicked to her elbows, and peered into the dark. Several hundred feet below, she glimpsed his body smashed on the rocks as a wave rolled in and smashed into the lava wall. When the wave receded, he was gone. There was no sign of him, not a flicker of movement, not a cry. Nothing but the storm, gnawing at the world with wind and water, like a dog with a fresh bone.

She told herself it hadn't happened. That the vision of him lying on the rocks below was all in her imagination. She told herself he'd somehow grabbed a branch, or a ledge, or that the old luck would finally run in his favor. But she knew better. She'd felt the moment he slipped away that had he grabbed her hand he would have taken her with him.

She turned on her back, eyes skyward. The clouds boiled, white in the lightning and black everywhere else. She tried to scream, but the sound stuck in her throat, and what came out was a raw, strangled sob that the wind shredded and took away.

She tried to get up, but her body refused. She thought about David, somewhere below, broken. She thought about their son, and the story she would tell him, and the story she would keep locked away forever.

She tried to find something to anchor to, the city, shining weakly through the rain. The ridgeline, ancient and unchanging. But it all felt foreign. Like she'd been rewired for a world that no longer had gravity.

She blinked hard. Rain or tears, it didn't matter. She pressed her hands to the ground, digging into the rock, needing something to prove she was still here. Her fingers bled, mud wedged in the cuts, but it made her feel alive.

She heard his voice replayed in her thoughts. "It's the only way," he'd said.

It made her want to laugh, or curse, or vomit.

At the storm's peak, the wind flattened her

against the stone. She let it. For a minute, for an hour, for all of history, she stayed there, pinned to the mountaintop, a failed savior mourning the man she loved and hated in equal measure.

She thought about letting go herself. About tumbling after him, becoming part of the same story, the same spiral, forever. But she didn't. She pushed herself up, bones aching, and her side on fire.

She inched forward on her knees, to the very rim, and screamed his name into the void. The echo came back, warped by distance and thunder and time. She didn't know if it was him or the mountain laughing at her. She sat there and watched the storm wash everything away.

Lightning split the sky, and for a split second, she saw her shadow on the rocks below. She kneeled, her hands empty, and let herself cry. She didn't move for the longest time.

CHAPTER FOURTEEN

Aftermath

The morning three days later was like surfacing from a week-long blackout, a hollow ring in the skull where the world's volume used to be. It was still raining when she woke up, but it was the soft, normal kind. The kind that made the house feel smaller but also safe, even when the roof leaked in three places. Leilani sat on her bed and watched the bruises blooming along her thighs and arms. The biggest one, a dark red-brown the size of a man's palm, wrapped her right side below the lowest rib, a fading echo of where David's elbow had landed, repeatedly. She touched it, tracing the outline, wondering if it would ever return to normal skin.

She found her uniform, stiff from air-drying, and moved through her morning like a ghost. The clock said 6:35, but her body ran on a time that didn't track with sunrise or traffic or anything but the beat of her own heart. She could've called in, claimed injury, bought a day or two of rest. But she didn't. She would face whatever awaited her at headquarters, and if it was the end, she would deal with that, too.

She barely remembered the drive. The morning traffic was mercifully light, the regulars all late, the cops with sirens off so as not to wake the neighborhood. At the department parking garage, she found her usual space blocked by a white van, the words HONOLULU CORONER stenciled in crooked letters across the back. She squeezed the Explorer in two slots down, avoiding eye contact with the morning shift rolling in behind her.

Inside, the station was less a workplace than a shrine to denial. The same photos of old brass and former mayors lined the corridor, the same twin vending machines hummed down the hall, and the same three detectives from night shift nursed the same brown coffee in the break room, as if time only advanced when nobody was watching. Her own office, a glass cube, fake fern in the corner, family photo with half the faces blurred out, was untouched since she'd left for the mountains. On her desk was a single yellow sticky, the handwriting unmistakable.

Report to IAD, 7:15. Wear your badge and full dress.

She checked the clock again. 7:08. Seven

minutes to decide if she was going to run.

Her badge weighed heavily on her chest as she limped down the corridor. Each step fired a warning from her side, but she forced her posture upright. The IAD suite, usually locked down and silent, was alive with voices, too many, she thought, for a standard complaint review. The entire department wanted a front row seat to her flameout.

The conference room had been set up for the kill. At the far end of a long faux-wood table sat three investigators, each in the same off-the-rack suit but with different tactics of aging. One with a horseshoe of white hair, one with a tight face and eyelids that never seemed to close, and one with hands so thin they looked surgical. A file folder for each, and one for her at the end, next to a carafe of untouched coffee and two stacks of sharpened pencils. On the whiteboard, a timeline in blue marker traced the arc from surveillance started, to officer injured, to suspect deceased (unrecovered).

She took her seat in silence.

"Detective Kealoha, you are aware this is a formal review of the events occurring at approximately zero four hundred hours on—" The tight face investigator didn't wait for a reply. "We'd like you to walk us through the events leading up to David Kekoa's death, from the last known radio contact, in your own words."

She blinked and forced herself to meet his dead eyes. "The raid on the warehouse came off as planned until it didn't. While we were effecting the arrest of David Kekoa, parties unseen staged a second attack. Several smoke canisters and flashbangs were set off, and in the melee that followed, David escaped into the subbasement and headed into the mountains. I spotted the escape and gave chase. David Kekoa, aka the Mastermind, was a prime suspect in multiple homicides, armed robberies, thefts, and corruption. He was armed and considered a threat to civilians. I moved to intercept."

"You were alone," said the investigator with the hands.

"There was no time. Air support couldn't get clearance because of the storm, and the creeks and rivers were flooding rapidly. He'd already killed two people in the previous forty-eight hours. I had to move, or he would have escaped."

White Hair scribbled something in the folder. "At what point did you lose your radio?"

"Right after I started up the trail after him. The mountain and the storm blocked all signals. After that, it was visual."

Tight face raised an eyebrow. "You're saying you pursued a homicide suspect alone, with no backup, and no radio contact?"

"That's what the file says," she replied, feeling the edge slip into her voice.

There was a pause, the kind that lasted long enough for a person to drown in it.

"And what happened next?"

She remembered the wet slap of the wind, the grip of his hand around her wrist, and she realized he wasn't trying to kill her, not really. She remembered the appearance of the rocks, green and slick, and the way he'd tried to tell her that what he did was necessary to protect the island and his family.

She told the story in bullet points, careful to keep her face flat. "He was limping. I gained on him at the third switchback. He attempted to run, lost his footing, and we rolled over the ledge together. I dislocated my shoulder and lost my weapon in the slide."

"We were both able to pull ourselves up, and he tried to escape again. I gave chase, and we fought. He was stronger, and he got the upper hand."

"Did you fear for your life, Detective?"

"I did."

"And is that when you fired?"

"I fired once," she said. "The round was off target. After that, it was hand-to-hand. I had no other weapons."

The silence returned. White hair shuffled a paper, found the line he wanted. "There is some confusion in your report. You say the suspect fell from the ridge, but there's no physical evidence of the body. No blood, no tissue, not a torn shirt."

She fought back the laughter. "It was a three-hundred-foot drop. The tide was at peak. The waves washed everything out to sea. If you'd like to look for him, be my guest."

Tight face leaned in, voice low. "You admit to pursuing a suspect outside protocol, with no backup, and using lethal force after failing to subdue by standard means. That's... convenient."

She stiffened. "I never used lethal force on the suspect. The entire time we fought, my goal was to bring him in alive, to stand trial and hopefully get more information about the people he corrupted over the last decade. I gave him multiple chances to surrender. Each time he attacked, I was forced to defend myself. You think I'm lying?"

"We think you may be protecting yourself from culpability."

A sound at the door. She turned. Agent Isaac Torres, Bureau tie loosened but still presentable, entered without knocking. He carried a tablet, and in his wake came the faint chemical scent of citrus shampoo and too many sleepless nights.

He nodded at the panel. "Apologies. Detective

Kealoha is still under a joint federal/ HPD task force. As such, she was under my command during the raid."

The investigators bristled, but tight face gestured for him to sit. "Agent Torres, we're clarifying some irregularities in the official narrative."

"Good," said Isaac. "Because the Bureau is ready to close this. We had a debrief immediately following the raid, with all the members of the team, and after careful consideration of the facts, Detective Kealoha's injuries and her timeline of events, we are prepared to close the Mastermind file. I will also state that with the information we recovered from the warehouse, we will file for multiple arrest warrants. The death of Mastermind is the end of his saga, but it is the beginning of the next chapter."

A click as Isaac opened his tablet, screen already queued to a list of files. He slid it across the table, the gesture tight, almost hostile. "You'll see here that your Internal Affairs server was breached two nights ago. Kekoa's people knew about your plan to undermine Detective Kealoha no matter what the outcome was. They were prepared for the day David Kekoa was arrested. The one thing they hadn't planned on was his dying on a cliff over the ocean."

Hands sat back, eyes gone hard and mean. "Are

you representing the Detective?"

"No," Isaac replied. "But you're not going to paint her as the villain here, not when the real bad guy is crushed on the rocks and every lead she chased was on the money. What Detective Kealoha did was dangerous and against protocol, yes. Her actions were reckless and could have cost her, her life, but what she did was one of the bravest things I've ever seen in my career. Had David Kekoa been allowed to escape on that rain-soaked mountain, the plans we discovered for his next conquest would have left this island in dire shape. Detective Kealoha may not deserve a medal for her violation of standards, but she deserves your respect for doing a job no one wanted to do."

The table fell silent. The three members of the panel spoke quietly among themselves for a few minutes while the audience held its breath. White hair closed his folder, crossed his arms, and stared at Leilani. The only sounds were the buzz of the fluorescent lights, the distant rattle of a passing cart, and the low thud of her own heart.

"Detective," said tight face, voice softening a notch. "We'll make our recommendation to Chief Mori and the police board that no further action is required, but a note of procedural caution will be placed in your file."

She waited for the trap. When none came, she nodded.

They rose as a unit, and the room seemed smaller. As the three investigators filed out, Isaac shot her a look that, in a different universe, could have meant relief. She matched it, turning away before she cracked and spilled.

Isaac waited, arms folded until the door shut. "You holding up?"

She gave a ghost of a smile. "They couldn't break me. At least, not in there."

He held her gaze. "You know he was dead before he fell, right? From your description, he'd lost significant blood. If you hadn't fired, if he'd made it off the mountain, he was done."

She shrugged, the motion sending a red spike through her shoulder. "I didn't want him to be dead. I wanted it to be over."

Isaac stared at the tablet. "They'll try to spin it. But nobody's coming after you, not after what you did. The Bureau is going to close the case as a justified homicide."

She sat back in the hard plastic chair and glanced at the badge in front of her. The gold had lost its shine; the center spiral was smeared with something she hoped was mud.

"You can go home now," said Isaac, voice suddenly kind.

She didn't trust herself not to walk until her legs gave out. She studied the room, the blank walls, the dead coffee in the carafe, the unused pencils never needed. She wondered whether any of it would mean anything tomorrow.

"Can I ask you something?" she said, not quite looking at him.

"Anything."

She drew in a breath, slow and measured. "Do you ever tire of covering for other people?"

He considered this, then smiled. "It's the job. But sometimes you get to pick the people worth covering for."

She let the compliment sit, then forced herself upright. The chair scraped a long, lonely line across the floor. As they stepped into the hallway, Police Chief Mori was waiting along with the new Chief of Detectives, Robert Mullens, a tall man with a full head of white hair and thirty years as a HPD detective under his belt. Chief Mori stepped forward. She reached out her hand, and Leilani shook it.

"Agent Torres was correct in there," she said. "What you did was reckless and dangerous, and I can't give you a medal, but you damn sure deserve one. If I had more officers with your drive, I'd have a great police department. Well done, Detective."

Chief Mullens stepped forward and shook her hand. "Detective, you made us all proud, and you lived up to the highest standards of this department. I'm glad you're one of us."

Leilani choked back tears, and as they walked towards the entrance, many officers stopped her to shake her hand and give her a well done.

They walked the corridor together, the silence companionable. When they reached the lobby, Isaac's phone buzzed with a call from an unmarked number. He glanced at the screen, then killed the ringer.

"Federal?" she asked.

"Yeah," he said, with a hint of mischief in his eye. "But they can wait."

Outside, the rain stopped. The city was shining, gold and wet, the streets washed clean and the air thin and light. Leilani believed she could start again.

The U.S. Attorney's conference room was never meant to hold this many bodies at once, not living ones anyway. It felt more like a holding cell than a war room, every chair filled, every patch of table covered with binders, phones, or half-drained cups of coffee. The air stank of printer ink and fear sweat, with a faint top note of industrial carpet cleaner that said, yes, this is where the real work gets done.

Leilani sat against the wall with her face to the glass. Beyond the window, the city shimmered in the pale light of an oncoming dawn, but in here, it was all shadow and nerve. Her knuckles were red from too much typing, her eyes ringed with black so deep it looked permanent, and every time she reached for a page or a cup, the ache from her ribs made her wince. She could feel the stares, some sympathetic, some with respect or admiration, but mostly, people kept their eyes on the files.

At the head of the table, Agent Torres led the briefing. He hadn't changed his shirt since the last one; the pattern was two days old, and he wore it like a badge. "We've isolated payment chains for fourteen officials," he said, scrolling through an evidence spreadsheet that looked like a hedge fund manager's nightmare. "Six are sitting judges. The others are on the city payroll, including a deputy mayor, two prosecutors, several high-ranking police officers and a retired captain from HPD's own anti-corruption squad."

Nobody laughed. It was too close, too obvious.

"Every dollar," Torres continued, "is linked to front charities or offshore shells controlled by Kekoa, Kapua, or the dead guys in their crew. The pattern matches exactly what Detective Kealoha and I flagged two weeks ago."

He glanced down the table at Leilani. The look was professional, but in the microsecond he let his guard slip, and she saw relief and respect. She didn't smile, but she sat a little straighter.

Someone else asked about the missing evidence in the warehouse, the artifacts table that got torched before they could inventory it. "Gone," said the tech, flipping through condition stills from a busted cell phone. "Most of the files were transferred out by satellite before the raid. We traced the upload to an offshore node, probably Fiji or Tonga, then dead-ended." A beat, then, "No way to know if the rest will ever surface."

Leilani's head pounded. She should have asked about the server bank, or the missing ledgers, or the low-level goons who'd scattered after the raid, but she couldn't make her mouth work. Everything she'd wanted for the last year was happening, right here in this room, and all she could do was nurse her coffee and pretend it didn't feel like losing.

She zoned out on the minutiae, the click and drag of evidence, the shuffling of bodies as more investigators squeezed in. People jostled, traded rumors in whispers, but the work kept going, unsentimental and steady. She watched Isaac navigate the chaos, trading sarcasm with the feds and fielding questions with the calm of a man who'd seen it all twice.

At one point, he came over and set a folder by her hand, marked in big letters: KAHANA CASE, FINAL. "Don't let them eat you alive out there," he said, voice pitched for her alone.

She almost smiled. "That's what I have you for."

He shrugged and was gone, lost in the thrum of printers and angry phone calls.

The meeting continued until noon, and by the end, most of the task force looked like they'd aged a decade. When Torres disconnected a call and stood to announce, "The warrants are signed," a tension snapped that no one had admitted was there.

The arrests started within the hour. Teams moved out in unmarked cars, feds and HPD riding together for the optics. The courthouse steps, normally a desert of crumbling concrete and stray pigeons, became a press pool in minutes. Vans from every station in the city arrived, cameras and tripods and sunburned reporters fighting for the best angle.

Leilani and Isaac watched from across the street, shields tucked under their jackets, heads low. It was better that way, less chance of being painted as heroes or villains, at least for now.

The first judge came out in handcuffs, white hair shining, suit pressed. The cameras went nuts. Leilani felt a pulse of satisfaction, plus a little guilt, followed by nothing at all. She recognized the man, remembered his kindness to her during a custody dispute years back. He looked smaller now, as if the act of being caught had shrunk him.

Next came two more officials, wrists chained, faces gray with exhaustion. The press shouted questions. "Did you take bribes?" "Do you deny the charges?" But nobody answered, not the suspects, not the agents leading them away.

Suddenly, a familiar face. The former captain from Internal Affairs. Leilani had once bought him lunch, years before. He glanced up and met her eyes, and she thought he might try to run. But he didn't. He let himself be led, shoulders hunched, face gone to stone.

Isaac leaned in. "Still think justice is simple?"

She smiled. "Never did."

On the courthouse steps, a junior reporter with too much hair gel and too little sense thrust a mic at her. "Detective Kealoha, you were the one who broke this case wide. What's it feel like to bring down the most powerful ring in city history?"

She tried to find the words, but none came. All she could think of was David's voice, calling from the darkness, the last moment on the cliff before the wind took everything.

Isaac stepped forward, hand out. "No comment," he said, deadpan. "We're happy this day has arrived and the people of Hawaii can feel safe."

The reporter frowned, but the camera still rolled. Leilani peered through the lens, and the world shrank to that single, unblinking eye.

She ducked away, her ribs protesting with every step. Isaac caught up, and together they threaded through the crowd, emerging at the far side of the plaza, the ocean breeze washing over them in a sudden, clean rush. She fished her badge from her pocket, ran a thumb over the dull metal. The letters meant nothing now, not after what it had cost her. She gazed at Isaac. "You think we made a difference?"

He considered this. "I think we tried. Sometimes that's all the city gets."

She nodded and turned her face to the wind. Behind them, the courthouse was a circus, a thousand stories being spun at once, but none of them could touch what she still carried. Not the badge, not the job, not the promise of justice. The memory of a man, and a spiral that kept spinning, no matter how many times you tried to break it.

She let the wind take her answer, and together

they walked away from the noise.

She drove home with the windows down, the city's early summer humidity a thick pelt on her arms and neck. The salt smell had shifted, less brine, more rot, like something left behind at low tide. The street she lived on, four blocks above the old Ala Wai, was empty except for the porch light two doors down, a mothballed TV hissing white noise through a neighbor's front window. She killed the engine and let herself sit in the dark, hands refusing to leave the wheel for a solid minute. She half expected to see a tail in the rearview, a shadow behind the mailboxes, but the night was unremarkable. No threats, no messages, not a hint of rain.

Inside, the house was exactly as she'd left it. Dishes in the sink, an old crossword half finished on the breakfast bar, and three pairs of Kai's shoes lined up like ducklings by the front door. The one change was the answering machine blinking with five new messages, each timestamped within the last hour.

She flicked the switch and listened, shoulder pressed to the wall. Her mother's voice came first, light as always but edged with worry: "Lani, call us when you're back. Kai is asking about you." The next two were almost the same, her mom trying to keep the boy busy, baking, gardening, and watching a TV hula special. In the background of one, she heard her own son's voice, thin but happy. "Tell Mom we're safe!" The last two messages grew more urgent, a rising panic in Naalei's vowels: "Are we coming home soon? It's not the same here with Uncle Kimo."

Leilani allowed the guilt to settle in. She should have brought them home as soon as the task force wrapped, should have set the world right with a phone call and a simple, "I'm here." Instead, she'd stayed at headquarters until midnight, hunched over evidence folders, reading and re-reading the same four lines about the body never found. As if by not letting herself off the hook, she could bring him back.

She walked through the house in silence, doing the routine she'd perfected after the spiral had reached their doorstep. Double-lock the doors, check the sliding glass in back, and run the lights off in reverse order so no one outside could track her movement. She cleaned her sidearm at the kitchen counter, field stripped and reassembled in less than two minutes, then checked the safe where she kept the badge and old medals. The gold was still tarnished from last week's rain; she didn't bother to polish it.

On her way to bed, she stopped at the family photo that had survived everything. She and Kai, on the sand at Waimanalo, squinting at the sun, no pretense of posing. She touched the glass, wiped away a smear, and lingered on the shape of her own arm draped across the boy's shoulder.

He looked so small, and she looked so... normal.

Sleep came on like a hangover, sudden and deep. But it didn't hold. Somewhere before dawn, she jerked awake, tangled in sweat-damp sheets and unable to breathe. She thought the old pain in her ribs had come back, or the air had thickened, but it was nothing more than her heart, pulsing at double speed.

She rolled over and forced herself to breathe slowly, like her mother taught her after the worst nights of the first spiral. But instead of calm, her breath brought her to the cliff, David's hand reaching for her wrist.

She punched the pillow, hard enough to sting, kicked off the covers and wandered to the living room. She turned on the TV for company, muted, and watched the late news cycle through the courthouse shots. Judges in cuffs, politicians hiding from the press, and the brief, unflattering frame of her and Isaac on the courthouse steps. The anchor called it "an unprecedented day for justice in Hawaii," but the words felt brittle, like the case was already fading into yesterday's violence.

The sky outside the window was going pale with dawn, a thin line of blue along the black. She checked her phone, one new message, from Isaac. "You awake?" She stared at it, her thumb hovering over the reply button, then put the phone down.

It was barely five when she pulled on the first clothes she found, clipped her badge and gun to her belt, picked her father's badge off the counter and walked out the back door, barefoot. The grass was cold, wet with old rain, and she walked across the sloping yard all the way to the berm, where the yard stopped and the beach began. The surf slammed against the rocks in white bands; the tide was coming in high and angry. She stood there, her toes digging into the soft dirt, watching the ocean work itself into a frenzy and then settle, wave after wave.

When the sun cleared the horizon, it was almost too bright to face. She blinked, squinted, and then, unable to help herself, laughed. It was a broken sound, loud and wet, but it was honest. She laughed until her knees gave out, and she sank to the sand, tears streaming down her cheeks.

She sat there, doubled over, her father's badge clenched in her hand, until the waves stopped mattering and the sun had risen well into the morning. It didn't feel like closure, or a clean start, but as the wind dried her face, she realized it was enough to have survived.

CHAPTER FIFTEEN

Healing Wounds

L eilani drove east along the coast, windows down, salt air lancing the backseat like a punishment. She took the corners slower than usual, not because of the wet pavement, but because the left turn of the wheel bit deep into her bruised side. The act of breathing stung, as if something in her lungs had cracked and never quite put itself back together.

She rolled through neighborhoods that still slept; the streetlights pooled in their little islands of safety; the houses shuttered against the night no one wanted to talk about. At this hour, the only movement was feral cats, a couple of joggers who kept their distance, and the last batch of drunks dragging themselves off the seawall to beat the sunrise home.

She pulled up to her mother's house at first light. The cottage had been in the family for four generations, never truly finished, always mid-repair. The plumeria tree out front leaned a little farther every year, threatening the power line, but still loaded with white and gold flowers in June. The front gate stuck, same as always. She put her shoulder to it and hissed at the contact with the frame.

Inside, the air was rich with coffee and the fatty perfume of Spam frying on the skillet. She heard voices from the back, muffled, her mother, and a boy's feet skipping on the tile.

The sight of him, Kai, froze her in the entryway. He was barefoot, still in last night's basketball shorts and a ratty tank, his hair a wild tangle on his forehead. He ran at her, arms open, but stopped short when he saw the way her hands raised up, protective. He looked at the cuts and scratches on her arms and legs, at the dried blood on her knuckles, the scratches, and bruises on her face, and his face twisted into something too complicated for a ten-year-old.

"Mom," he said, his voice broken.

She reached out anyway, pulled him in, careful to brace him with her good arm. "Hey, bug. I missed you," she managed, and held on, willing her body to remember this, not the violence.

Her mother stood in the kitchen, spatula in one hand, eyes sharper than any badge. "Are you hungry?" she said, as if nothing at all was out of place.

Leilani tried to smile. "Always," she said, but

she could hear the tremor.

They moved to the lanai, the three of them, breakfast on mismatched plates. The ocean crashed thirty yards away, visible over the hedge, and the sun threw gold bands across the deck. Kai picked at his food, poked the eggs until they bled yolk over the Spam, but barely touched a bite.

Naalei poured coffee for them, her own cup a chipped mug from the nineties that had outlived four blenders. She settled into the wicker chair, feet tucked up, watching Leilani with a patience that was comforting and merciless.

"You're going to have to tell him," Naalei said. "He already knows something happened. He's been waiting all morning."

Leilani felt the nerves fire in her jaw, a warning of the headache to come. "I know," she said. She studied Kai as he traced the outline of his fork on the plate, careful not to meet her eyes.

She waited until her mother moved inside. She scooted her chair closer. The deck boards gave a soft groan under the shift. She leaned in, voice low. "Do you remember the case I told you about? The spiral, the one that kept coming back?"

Kai nodded, not looking up.

"There's something I never told you. About the man behind it."

He looked up, and she saw herself in the set of his mouth, and how he prepped for bad news. "Is it Dad?"

She felt the world drop out, a bottomless hush in the morning. "Yeah," she said. "It was him."

Kai blinked, as if fighting through the stack of lies he'd heard over the years. "But you said he died. The sharks—"

"I thought so, too. Everyone did. But he made it out. He was hiding, and when he came back... he wasn't the same."

Kai was silent. She watched his hands. The left was fisted, the right flat and trembling. When he spoke, the words came out small, almost lost.

"Is he dead now?"

She nodded and said it out loud. "Yes. He's gone. This time for real."

He pressed his palm to his eye. When it came away, his eyelashes were wet, but he didn't make a sound.

"What happened?" he asked.

She didn't want to tell him about the cliff, about the fight, about the sound a body made when it hit the rocks below. Instead, she told him the cleanest version she could.

"He did a lot of bad things. Hurt a lot of people. I tried to stop him. We fought, and he...he ended it."

She reached for his hand, but he pulled it away, let it fall into his lap. She was trying to tell him it was okay to cry, but she couldn't find the right words. She hoped to say something that made it all make sense, but there was nothing.

"I wanted him to be good," Kai said, voice sharp. "You always said he was a hero."

"He was once," she said. "But sometimes people lose their way."

He grew quiet again, this time for so long she thought he might never come back.

Naalei reappeared, a plate of fruit in one hand. She studied her grandson, saw the wet eyes, and didn't flinch. She put the plate down and sat beside him.

"We can do something if you want," Naalei said. "A small thing, for letting go."

Kai shook his head, but after a moment, he stood up. He walked to the end of the deck and looked out at the surf, arms wrapped tight around his belly. She saw the way his shoulders hunched, as if the truth was an actual weight he carried. He stayed like that until the fruit flies found the papaya, and the sun had climbed high enough to burn off the dew.

Leilani watched him, feeling both proud and ashamed, and wondered if she'd broken the last piece of him that still believed in heroes.

When he finally turned back, his face was blank, scrubbed clean by salt and sun. He walked down the stairs to the beach, feet sinking into the soft sand, and kept walking, all the way to the water's edge, where the ocean would take whatever he gave it. She let him go. She'd done enough for one lifetime.

By the time the day caved in on itself and the sky changed to purple, and the air had lost the burn of the afternoon. It was Naalei's idea, of course, to do the ritual that night, old ways, she said, for new hurts. She wore a muumuu that trailed like ocean foam and carried the supplies in a battered canvas bag, the kind you used for groceries or funerals, depending on the mood.

She led them down a stretch of beach west of the cottage, away from the condos and the joggers and anyone who might remember them from before. Here, the sand was thick with driftwood and the tangled legs of naupaka, its bitter flowers littering the tide line.

At the appointed spot, Naalei made a place for them, scooping out a low bowl in the sand and laying out three broad ti leaves, washed and de-spined. She set a fistful of sea salt in a cracked shell, a dish of kukui nuts, and two bamboo styluses, their tips dark with ink. The altar was nothing, but also everything. The sum of a thousand little meanings, none of which needed to be said aloud.

Kai trailed, reluctant but obedient. He hunched his shoulders against the breeze, hands stuffed deep in his pockets. Leilani came last, taking the steps slowly, her hip locking at odd moments, her body still foreign and tight from the last week.

They sat in a rough triangle, knees touching if anyone cared to notice, but nobody did. Naalei gazed at her daughter, then at her grandson, and then out at the waves, which crashed in sets, a heart still beating when everything else had quit.

"This is what we do for pain," Naalei said, her voice level but not unkind. "You write it down, you give it away, you let the sea take the rest."

She took one stylus and handed it to Leilani, offering the other to Kai, who stared at it like it might turn into a snake in his hand. He took it but said nothing.

The oli began as a hum, loud enough to mark the space as sacred. Naalei's voice wasn't the strongest, but it had a kind of backbone, a spine that ran from the soles of her feet to the tip of her tongue. The chant rose and fell, riding the rhythm of the tide, every syllable a small stone tossed into a bigger ocean.

Leilani looked at the leaf, at the stylus, and then at the sky, where the light cut the horizon to ribbons. She tried to find words for what she desired to leave behind, but nothing fit. The need to edit herself, to make the pain tidy, was strong. Instead, she wrote what she could:

ANGER.

GUILT.

LOVE.

BETRAYAL.

HOPE.

She pressed the tip until the green surface bruised and bled a little pigment.

Kai watched her, not directly, but out of the corner of his eye, the way kids do when they're afraid they're about to cry. His hand hovered over the leaf for a full minute, fingers twitching. When he finally wrote, it was all at once, long angry slashes and big block letters, like he was trying to stab the words through the plant and into the sand below. He didn't show her what he wrote, but she saw the indentations, the lines that nearly tore the leaf in half.

When they were done, Naalei reached for the kukui dish and dabbed a drop of oil on her thumb. She drew a line down each forehead, the way she'd done when Leilani was little.

When scraped knees and lost toys were the only tragedies in the world.

She spoke then, half in English, half in Hawaiian. "The light of the kukui shows the way. In the darkness, it keeps burning. We all need that sometimes. Especially when the world doesn't care if you go out."

Kai's face screwed up as the oil touched his skin. But he let it happen.

Naalei gathered the leaves, careful not to mix them, and tucked them side by side in a shallow depression on the altar. She swept a line of salt around the mound, sealing it, and stood, brushing sand from her knees.

She motioned for them to follow, and they walked together to where a small, battered outrigger rested above the high tide mark. It was old, with paint flaking, but it was seaworthy. White flowers, gardenias, with a few clipped plumeria, ringed the hull, woven through the lashings. Naalei laid the bundle of ti leaves inside, on a bed of dry pandanus, and gestured for Leilani and Kai to steady the canoe as she slid it toward the water.

The tide was rising, fingers of foam reaching higher with each wave. Together, they pushed the outrigger into the shallows, Naalei guiding it by the stern, Kai, and Leilani by the ama. The flowers bobbed and rolled, scattering in the first swell.

When it was deep enough, Naalei let go. The canoe rocked in the surf, took a hard right, then drifted out, moving faster as the current found its purchase.

They stood at the edge, bare feet in the water, watching the little craft make its way. No one spoke. The sky had gone from purple to gray-black, and the line of the horizon was less a promise than a threat. Still, the canoe kept moving, flowers trailing behind, the leaves inside holding steady.

Kai reached for Leilani's hand, squeezed it once, and let go. They waited until the canoe was a dot on the water, and the darkness came up all at once.

When the last of the light was gone, they turned back up the beach, moving together, every step a little less weighted than before. At the top of the path, Naalei looked at them and nodded, as if to say, it's not done, but it's better.

They headed home, and the sea, for a night, kept the rest.

Later, back at her house with the churn of the sea to mark time, Leilani found Kai on the steps of the cottage, knees drawn to his chin. He'd changed into dry clothes, the old T-shirt two sizes too small, letters peeling from the chest. The porch light caught his silhouette, and he looked like a child again, small, uncertain, the world suddenly too big for his bones.

He didn't look up when she sat down beside him. The stairs creaked under her weight, and she eased herself down with a grunt. She waited, not speaking, the way her mother had taught her. Let the silence do its work, and the truth will walk in on its own.

Kai had a notebook open on his lap. He flipped through the pages as if each one cost something to turn.

"I don't want to do detective stuff anymore," he said, voice flat. "It's stupid."

She didn't answer right away. The smell of the ocean was sharp, iodine, and sand and something electric. Far off, a barge's horn called out, lonely and low.

"I mean it," he said, closing the notebook with a slap. "I was always trying to solve things, like if I paid attention enough, it would fix stuff. But it didn't, so I'm done."

Leilani reached for the notebook, not grabbing it, but placing her palm near it on the step.

"You were never trying to fix things," she said. "You were seeing. That's a gift, not a curse."

He squinted at her, angry or tired, it was hard to tell. "Grandpa used to say that. That I had cop eyes."

She smiled, the ache blooming into something softer. "He wasn't wrong. But there are better things you can do with them."

Kai snorted. "Like what? Be a lookout for the next criminal in the family?"

"Like noticing things other people miss," she said. "Writing them down. Remembering. One day you'll help your grandma record the old chants, or help neighbors find their lost cats. You'll be the first to spot a new shell on the beach. You can be a different detective."

He mulled this, staring at the notebook, turning it over in his hands.

She tapped the cover with one finger. "Can I see?"

He shrugged and handed it to her.

Inside, the pages were a storm of notes. Lists of what he'd seen that day, the colors of the sky, the names of fish in the tide pools, a detailed map of the cottage. There were pages of things he'd overheard, exact phrases in quotes and sketches. There was a rough but true picture of her mother's hands, the outrigger canoe at sunset, and the bandage on her wrist.

She flipped a few more pages, not lingering on the ones marked with dark, angry scribbles. She shut the book and handed it back. "You're good at this," she said. "Really good."

He didn't answer, but his grip tightened on the notebook. A cool wind rattled the eaves. Leilani stretched her legs, wincing, and looked out towards the line where the ocean met the stars.

"Dad wasn't all bad," Kai said, quiet now. "He wanted to do something good. He… got lost."

She nodded. "Sometimes the best swimmers get pulled out by the current."

They sat together, letting the waves wash the rest away.

After a while, she stood, brushing sand from her shorts. "Come inside," she said. "We'll make some tea."

He hesitated, got up, following her through the open door and into the warm, lighted house.

Leilani set out two cups, steam curling from the top. She poured, no ceremony, just the clink of a spoon against porcelain. They sat and let the tea fill the empty spaces.

They didn't talk. They watched the dark through the window, the ocean a restless thing, alive and always moving. Leilani felt the spiral loosen. Not broken, but bent in a way that let the air move through again.

She sipped her tea and reached for her son's hand, and together, they let the night hold them, quiet and whole.

CHAPTER SIXTEEN

Rebuilding Trust

A t 8:05 a.m., the fourth floor briefing room of Honolulu PD headquarters was an oven, with a boxy volume low ceilings, dirty carpet and humidity that turned polyester uniforms into shrink wrap. Two dozen men and women crowded around the long U-shaped table, rank denoted by the shade of blue on the shirt and the width of the badge. At the bottom of the U stood Leilani Kealoha, blazer on over her dress shirt despite the weather, eyes red-rimmed and hair clipped back in a style meant to project both authority and the possibility of going feral if provoked.

Behind her, the whiteboard was prepped for war with charts, timelines and a couple of stick-figure cartoons she'd left in the corner as a psychological experiment. The next fifteen minutes were going to make her the most hated cop in the state, or the one who could still face a crowd without breaking into hives.

She clicked the remote. "Thank you for coming on short notice. I promise not to waste your time." There was no attempt at small talk. Instead, she dove in, moving through the first set of slides with a dry precision, outlining the spiral of corruption that had pulsed through the department over the last decade. From the earliest payroll leaks to the six-year run of lost evidence that had ended three weeks ago, with a warehouse raid and the death of the Mastermind.

As she gestured to the projected org chart, red lines connecting judges, cops, and three local politicians she'd never voted for, her side flared, the wound reminding her you could clean the surface and still fester underneath. She didn't flinch. The senior brass on her left, mostly Internal Affairs and a couple of city prosecutors, were watching for that, the micro-twitch, or the voice break that would make her seem fragile, damaged, unreliable.

A detective captain, mustache like a badger pelt, was first to speak. "If you're saying half the department is dirty, talk to the feds. Not here."

Leilani thumbed to the next slide, a matrix of arrest records and payout dates, columns highlighted in careful pink and acid green. "I'm not saying half. I'm saying we have a pattern that makes sense if someone inside is feeding information. The Mastermind wasn't working alone. He had help."

Two officers shifted in their chairs. One, a burly sergeant, crossed his arms over a chest that looked bulletproof, but his eyes darted to the door. Another, a woman with a patchy streak of gray in her bun, leaned forward, hands folded, interested.

Leilani gripped the whiteboard, letting her fingers go white. "Here's the proposal. New intake on every major case, outside audit every six months, and—" she let it hang, waiting for the next wave of resistance.

It came on schedule, from a civilian in the back, a judge, in retirement but still kingmaking from the shadows. "And you, Detective Kealoha, would be in charge of all this oversight? After the last three weeks?"

The smile she gave him was both a courtesy and a warning. "The investigation into my conduct was closed yesterday. I was cleared. If you have a different complaint, Judge, file it. Otherwise, I'd like to finish the briefing."

The judge's face pinched, but he sat back, satisfied in the way men are when they think they've forced a woman to prove herself one more time.

She worked the next part like a judo hold, pivoting from defense to offense. "The audit is run by the state. The anonymous reporting system is run by an outside contractor." She clicked to a slide with the company's logo, a cartoon squirrel clutching a whistle, "and the oversight panel is community led. I'm not the sheriff. I'm the one giving you a toolkit so nobody has to play lone hero again."

A beat. The two sides of the room regarded each other, recalibrating.

A lieutenant at the end raised his hand, sheepish. "Why anonymous reporting? Wouldn't that clog us with bullshit calls?"

Leilani nodded. "There'll be bullshit. There always is. But for every ten crank calls, one will be real. Right now we have zero because no one trusts the system. If we want the public to trust us, we have to prove we trust each other first."

The words were nothing new. Every rookie heard the same line in orientation. But in this context, delivered in the same room where, a year ago, she'd nearly been fired for speaking out of turn, it landed differently.

She switched the slide again. "Every department on the mainland that's tried this has seen a thirty percent drop in internal investigations within two years. Not because the crimes stop, but because the reporting moves upstream. We get to the cancer before it metastasizes."

A low whistle from the captain with the

mustache. "How do you keep it from being weaponized? You know what it's like when you get two officers who hate each other."

She shrugged, careful not to let the motion pull her bandaged side. "We don't. But we balance it with transparency. For every accusation, there's a record. We track retaliation, and we publish findings. The moment the data stops matching reality, you know you have a problem."

By now, a third of the room had shifted their body language. Arms uncrossed, faces less hostile, and the general feel of a place bracing itself for something big. There was a joke or two that didn't carry, but for once it didn't have the charge of a kill shot.

Police Chief Mori stood. She was old-school, built like a linebacker, and her uniform covered with twenty years of medals. Her presence was not a request. When she spoke, the room shut up.

"This plan has the full support of my office," Mori said, voice calm but iron. "And I expect each of you to treat it as the law of the land starting tomorrow. If anyone objects, you can take it up with the mayor, or with me. But do not waste Detective Kealoha's time, or mine, with petty politics. We've got enough enemies outside the department."

That was the moment it was over. Not

officially, not on paper, but in the minds of everyone watching. If the old warhorse was signing off, the rest would follow.

Leilani clicked the last slide, a cartoon squirrel saluting, a holdover from the outside contractor's idea of humor, and turned off the projector.

"Questions?" she asked, but there were none that mattered.

As the meeting adjourned, the crowd broke into clumps. Some congratulated her. Some, more likely, plotted their next move in the shadow war that never really ended. But for once, she didn't care. She felt the tightness in her side loosen and allowed herself to believe that it was possible to change something in this city that lasted more than a week.

She gathered her files, clumsy with fatigue, and noticed the one body that hadn't moved the entire hour. Agent Torres, leaning against the back wall, arms crossed, tie gone and shirt unbuttoned at the neck, watching her with the pride that didn't need an audience.

She allowed herself a second to meet his gaze before she turned away, the faint smile already gone by the time she reached the door.

◆ ◆ ◆

The squad room was alive, with a continuous dribble of voices and phone bells and the underlying grind of the printer that never slept. The place still smelled of burned coffee and decades of blue ink, the same air she'd breathed since rookie year. There were small signs of change, a new pot of succulents by the window, a poster advertising yoga for stress relief, but mostly, it was the same hive of nervous energy, grudges, and dead-end paperwork.

Leilani took the main aisle, tracing the path with the muscle memory of a hundred late nights and a thousand fights with the copy machine. Most of the desks were manned in the lull between shifts, and she was conscious of eyes tracking her, not hostile now, but cautious, measuring whether she was still the same after the week that nearly cracked her open.

She made a deliberate stop at Detective Akana's desk. Akana was old-school, hair buzzed to the bone, shirtsleeves rolled to the tattooed biceps, and a wedding ring made of black tungsten and heavy enough to double as brass knuckles. He was reviewing a printout when she approached, and he didn't look up until her shadow crossed the paper.

"Morning, Lani," he said, voice low, a holdover from too many overnight surveillances. "Word is, you're running Internal now."

She sat on the corner of his desk. "Hardly. I'm helping the Chief not get run out of town."

He grunted, scanning the printout. "I saw the broadcast from upstairs. Didn't expect you to pitch the ratline."

She nodded. "Neither did I. But it's what we need."

Akana looked up, eyes sharp but not unfriendly. "People won't use it. Not unless it's about someone they already hate."

"That's true, for now." She let the silence sit, then added, "It's not about catching bad cops. It's about protecting the ones who are good. The ones who end up next to a body and realize they're suddenly on their own."

Akana's gaze softened. "You think this would've saved Palu?" He meant the detective from two years ago, the one who got burned as a scapegoat when a shakedown went sideways.

"Probably not. But it would've made it harder to bury him," she said.

Akana turned this over and nodded. "If anyone can sell it, it's you. They'll follow your lead."

She thanked him by squeezing his shoulder, a gesture that said everything and nothing, and moved down the line.

At the bullpen's edge, a knot of younger officers watched her approach with the wary respect usually reserved for parole board interviews. One, a rookie with pressed creases and a badge number still sharp around the edges, tried to hide a Reddit thread behind a spreadsheet.

She stopped and faced him, arms folded. "Menehune, you ever think about what you'd do if you caught your partner cutting corners?"

The rookie startled. "I'd call it in. That's policy."

She almost smiled. "Easy to say. Harder when it's a guy you share a patrol car with."

He flushed, then looked past her. "How do you make it work?"

Before she could answer, Torres appeared, as if conjured by the question. He'd swapped his suit for a borrowed HPD windbreaker, and somehow it fit, the navy blue softening his usual sharp-edged presence. He leaned on the desk next to hers, hands loose.

"You build habits," he said to the rookie. "Small ones, every day. Like calling out your mistakes before someone else does."

The rookie nodded, grateful for the lifeline.

"And you don't forget why you started," Leilani added. "It's never about the system. It's about the people."

Torres grinned. "The system's a mess. But the

people are worth it."

There was a beat, then a new question from the rookie. "How do you get the public to care? I mean, the forums are already joking about the new policy."

Torres fielded it. "You show up. Every time, especially when it sucks. Especially then. Community isn't the enemy; it's our best resource."

He caught Leilani's eye as he said it, and she saw what the others did. Someone who could bridge the gap between outside authority and homegrown stubbornness. He belonged here, in a way that made her jealous, but also strangely proud.

The phone at the corner desk rang, and the moment snapped. Leilani reached for a case file as Torres did. Their hands brushed, and she pulled back, sudden and hot, as if she'd touched a live wire. He didn't react but slid the folder her way and kept talking.

"There's a community meeting tonight, right?" he said.

She nodded, trying to steady her breath. "I got final approval. They want us to field questions, take heat, and smile for the news cameras."

Torres made a face. "My specialty."

A notification buzzed on her phone. She

glanced at it, saw the message: Forum at 1900. The press will be present. Come prepared.

She sighed. "It's going to be a shitshow."

"That's the job," said Torres.

She stacked the files, prepping for the next fire. As she turned to leave, he stopped her.

"You doing okay?" he said, voice lower than before.

She paused, not sure if the question was professional or personal. "Depends on the day."

He smiled. "That's honest."

She matched it. "You sticking around for this?"

He hesitated. "I've put in for a transfer. Permanent, if the Bureau lets me."

She blinked, surprised. "You sure? It's not exactly a promotion."

He shrugged. "I don't need a promotion. I need to be where I'm useful."

She let that sit, not sure if she was hearing what she wanted, or what she needed. They moved down the hall.

They reached the exit. The squad room behind them was still humming, a machine built to survive on muscle memory and the hope that things could get better. She glanced at Torres as he fit into the new rhythm, and let herself imagine a future where this wasn't all on her.

He held the door for her, and for once, she didn't rush through it.

The lanai at the Waikiki Community Center was built for luaus, not truth commissions. Folding chairs curved out from a makeshift dais, the line of them broken by the paths of breeze that found their way in from the ocean and left the scent of plumeria and cigarette butts in the crowd. The light was that perfect hour, gold, and pink, the city's high rises glowing in the distance while here, the world shrank to a manageable patch of concrete and string lights.

Leilani sat on the lip of the dais, holding a clipboard, already sweating through her blouse. Torres stood to her left, in the same HPD windbreaker from earlier, hair tousled in a way that seemed more honest than any badge. In the first row, Naalei was flanked by three aunties and a couple of kids who looked like they'd rather be anywhere else. The crowd was a mosaic of old uncles, small business owners and young parents with their arms folded like shields.

She waited until the last batch of latecomers had found seats. Then, using her cop voice but none of the cop posture, she started.

"We can all see the problem," she said. "It's

why you're here instead of eating dinner with your family." She let her eyes move through the crowd, pausing at the faces that looked least friendly. "The department hasn't always earned your trust. I know that. I'm not here to talk over you. I'm here to listen, and if what you say makes sense, to put it into practice."

A tight silence. She could hear the cars on the avenue below, the scrape of a metal chair foot on the lanai.

She tried again. "We want to know what isn't working. What scares you? What do you think we could fix if we weren't too busy trying to look good for the cameras?" She nodded at the News 8 van idling by the curb, earning a low laugh from the crowd.

The first speaker was an old man, rail-thin, trucker cap at least a decade out of date. He stood, voice already quavering with the energy of it. "My house got robbed last year. I called three times. Not once did a real cop show up. You sent the haole intern. He wrote my name down; nothing happened."

Leilani wrote the words down, careful to get it right. She didn't interrupt. The old man, seeing that he was being taken seriously, sat again, but not until he'd made eye contact with at least five people near him.

The next voice belonged to a young mother.

She had a toddler in her lap, one hand wrapped tight around the child's ankle to keep him from bolting. "They teach you in school that the cops are your friends," she said, "but the last time someone got pulled over on our street, there were three cruisers and they acted like the block was out to kill them. My kid gets scared every time he sees you now."

Another hand shot up, then another. In five minutes, the lanai was a low tide of complaints and small histories. Some legitimate; delayed response times, lost paperwork, a city councilman's cousin getting out of a DUI. Others, less so. Aliens, secret cameras and a rumor that the department was tracking cell phones for the Chinese government. Torres fielded those with dry grace, sometimes redirecting, sometimes listening, always keeping his tone shy of sarcasm.

She noticed her mother's face in the front row, neutral but alert, eyes flicking from her daughter to each person who spoke as if weighing every word for truth and threat.

As the stories started repeating, six complaints about a speeding ticket, four about the same uncollected junker on the street, Leilani used the lull to reset the room. She stood, let the clipboard dangle at her side.

"Here's what we're doing, starting now.

Anonymous reporting system. Not for cops, but for anyone who feels like they can't get heard. We'll read every one." She gestured at Torres. "And we have people from the federal side, too, so nobody's playing favorites."

Torres stepped in, his voice carrying. "We'll also be publishing response stats, how long it takes to get to a call, what happens after, and who's responsible when it doesn't go right."

That got a murmur from the room. People didn't trust numbers, but they liked having someone to blame when things didn't turn out as planned.

She continued. "We'll host this forum every month. If you see the same face screwing up each time, you'll know. If it's me, say so. If it's Chief Mori, she'll be here next time, and you can tell her yourself."

A kid in the third row, a teenager with a skate tee and headphones around his neck, raised his hand, but thought better of it. Leilani caught his hesitation. "You've got a question?"

The kid shrugged. "Will anything actually change?"

She paused. "I don't know. But I'm going to be here every month until it does."

It wasn't a promise, but it was honest. That seemed to land with at least a quarter of the crowd.

The forum went long, an hour, and a half of people working out old injuries. The light faded, lanterns kicking on one by one, and by the end, the complaints were thinner, replaced by nervous optimism. A shop owner offered to organize a neighborhood watch. Two old women compared notes on the best time to call in vandalism. The old man, who started the night with a rant, waited around to shake her hand. She felt the muscles in her back relax.

As the crowd dispersed, she looked for her mother, but Naalei was gone, probably to avoid any overt sign of support. Instead, Leilani found herself on the lanai, looking out at the city, clipboard still in hand. Torres joined her, two paper cups of coffee in hand. He handed her one, then leaned on the rail, shoulder barely an inch from hers.

"Nice work," he said.

"Most of them still hate us," she replied.

He smiled. "That's progress. It's when they stop talking that you worry."

She sipped her coffee, let the quiet stretch.

Torres was the one who broke it. "You ever think about what comes next?"

She glanced at him, then out to where the surf broke against the dark. "I don't know what tomorrow looks like."

He nodded. "That's how you know you're in the right place. You're not trying to control it anymore."

She thought of the spiral, how it never really ended, but shifted direction. She wondered if that was enough.

She set the cup on the rail; the foam catching the last of the evening light. "This might actually work," she said, softer than before.

Torres shifted closer, his hand resting on the same rail, fingers nearly touching hers. "It already is," he said.

The last of the crowd filtered out. The city behind them pulsed with traffic, but up here, it was nothing but the warm air, the hush of distant waves, and the slow thud of her own heartbeat.

They stood there, side by side. Neither moved. Neither needed to.

CHAPTER SEVENTEEN

Family Redemption

I f the city woke early, the hills above Kaimuki woke earlier. The dawn light skated down the ridges, slipping through battered window glass and beating the roosters to their job. In a converted garage painted soft green, Naalei moved from shelf to table, trimming ti leaves with a fishbone knife that looked older than any living member of the family. She arranged each cut stalk into a neat pile on a woven mat, fingers moving by memory, unhurried by the world outside.

A mound of plumeria waited in a cardboard box lined with old supermarket ads. The flowers had been picked the day before, still slick with dew at the base, a perfume that clung to her hands and wrists. She took three at a time, spun the stems, and laced them onto the string, never snapping a petal or breaking stride. If the rain from last night had knocked any blooms loose, she didn't show disappointment; she worked the blemishes in, invisible as old scars.

Through the open garage door, the street was mostly silent except for a delivery truck exhaling somewhere up the hill. The city's humidity was already rising, making the air heavy and close, but inside the studio, everything felt ordered, deliberate, a pocket of clarity before the day's complications.

A car door thudded at the curb. Footsteps on the gravel, followed by the scrape of a flip-flop at the threshold. Leilani's silhouette, a little hunched from years of wearing a badge and a chip on her shoulder, filled the doorway. She held a tray with two coffees and a paper bag from Leonard's.

"Mom, you should see the line for malasadas at seven a.m.," Leilani said, but set the treats down with a care that made the complaint sound like a prayer.

Naalei snipped the end off a leaf, didn't look up. "Good thing the old people let me cut in. I have a community event," she mimicked, voice thin and sharp, not unkind.

"Abusing your status with the kapuna," Leilani said. She smiled, and this time it moved to her eyes. "That's how you get the good kind. Cinnamon and sugar, not plain."

The joke floated, light as a plumeria, and settled. They stood together over the table; the mother threading and the daughter peeling back the cup lids, pouring cream and sugar into the mix. There were words waiting to be said, but neither woman rushed. They'd spent too much of their lives in a hurry, and this was a morning to let the time stretch out a little.

Leilani glanced around the studio, noting that nothing had changed. The same battered folding chairs, the same cooler with "PROPERTY OF NAALEI" in Sharpie on the lid, and the same glass-fronted cabinet with bowls and bundles of dried kukui. But something in the room felt different. It could have been the memory of how, last night, her mother had led a ceremony on the beach that stitched together pieces of their family she hadn't realized were loose. Or it might be the way her mother's hands never shook, even with the neighborhood riding on her voice.

Leilani nodded at the lei in progress. "Is that for the center? Or for the TV crew?"

Naalei gave her a look, equal parts pride and reprimand. "For the altar first. I'll see who deserves one." She slipped the string around her neck, held the weight for a beat, then laid it down.

The scent of coffee filled the small space. They sat on mismatched stools, the silence less a void and more a shared garment, something worn in and comfortable. After a few sips, Leilani cleared her throat.

"I was thinking about what you said. About today. How it's the first time anyone's bothered to get cops and cultural people in the same room without a judge in between."

Naalei shrugged, but her fingers slowed on the string. "First time for everything," she said.

Leilani watched her mother's hands, how the thumb and forefinger moved, a choreography so efficient it seemed choreographed by the gods. "Do you think it'll make a difference?"

A small smile ghosted across Naalei's mouth. "Not today. Not in my lifetime. But you don't plant a tree for yourself."

Leilani turned the idea over, found a place for it near her own battered hope. "If it goes sideways, you know I'll be the first one they blame."

"I know." The older woman's tone was flat, but her eyes were soft. "That's why you have to make it look like you're not trying."

"I'm still working on that part," Leilani said. She sipped her coffee, and let the sweet burn settle in her throat. "You ever wonder what you'd be if you didn't have to hold it together for everyone else?"

Naalei snorted. "I'd be in the mountains. Grow sweet potato. Listen to the rain." She leaned back, looked her daughter up and down, and for once didn't hide her pride. "But who would show you how to braid a proper lei?"

The laugh that followed was gentle, but edged with something old and sharp. They knew the answer to that one. They sat there, letting the world do its own thing outside.

From the hallway, the slam of a bedroom door was followed by the rush of small feet. Kai entered at full speed, clutching a battered manila folder covered in stickers and the pen-marks of earlier grades. His hair stuck out in every direction, like he'd spent the night fighting off wild boars instead of sleeping.

He waved the folder above his head. "Mom! Nana! I got the map!"

Leilani hid her smile, but Kai barreled straight to the table, flipping the folder open. Inside, a piece of construction paper, covered with hand-drawn outlines and little flags stuck at random intervals. The colors bled a bit, but the detail was impressive, ridges, rivers, and what looked like abandoned military bunkers.

"Check it out," he said, pointing at a clump of blue dots near Kaneohe. "That's all the old heiau. I put the sacred sites in red."

Naalei peered at the map, fingers gentle as she traced the lines. "You did all this yourself?"

"Uncle Kimo let me use his laptop for the satellite stuff. But I did all the drawing."

Leilani ruffled his hair, an old habit she'd never lost, and looked at the map with a cop's eye. "You're sure this is okay to show everyone?"

Kai's eyes grew wide. "That's the point, Mom. If everyone knows where the sacred places are, they'll stop painting over them or littering there." His voice got quiet, with an edge of old pain. "Nobody likes when their stories get erased."

The table was still. Naalei reached for a small bowl, set it before Kai, and filled it with the best of the plumeria. "For you. To offer when we get there."

The boy beamed. "I'll do it right."

Leilani watched her son with a wonder she'd thought had died in the last year. Hopefully, it was coming back to life. She let herself believe it for now.

The clock on the wall ticked louder as the morning wore on. Outside, the traffic picked up, and the city resumed its hustle. Inside the garage, they worked together, the three of them. Leilani rolling up the lei and storing it in the cooler. Naalei double-checked the ceremonial bowl and shells, and Kai packed up his map and a few dog-eared books about Hawaiian legends.

They loaded everything into Naalei's minivan, Kai in charge of wedging the boxes so nothing crushed the flowers. Before they locked the garage, Naalei lingered at the little altar by the door. It was barely more than a shelf, with a faded family photo in a dollar store frame, the faces younger but the poses the same. She ran her thumb across the glass and then pressed her palm to the wood.

Leilani watched but didn't comment. There were still some things too personal to bring into the daylight.

Naalei straightened, brushed her hands on her dress, and smiled at her daughter, then her grandson. "Let's go," she said. "There's no point in waiting for history to fix itself."

They stepped out into the morning, three generations and a trunk full of hope, ready to see if the world could do better than yesterday.

The parking lot was already half full by the time Leilani turned into the community center. The sign out front, WAIMANALO MULTI-USE PAVILION, rattled in the trade wind, and someone had rigged a garland of ti leaves across the entrance, the green pops of color flapping like flags on parade. In the hour since sunrise, the space had morphed from a recreation league gym to a hive of movement. Volunteers lugging folding chairs, old uncles in slippers directing traffic, and two teens taping butcher paper over every exposed cinderblock wall.

Inside, the air was three degrees cooler than out, but at least ten times more electric. The main room, usually host to Zumba classes and Friday night bingo, was now divided into quadrants, each claimed by a different tribe. Keiki craft tables stacked with paint sets and coloring books; a buffet line waiting to be filled with steam trays and aluminum pans; a set of low platforms ringed by fresh lauhala mats; and a cluster of city officers, most in off duty polos, looking out of place amid the backdrop of ti and tinsel.

Naalei was everywhere at once. She orchestrated the garland hangers, policed the arrangement of food platters ("no, no, those come last, or the ants will riot"), and still found time to adjust the angle of the altar in the center of the room, fussing with the offerings so nothing looked too studied. She wore a faded T-shirt, plumeria print at the collar, and moved with the careful authority of a kumu who'd long ago mastered the art of organized chaos.

"Here, put this by the registration table," she called, handing off a bundle of white flowers to the first person she saw. "Don't crush the stems, or we'll have nothing to work with by noon."

Kai trailed behind her, arms full of poster

board and folders, his map from the morning already set up on a trifold. He'd labeled it OAHU SECRETS: Sacred Sites and Stories, and in sharpie underneath, Ask Before You Go. He tested the sign twice, then stepped back, assessing his work with a scientist's skepticism.

Leilani took it all in, her hands on hips. A few feet away, two officers debated whether to set their pamphlets on crime prevention before or after the health and safety ones.

She walked over, sized them up. "Guys, we have to blend in, not stand out like a cop shop. And for God's sake, do you see the shoes? This is a barefoot event, so play along."

The younger of the two looked down. "What if we step on a staple?" he asked, half joking, half terrified.

She grinned, the mean edge dulled. "Well, you tell Officer Akana, and he'll patch you up in first aid. It's tradition."

Behind her, a heavyset man in an aloha shirt tried to hang a flag from the far wall, but his ladder wobbled. "Careful!" Naalei called, materializing at the base and steadying it with both hands. "If you break your neck, nobody gets lunch."

Leilani watched her mother work the room, her voice not loud but perfectly pitched, her gestures always this side of dramatic. Within fifteen minutes, three disputes were resolved, five tasks completed, and the entire back wall lined with paper orchids made by the third graders at the elementary school up the street.

At exactly nine, the door cracked open, and a line of women in matching muumuus streamed in, arms loaded with bowls, drums and potted ferns. The first of the cultural practitioners, Leilani thought. She scanned the faces, none angry, but most suspicious, eyes flicking from the police to the buffet table to the banners on the wall.

The lead dancer was a woman about Leilani's age, with long black hair slicked into a perfect bun, every movement controlled and poised. She made a direct line for Naalei, who greeted her with a kiss on each cheek and a quick inventory of the containers in her arms.

"Mandy, you remembered the kalo! The kids will love you."

The dancer shrugged. "I'm hoping they eat something besides cupcakes." She looked past Naalei at Leilani. "You're the detective?"

Leilani nodded, bracing for whatever came next.

"Big shoes to fill," Mandy said, but not unkindly. "We all heard about last week. Your mom lets nothing slip."

Leilani winced. "Word travels."

Mandy laughed, and slipped away, directing her own crew to the staging mats. The tension eased a notch.

Another arrival, a man in a white button-down, sleeves rolled up to the elbows, arms filled with boxes marked Safety Outreach. Leilani spotted the sharp jaw and the way his hair refused to obey the weather and fought with the wind. Torres, running late as usual but pretending he wasn't. He set down the boxes by the door, flashed a look at Leilani that could have been a whole paragraph if anyone else was paying attention.

She raised an eyebrow. "Thought you hated community events."

"The ones with bad coffee," Torres said. "This is a major upgrade."

She grinned, gestured at the boxes. "You're not here for the PR, right?"

He leaned in, dropped his voice. "The new Chief wants pictures for the website. Says we need to show the people we can play nice, but I'd come anyway. Wouldn't miss it."

She caught the slight pulse, but ignored it. "We're on lei duty in ten. Don't embarrass me."

He saluted and joined the flow.

On the far side of the room, Kai arranged his

map and laid out a set of Sharpies and Post-its. The first wave of kids came by, and he introduced them to the sacred site markers, telling stories he'd memorized from his grandma and the internet, in that order. The older boys, who usually cracked wise at anything touristy, stood quiet, listening as Kai explained why the stones on the North Shore weren't rocks, but places where our ancestors stopped to rest.

By ten, the room was near capacity. There were officers at every station, from the neighborhood watch signup to the lost pet desk. Leilani made her rounds, stopping to remind each group of the protocol, accept food with both hands, never refuse a lei, and if you forget a name, say "aloha" and smile.

The first awkward moment came when an old uncle, barefoot and shirtless, wandered over to the police table and started lecturing the sergeant about the time his cousin got pulled over on the H-1. Instead of bristling, the sergeant listened, offered a plate of lilikoi bars and a handshake. The moment passed, and with it, a little more of the line that divided the room.

Another flash of drama. Two hula dancers needed a last-minute fix on their pa'u skirts. Naalei dove into the fray, borrowed safety pins from the registration table, and cinched the skirts herself, making both dancers laugh and call her auntie when she was barely a decade older.

By mid-morning, the distinction between the groups was who wore a uniform and who wore print. The lines had blurred, not erased, but smudged enough that it no longer felt like us and them. Between assignments, Leilani leaned against the snack table, sipping a guava juice and watching the room reset itself with every new arrival. Torres joined her, handing her a napkin.

"You see that?" he said, nodding at Kai, now deep in conversation with a detective who looked genuinely interested in the map. "He's a natural."

Leilani looked a little awed. "I think he wants someone to listen for a change."

Torres nudged her shoulder. "Remind you of anyone?"

She snorted. "I was never that cute."

He raised an eyebrow. "You're still pretty cute when you get passionate about something."

She almost spat out her juice. "Wow, is that an FBI pickup line?"

He laughed, shifting his gaze. "Your mom is working miracles."

They both watched as Naalei, never still for more than a minute, wove through clusters of dancers and officers, making introductions, trading jokes, and every so often stopping to touch a shoulder or offer a correction in the softest possible way.

When she reached a group of three women in floral dresses, the tension was high. One woman's face was set, arms crossed. Leilani recognized her as a kumu from the news, someone who'd openly criticized the police for years.

Naalei didn't flinch. She spoke and pointed across the room at one officer. "Did you know Officer Keahi's grandmother was my hula sister? She used to make the best laulau and taught the class how to chant." The kumu's arms relaxed. "And Chief Mori's family," Naalei continued. "They protected the Waimea heiau during the last flood. Risked their lives. That's what aloha means."

The mood shifted. There were still things to fix, always would be, but the wall was cracking. Leilani watched the lightness ripple through the room, the way laughter traveled faster than gossip, the way people found reasons to linger instead of reasons to leave.

She glanced at Torres. "You think we'll ever get it right?"

He shrugged. "We're closer than yesterday."

She let herself believe it.

As the clock neared eleven, the organizers started shepherding people toward the mats in the center of the room. The kids carried bundles of flowers; the officers brought their chairs, and the old uncles led the way with their own kind of stubborn grace.

On her way to the center, Leilani passed Kai, who was packing up his station. She stopped, kneeled to his level. "You did good, bug."

He grinned wide and true. "Everyone wanted to know about the map. I think I'm gonna make a website."

She laughed, ruffling his hair. "You're a born organizer."

He looked up, mischief in his eyes. "I get it from you."

She hugged him, and they joined the crowd, ready for the ceremony to begin.

If the event had a start time, nobody believed it. When Naalei stood at the front of the room, a hush swept over the crowd so sudden that the toddlers stopped fidgeting. It wasn't the silence that fell when people were being polite; it was the kind that settled when something sacred was about to start, and everyone could feel it in their lungs.

She began the oli without preamble. The first notes were deep, lower than her speaking voice, and they rose in slow spirals, climbing and tumbling in a pattern older than any calendar.

She called to the gods of wind and rain, to the ancestors whose bones lined every ridge, to the living and the unborn. The words were Hawaiian, full of guttural breaks and soft vowels, the kind that could gut a grown man if he listened with his heart instead of his ears. Every time her pitch changed, the echo in the rec room made it sound as if the building itself had joined the chorus.

Leilani watched her mother. Not the woman who corrected homework or paid the bills or scolded her for letting the laundry sour in the basket, but the keeper of something raw and essential, a conductor channeling voltage straight from the source. The chant ended on a single unaccompanied note, and for one breathless moment, nobody moved. The kids started clapping, and it was as if the whole place remembered how to breathe.

The interactive stations opened with a rush. The first was the hula basics, where the dancers showed volunteers how to move their hips and tell a story with their hands. The officers, who hours earlier had stood rigid and wary, were now lining up to learn the four basic steps. When Sergeant Reyes tried to keep time, he failed so spectacularly that the sternest auntie couldn't help but laugh. Instead of looking embarrassed, he took a bow and offered a high five to anyone who'd join.

Nearby, the table labeled Tools of the Trade drew a crowd of aunties and uncles, who marveled at the plastic handcuffs and pepper spray. One kumu asked if the radio was tuned to the same channel as on Hawaii Five-O. The officer working the table grinned and let her try the mic, which resulted in a brief, highly inappropriate exchange in pidgin that had the room in stitches.

Kai found his place as a tour guide, leading groups of kids and adults from his map station to the various displays. He pointed out which rocks were real and which were fake, which stories you could tell to tourists and which ones you had to keep for family. His confidence grew with every group, and by midday he was giving the closing remarks for each stop, always remembering to say thank you in both English and Hawaiian.

Outside, food was served. Plates of kalua pork and chicken long rice, bowls of poi and lomi salmon, and trays of sweet bread and mochi. Leilani took a turn at the buffet line, handing out plates and joking with a couple of retirees who claimed they only came for the haupia. Torres drifted over to help, working the crowd with that FBI charm that could turn an audit into a luau if he set his mind to it.

The formality of the event never overpowered the joy. When Chief Mori took the mic, her words were brief, focused not on accolades but on respect. "We're here because we owe a debt to the people who came before us," she said, her voice carrying over the chatter. "Hawaiian culture is not a museum piece. It's a living thing. If we can't honor it, we have no business wearing these uniforms." She nodded at her officers, who for once stood a little taller.

Now, it was Naalei's turn. She didn't use a mic, but nobody missed a word. She spoke of stories and secrets, of how things passed from one hand to the next, sometimes changing, sometimes staying stubbornly the same. "We talk a lot about preservation, about holding on to what is precious. But to do that, we must first trust each other. It's hard. It's never going to be easy. But if we try—" She held up a half-finished mat, the strands uneven but woven tight. "If we try, what was once broken can be rewoven. We start again, and this time, we make it better."

She set down the mat, and everyone knew it was time for the lei.

The final activity was simple. A lei of ti leaves, plumeria and bits of lauhala, long enough to encircle every person present, whether they wore a badge or muumuu, or faded denim. The volunteers passed it along, each person adding something, a flower, a shell, a wish whispered to the inside. When the circle was complete, it closed the old wound or at least drew a line around it.

At sunset, the crowd walked together to the beach. The tide was high; the waves frothing pink in the last light. They formed a circle; the lei stretched across outstretched arms, and Naalei started a chant, low and rolling, joined by the other practitioners one by one. This time, the officers joined too, not in pitch, but on purpose. The lei was set in the water, where it bobbed and spun before the current carried it out to sea.

Leilani stood between Kai and her mother, her arm resting on the boy's shoulder, her own shoulder warmed by the press of Naalei's hand. Torres lingered a respectful step away, but he didn't hide his smile when he caught Leilani's eye. The future seemed wide open, as bright as the sky after a storm.

They stood until the lei vanished from view, turning to face the city lights coming up behind them. If the world wasn't fixed, it was at least changed, a new pattern, a fresh story, one worth telling again and again.

As the crowd drifted back up the path, Leilani hugged her son, hugged her mother, and let Torres put an arm around her waist. The salt wind dried the last tears on her face, and the ache she'd carried for so long seemed lighter, almost gone. They walked home together, the old pain woven into something softer, something strong enough to last another day.

CHAPTER EIGHTEEN

Lingering Shadows

The morning was a bandage, white and clean, wrapped tight around the last week's wounds. The trade wind slipped through the slats of the kitchen windows, billowed the faded curtain, and pulled the salt off the surf to layer everything with its thin, sharp taste. The house was still, with no shoes scattered in the hall, no clatter of cartoons from the TV. The hush that comes before anything bad or good starts.

Leilani stood at the stove, left hand bracing the pan, right hand sifting Spam slices into a slow sizzle. She'd woken early, not because of nightmares (for once), but because her body refused to believe it had survived the week. She watched the Spam crisp, a brown tide advancing across each pink island, and tried to match her breathing to the rhythm of the popping fat. She was almost successful.

Behind her was evidence of progress. Kai's

latest notebook, a spiral-bound job, lay open and annotated in three colors of pen. Two new drawings of Kaimuki's ancient heiau, rendered in an eleven-year-old's brash lines, took up most of page one. On the fridge, last night's shopping list, which she'd remembered to finish, was hanging beside the picture of her father in uniform, and beside that, a snapshot of herself, Kai, and her mother, all windblown and mid-laugh on the bow of a whale watching boat. The house seemed to exhale, letting the lines between past, present, and after bleed a little.

She took the Spam off, plated it, and cracked three eggs into the same pan. The sound was a balm, bright, ordinary, and unremarkable.

Her phone buzzed once on the counter. She reached without looking, thumbed it open, expecting some last-minute update from HQ, a text from Isaac, or at worst, a payment due reminder from her least favorite utility. Instead, it was a number she didn't know. No name, a local area code and a timestamp one minute before sunrise.

The text contained two things. First, a simple black spiral emoji, the one with the curl a little too tight, the vector graphics clean and sharp, like a razor laid on a fingerprint.

Second. *Not all branches wither when the trunk falls.*

For a long moment, nothing happened in her brain except the thud of her pulse behind her eyes. Piece by piece, it came back. The spiral was the mark, David's mark, or more accurately, the mark of the network that had burned through the city for a decade and supposedly died with him.

She read the message again, this time cataloging every detail. The sender's number was a throwaway, or at least not in her contact list or the department's records. The font was standard, but the emoji code was one digit off from the default. Someone had gone to the trouble of tweaking the spiral, adding the sun at the end, like a flourish or a dare.

Her fingers felt cold, but her mind ran through the checklist. Who had access to her number? Who still ran ops after last week's arrests? Was this a leftover cell, some zealot too far downstream to have caught the collapse, or a sick joke from an old enemy? The wording gnawed at her. The way, trunk and branches could mean one thing, and how wither implied she was the tree, and not, as she preferred, the ax.

She locked the phone and set it face down. The sizzle of the eggs had turned into a dull hiss, the yolks blooming and going glassy. She shut the burner, slid the eggs onto the plate, and forced herself to move with an efficiency that read as confidence to anyone watching.

The footsteps came soft, but the door slam was classic, a miniature hurricane, followed by a long pause and a half-whispered, "Ow." Kai shuffled in, T-shirt from yesterday (the one with the glow-in-the-dark skeleton), shorts backwards, hair in a swirl that would shame any natural disaster.

He dropped his crime notebook on the table, gazed at the food, and at her. "Mom, can I show you something before school?"

She forced a smile. "Always."

He sat, started in on the Spam with a single-mindedness that belonged to kids and criminals. "You know how you said we shouldn't ever make a map of our house, because bad guys might use it?"

Leilani tried not to look at the phone. "I remember."

"So, I made a map of the entire neighborhood instead. That way, if anyone tries to break in, we can see all the ways they'd try to escape." He said this with the pride of a child who had no idea how true the words were, or how much his own parents had run that same play, decades earlier, for much darker reasons.

He flipped open the notebook. The map was good, showing all the alleys, fence gaps, and the one drainage ditch that cut through the neighbor's yard and out to the canal. Each escape route was marked, color-coded, and annotated with time estimates for someone fast, average, or old. In the margin there was a legend; S = suspicious. X = super suspicious. He'd tagged three houses and a van down the block.

Leilani felt a laugh trying to break through the knot in her stomach. "You really want to be a detective, don't you?"

Kai looked up, mouth full, unashamed. "I already am. I don't have a badge yet."

She tousled his hair. "You'll be a better one than me, for sure."

He beamed and returned to his project. As he ate, he recited a list of the day's goals. "Turn in the volcano report, don't forget shoes at PE, and try to get a picture of that one bird for Nana." He was, as always, operating on multiple channels at once. She envied it.

Her phone buzzed again, one new message, same number, no text. The spiral alone, as if to say, Did you get it? Are you watching?

She didn't flinch, not while Kai was there.

She watched him for another minute, memorizing the set of his jaw, the small confidence he carried when he thought the world was safe. She ruffled his hair a second time and told him to brush his teeth before school, despite it being an hour early and he hated that part of the routine most.

When he left, she picked up the phone, unlocked it, and stared at the spiral. This time, she let herself think like a cop. Professional. Precise. Patient. Not a prank, not a leftover. This was a challenge, a test of whether she was still on duty, or whether she'd truly started over, as everyone had begged her to.

She thumbed through her contacts, searching for old enemies. There were five people left in the city with the means and the balls to pull something like this, and she'd already arrested three, testified against another, and buried the fifth herself, three years back.

She ran through the list twice. Each time, her mind added more suspects instead of subtracting. She gripped the rim of the table, felt her pulse in the heel of her hand. The old paranoia wasn't gone; it was on lunch break.

Kai called from the other room: "I'm making a backup map for Nana's garage, is that okay?"

"Don't use the red pen for everything," she said.

He laughed, and she let it calm her.

She copied the spiral, saved the number, and set a calendar reminder to check for new pings every hour. The techs at the station could trace it, or at least get close. But she wouldn't let herself call Isaac until she had something more than a ghost and a feeling.

She cleared the plates, wiped the table, and glanced at the fridge. The photos looked back at her, silent, nonjudgmental, exactly as they had the morning after the last war ended. She squared her shoulders, checked the locks, and began the day.

Two hours later, the inside of Surfside Beans was louder than a squad car radio, but the noise had its own logic. Grinders roaring, blenders howling, the clatter of mugs, and underneath it all, the din of locals cycling in and out, sleep-deprived and desperate for the day's first fix. The air was thick with espresso and banana bread, and the tables were already half filled with laptops and legal pads. Leilani threaded her way to the back, bypassed the cop cluster that always formed near the cream station, and found Isaac at their usual corner.

He was in civilian mode, jeans, a University of Hawaii T-shirt, and a dark windbreaker zipped enough to cover the holster. He looked like he belonged here, like he could be any guy finishing his dissertation, except for the way his eyes tracked the exits and how he always sat with his back to the wall. Some things you never shake. He smiled when he saw her, but it faltered as soon as she set her phone down and nudged it his way.

"Morning to you too," he said, half joking.

She returned the smile, tapped the screen awake, thumbed into messages, and rotated the phone so the spiral stared up at him, bright and oily on the black glass. "Got this before dawn," she said. "Number's not in my log, but it's local."

He studied it; the banter draining out of his face. The first thing he did was turn the phone over and check the make, like the device itself had secrets. He scrolled, flicked back and forth between the two messages, and looked up at her with a frown she hadn't seen since the night of the raid.

"I thought we got them all," Isaac said. He didn't whisper it, but the words landed hard.

"So did I."

He looked around, did a quick scan for anything that might be an open ear or stray lens, and leaned in, elbows on the tiny round table. "Anybody else know yet?"

She gave her head a shake. "You're the first. I wanted to see if you could run it through your Bureau toys before I loop in the brass. It's someone on the outside, or someone on the inside with a sense of humor I really don't appreciate."

Isaac grunted, set the phone down gently. "Could be a stray. Someone from the old network, panicking. Could be a copycat, some kid who found the archives."

"It's not a kid," Leilani said. "Look at the signature. They modded the emoji, offset the character code. You don't do that unless you know how to cover a digital trail."

He gave her the old, crooked smile, the one that said you're still sharper than any of us, even after the world tried to break you. "You run the number yet?"

She pulled out a slip of paper, written in block letters, and slid it to him. "Spoofs as a prepaid, but the tower ping was less than three miles from here. Kaimuki side."

Isaac nodded, already in hunter mode. He sipped his black coffee, no matter how many times she told him to lighten up, and started a low, steady drum of his fingers. "Okay. Let's break this down. Worst case, someone's rebuilding. It could be one of Kekoa's people, a cousin, a friend, or anyone with a stake in the spiral not dying. "Or," he added. "Someone's testing you to see if you'll flinch."

She snorted. "They'll have to try harder."

His eyes flicked over her face, searching for tells. "You okay?"

She shrugged. "I hate games. If someone's got a beef, they should come at me like a grown-up."

Isaac grinned. "You never were subtle."

She almost smiled. "That's why you love me, right?"

He didn't answer, but his hand reached across the table and covered hers for half a second, a squeeze so brief you'd miss it if you blinked. "I'll put our guys on it," he said. "Quietly. No need to kick up dust yet, especially if this is a fishing expedition."

Leilani nodded, focusing on the table's grain. "I thought it was done, Isaac. I really did."

"Yeah," he said, voice softer. "Me too."

The world shrank down to the ring of the coffee mug, the condensation pooling at its base, the shape of her hand under his. The shop's speaker squealed with a synthpop cover of "Hotel California," and the spell broke.

She took back her phone and pocketed it. "We keep watch for now?"

"Yeah. We cross-reference any hits on your number, and I'll put a hold on all outgoing case data from the last month. I'm guessing if they wanted a war, they'd have announced themselves bigger. This is small. It's almost polite."

"Polite's overrated," she said. "You should see Kai's new notebook. He's mapped every alley between our house and Nana's. Kid's prepping for the apocalypse."

Isaac looked up, and there was pride in how he did it. "He gets it from you."

She laughed, the edge catching in her throat. "That's not the compliment you think it is."

He drank his coffee, not arguing.

A silence stretched between them, not awkward, but full of all the things they didn't say. Leilani studied his face. The last few months had carved lines around his eyes, but also in the way he gazed at her now, less like an agent and more like someone who'd stayed.

She reached over, plucked a crumb from his shirt, flicked it onto the tray. "You know, if this is a sick joke, I almost want to shake their hand. They got the emoji perfect."

"You're not mad?"

She leaned in, voice low. "I'm mad that I have to waste my time chasing ghosts. I'm mad that people who get off on power never vanish. But mostly, I'm mad I can't drink my coffee and pretend I'm not looking for traps every time I sit down."

He smiled, set his mug aside and laced his

fingers together. "We've earned some peace, Lei. Even if we fight for it every day."

"I'll be ready," she said.

He nodded. "You got it. I'll call you if anything pings. And if you get another, don't open it alone."

"Deal."

They stood, bussed their own cups, and walked out together. She let him hold the door, and as they stepped into the blinding mid-morning light, she thought: let them come. Some things survived the pruning. She was one of them.

By evening, the house had shifted personalities: kitchen table scrubbed and cleared, dining room overheads on low, the whole place prepped for business. Kai buzzed from the hallway with the energy reserved for field trips and the opening of rare Pokémon packs. He skidded into the dining room, arms full of markers, a kid's digital camera (borrowed from Nana, allegedly for "nature shots"), and a folder with the beginnings of a homemade case file.

Leilani sat at the table, sorting evidence bags with the practiced neatness of someone who'd once lived out of a Ford Explorer for three years. Each item had a purpose, and she lined them up in the order any investigator would need. Gloves, bag, notebook, camera, index cards, a Sharpie, and, her nod to the evening's improvisational nature, a half-empty bag of Sweet Maui Onion chips for breaks.

"Ready for your forensic lesson?" she asked.

Kai didn't answer with words; instead he snapped on the latex gloves she'd laid out for him. They were a size too big, but he grinned, showing the teeth that were mostly second wave and already angling for an orthodontic disaster.

"I set up the scenario," he said. "Solve the case."

Leilani raised a brow. "What's the case?"

Kai cleared his throat and read from the index card. "At 1840 hours, the subject discovered a series of mysterious objects on the back porch. Suspect left them arranged in a spiral." He hesitated, looking up with a conspiratorial squint. "Coincidence?"

"Not in this house," she said. She smiled, but the sharpness in the words was an old reflex.

He beamed and launched into the first step, narrating as he worked. "Approach the scene. Observe but don't disturb." He crouched near the patio door, his sunglasses perched on his nose though the sun was down, and scribbled in his notebook. "There are five pieces of evidence," he declared, drawing the spiral on the margin for reference.

Leilani followed him, offering pointers when he looked about to wipe his nose with the glove, or step over his own shoe prints. "Remember, write exactly what you see, not what you think happened."

He nodded, careful now, and wrote in tiny block letters: 1. RED FEATHER. 2. USED BAND-AID. 3. PLASTIC COIN. 4. TINY TOY DOG. 5. STRAWBERRY GUMMY, HALF MELTED.

She let him bag each one and label the tag in Sharpie with the item, location, and time. "Chain of custody," she said, passing him the second notebook. "Never let it out of your sight and always document the handoff."

He took this seriously, inventing a plausible transfer to "Detective Nana," then scribbling her signature with impressive accuracy.

The photos came next. Kai snapped one for each object, another for the overall scene, and three of his own face in exaggerated detective mode. "Gotta have an ID for the file," he explained.

They returned to the table, evidence lined up on a folded towel. "Now," said Kai. "We solve the crime."

Leilani poured them a glass of water, set out the chips, and leaned in. "Interview time. You're the lead. What's your theory?"

He flipped open the folder, tongue sticking out as he checked his notes. "The red feather is from the cardinal outside. I saw it this morning." He spun the bag, pointed. "Used Band-Aid, gross, but also Mom, your left hand has a fresh cut."

She lifted her palm and saw the sliver she'd gotten slicing mango earlier. "You're good."

He grinned and examined the plastic coin. "Probably from the gumball machine at Foodland. Did you go to Foodland today?"

"For soda. But I didn't get a coin."

He shrugged, noted it, reaching for the toy dog. "This is from my old set, but I haven't seen it in months." He looked thoughtful. "The criminal could be a dog lover."

"Or you lost it, and someone found it on the porch."

Kai considered this. He scribbled: "Possible. Check the camera for prints."

Leilani stifled a laugh before she took the last piece of evidence. The gummy, now misshapen and sticky, smelled faintly of strawberry and defeat. "Final clue."

He sniffed it, not wanting to get too close. He wrote: "No bugs. Fresh?"

She watched him assemble the theory, stringing the evidence together, discarding bad ideas, circling back. It was beautiful and terrifying, the way his brain worked, a pattern that felt familiar and foreign, like seeing her own childhood in a funhouse mirror.

Finally, he sat back and pushed his notes to her. "I think it was the neighbor cat," he declared. "She brings stuff to the porch all the time, and the toy probably fell out of my backpack. The coin and gummy were bait, but she's not picky, so she took the feather instead."

Leilani read it over, impressed. "And the Band-Aid?"

He grinned. "Red herring. Or you, but mostly a herring."

They both laughed.

She let the moment linger; reached across and ruffled his hair. "You've got good instincts, bug. Promise me you'll use them for good."

He nodded. "Always. But what if the spiral comes back?"

She stared at him, surprised by the question's weight.

"We watch, and we remember the old cases. But we don't let them run the house, okay?"

He nodded, understanding more than most grown-ups did.

They packed up the evidence, stored it in the old cookie tin (chain of custody observed), and cleaned the table. Kai darted off to finish his report, promising to scan and send it to Nana by bedtime.

Leilani sat for a while, notebook in hand, and let her mind drift to the spiral message locked in her phone. It was a reminder that the world out there wasn't tamed, but contained. But inside this house, for one night at least, the case she cared about was already solved. She closed the notebook, switched off the lights, and listened to the quiet, punctuated by the gentle click of keys from Kai's room.

Some branches withered, but others, given time, grew stronger than the trunk ever was.

Leilani's phone chimed, and she glanced at the screen. The number belonged to the private cell phone of the U.S. Attorney. Her hand shook slightly as she wondered what news awaited her. She pressed the green button.

"Good evening, sir," she greeted, with a slight tremor in her voice.

"Good evening, Detective. I hope I haven't caught you at a bad time."

"No, sir," she replied.

"Very good," he responded. "I wanted you to hear it from me and not from some reporter."

Leilani held her breath.

"After reviewing all the evidence you presented on behalf of your mother and the other community leaders, we have decided not to pursue this matter any further."

Leilani was taken aback. "That is fantastic news, sir."

"Please let your mother and the others know and thank them for allowing you to bring the matter to our attention. Have a good rest of your evening, Detective."

"I will, sir, and thank you again." She ended the call and dialed her mother.

"What's wrong?" asked Naalei.

"Good news, Mom. The U.S. Attorney's office is not going to pursue your involvement with the spiral money any further. They are dropping the case."

Naalei was silent for a moment. "That's wonderful. I need to call the others and let them know. Thank you, Honey."

The call ended, and Leilani walked to the kitchen to pour herself a glass of wine in celebration. It was the perfect ending to a perfect day.

CHAPTER NINETEEN

Island Healing

B efore the sun found the horizon, the Kealoha family crept barefoot down a slope of loose rock and ironwood needles, each step a memory of an older world where ceremonies happened in the open, for the living and the dead and all the ghosts that hovered between. The path to the secluded cove twisted through guava and wild ginger, the branches close, and wet with night, the silence broken by the occasional crack of a twig under Leilani's heel or the whisper of Kai's notebook, thumbed for the hundredth time to make sure it was still there.

No cars passed on the old coast road. The surf was restrained, curling against the rim of black sand in soft, respectful exhalations, as if it too had something to atone for.

Naalei walked ahead, the first to step out onto the open crescent where tide pools glittered under the last of the stars. She wore her teaching dress, a simple dark cotton, hem faded by years of salt and sun, and on her shoulders draped the broad green of a freshly cut ti leaf, a cloak for crossing thresholds. The woven basket in her arms held the morning's work. Bundles of leaves and flower heads, small polished stones, and three wood-carved implements shaped like paddles but smaller than a hand span, their edges worn smooth as river pebbles.

Kai trailed her at a distance, caught between the need to witness and the fear of witnessing wrong. His usual running commentary had shrunk to a hush, his hands occupied by a single object wrapped in a kitchen towel. A gourd hollowed and sanded to a thin shell, the handiwork of last month's school project, now assigned a role in a ritual he half understood.

Leilani brought up the rear, the morning wind stinging against skin left raw by weeks of healing. Every step sent a pulse through her side, the old bruise now a faint yellow but no less insistent, as if her body remembered more than it let on. She kept her eyes on the sand, counting the steps to the water's edge, refusing to limp unless she thought no one was looking.

They met at the shoreline, where the slope evened out and a vein of driftwood cut across the black. The air smelled of crushed limu and the metallic brine of salt drying on rock. Naalei paused, surveyed the space, and nodded as if it confirmed something she'd been thinking since before sunrise.

"This is good," she said, voice low. "We'll use the curve for a bowl, keep the ocean in the backdrop."

Kai hovered, unsure of where to set his burden, until Naalei pointed to a dry patch of sand above the high tide line. "You can put it there, hon. But face it toward the water."

He did, hands shaking a little. The gourd rolled in place, and settled, pointing like a compass needle straight to the horizon.

Naalei set her basket beside it, and set about the business of arranging. Three bowls, each the size of a cupped palm, came first, nested in a line and filled by hand with coarse rock salt brought in a jam jar from her kitchen. Next, a fistful of plumeria blossoms, waxy and yellow at the rim, set in a crescent arc that mirrored the cove. She placed the paddles last, one at each end of the arrangement and the third at the center, handles crossed, blades facing out.

Kai watched her work, questions building behind his tongue, but this time he let them sit. His eyes darted from the implements to the salt to the line of shells, absorbing the pattern as only a child could.

Leilani stood a few paces back, arms folded against the dawn chill, her own bundle pressed hard against her ribs. She could taste an old ache in her lungs. The cliff was three weeks gone, and the bruising almost faded, but every time she exhaled, it seemed to come from somewhere farther inside.

Naalei motioned for her to approach. "You'll help," she said, the words an instruction but also a comfort. "Set your bundle on the left side. Kai, you're on the right."

Leilani obeyed. The bundle was nothing, a handful of ti leaves, but she placed it as directed, smoothing the sand where it landed. Kai did the same, using both hands, though his object was so light it barely dimpled the surface.

Naalei took her place in the middle. She crouched, folded her legs under her, and beckoned them to sit, knees to sand, forming a triangle around the altar. Kai glanced at his mom, uncertain, and mirrored her movement. The cold of the beach seeped up through their shins, a reminder that the world was always in contact, no matter how much you tried to float above it.

When they were settled, Naalei unwrapped a bundle of her own, revealing a single piece of kapa, the tapa cloth thin as parchment and inked with a spiral in ochre and charcoal. She set it atop the salt bowl, and let her hand rest on it, as if steadying the memory for what came next.

"We start with the oli," she said, the words gentle but carrying the command of ritual.

Leilani bowed her head. Kai copied her, eyes closed so tight the lids shivered.

Naalei cleared her throat, and the first note came out lower than speech, a vibration that made the hair on Leilani's arms tingle. The chant was old, probably older than any of their ancestors, but the melody moved with the ease of a childhood song. The words called the wind first, then the sea, then the ancestors whose names still clung to the island like lichen to lava. Each phrase was a wave, rising and spilling, never abrupt, always carrying forward what the last had left.

At the second verse, Kai relaxed his shoulders. He peeked through one eye to check and saw that his mom was not looking at him, but at the water, her face gone soft and unreadable. He let his eyes shut again and tried to catch the rhythm, mouthing the syllables under his breath.

Naalei's hands moved as she chanted, tracing the spiral, then gesturing in small, circular motions over the salt bowls, as if stirring something invisible into the mix. Her voice blurred with the surf, so that sometimes it seemed she was another current working its way around the cove.

When the oli finished, the silence that

followed was not an absence but a thickening, like the moment after a bell is struck and all you hear is the world remembering itself. Naalei kept her eyes shut, lips moving, silent now, but still working the air. After a breath or two, she opened them, and the look she gave her daughter was clear and bright, as if she'd returned from somewhere farther away than the cove.

"Do you have anything to say?" Naalei asked, not quite a challenge, more an offer.

Leilani swallowed. The words that came to mind were the kind that started and ended with names, and she wasn't sure if the names would help.

Naalei nodded, as if this was the answer she'd expected. "Let's get to work."

She reached for the leftmost salt bowl, scooped a pinch between her fingers, and sprinkled it into the tide line. "We start with the things we want to keep safe," she said. "We give up what needs letting go."

The sun was a pale coin above the sea, bright enough to blur the outlines of things but not yet mean enough to chase off the chill. Kai found a spot and began digging with his hands, scooping out a divot for his gourd, careful to keep the sides straight.

"Deep enough so it won't blow away," he said, more to himself than to the women. When it sat level, he dusted his palms and looked up, waiting.

Naalei strolled back to her basket, drew out a spool of twine, and unwound a piece for each of them. "Next part," she said. "We write it down."

She passed around the notepaper, ripped from a composition pad, the blue lines running faint and slanted where the pen had bled through from the sheet above. No ceremony in the materials. The meaning, she'd always said, was in the doing.

Leilani took hers and steadied her hand on her thigh. The tremor, a leftover from the injuries, hadn't come back in weeks, but now it returned, subtle but persistent. She pressed the pen to paper and contemplated the margin, waiting for the words to make sense. What do you call what's left behind? Was it guilt, or relief, or the space of not knowing which?

She wrote: *Fear of forgetting. Guilt for not wanting him back. Rage at what I let happen. A hunger for the city to go quiet, for a day.*

She folded the sheet twice; the edges aligning with a precision that felt almost bureaucratic.

Kai's turn. He stared at his page for so long that Leilani wondered if he'd blanked out, but he wrote with the intensity of a confession. *I don't want Mom to leave again. I'm scared that if she dies nobody will tell me the truth. I want to stop being afraid of the ocean at night. I want Nana to never be sad.*

His hand moved in hard, fast lines, printing each word in uppercase so there'd be no room for misreading. He folded the note into a tight square, then held it up to the light before pressing it to his lips and tucking it into the ti leaf.

Naalei's own note was the briefest. A single sentence, written with a stubby pencil and folded twice: For all that was left unsaid. She didn't show it to anyone, but Leilani caught the last word, slanting across the paper as the leaf curled around it.

Naalei showed them how to wrap the bundles. "Start with the backbone," she said, pointing at the thick rib of the ti. "Fold the pain inside, and roll it tight. The twine holds it until you're ready to let go."

Kai watched her hands and mirrored the motion. His leaf wasn't perfect, but it held together, the twine spiraled from stem to tip like a vine on a fence. Leilani's bundle came out lopsided at first, but she smoothed the corners and tried again until it sat level in her palm.

"Now you bless it," said Naalei. "With breath first, then with salt."

She held her bundle to her mouth and blew a long, slow stream across the surface. Kai followed, then Leilani, who felt ridiculous until she saw the focus on her mother's face. It was an old act, a way of marking boundaries, of sending away what you couldn't carry any further.

Naalei dipped a finger in the leftover salt, pressed it to her bundle, tracing a line along the spine. "The salt is for purification," she explained. "It keeps what's important and dissolves the rest."

She sprinkled the last of the plumerias into each of their hands. "Flowers mean new growth. If you are looking to plant a new story, you start with something that can root and spread."

Kai tucked the flowers into the hollow of his leaf, using the twine to anchor each petal. Leilani tried to do the same, but her fingers fumbled, and one blossom slipped out, landing on the sand beside her knee. She picked it up, brushed off the grains, and pushed it back in, forcing herself to care about the little acts, when the bigger ones felt like theater.

When the bundles were done, they set them in a line at the front of the gourd, facing east. Kai looked up, shading his eyes, and asked, "Do we bury them, or send them away?"

"We let them go together," Naalei said. "But first, we kneel."

They kneeled, the three of them, knees pressed to the damp, cold sand. There was a shiver, not quite a chill but enough to make Leilani aware of every inch of skin not covered by the old hoodie she'd worn. She placed her bundle down. The need to reach out and touch Kai's hand was so strong she almost missed Naalei's start.

Naalei's voice came low, quieter than the first chant, more a hum than a melody. This was the chant of release, of turning the story forward and letting the old roots rot beneath the surface. The syllables caught on the wind, spinning back at them from the rocks, but instead of bouncing, they seemed to be absorbed by the cove, as if the island itself had ears.

Leilani joined, off-beat but close enough. Kai mouthed the sounds, then found his own note and added it, high and clear, piercing through the two older voices like a third color in a spectrum.

They let the chant build, then taper off, until the only sound left was the gentle slosh of water in the pools below. Naalei placed her hand on the gourd, pressed down until it wobbled, and then waited.

"Ready?" she asked.

Nobody said yes, but all three reached forward, hands hovering over the bundles, waiting for the signal.

Naalei nodded once. "On three."

"One," she said, and Kai closed his eyes.

"Two," and Leilani's breath caught, but she didn't let go.

"Three." Together they picked up the bundles and stood, not rushing, but moving as if their bones had always known this would be the next step.

They walked to the tide, the sun now above the water. The sand was warmer here, softer, and the tracks ahead of them were bird prints and the spirals of sand crabs returning from a night out. Naalei led the way, turned, so all three stood in a row, their shadows long and doubled behind them.

She lifted her bundle and spoke, the words more breath than voice: "I give what I can, and I keep what is needed."

Leilani came next. She stood for a time, the offering in her hand, eyes fixed on the foam that surged and pulled and never quite settled. The brine stung her cuts, and the pressure of the sand beneath her feet was enough to remind her what it felt like to stand her ground.

She breathed in, let the salt burn her lungs, walked forward, past where her mother had gone, up to the thighs, the bruised flesh tight and hot beneath the cold slap of the wave. She found the sharpest memory, the moment at the cliff, the feel of David's fingers slipping from her wrist, her own hand refusing to hold on. She shaped it into a single word and pressed it into the leaf with all the force she had left.

She opened her hand. The bundle landed with a splash, bounced once, and was gone, sucked straight down by a second wave so fast she barely caught its leaving.

She didn't want to cry. So, she didn't. Instead, she turned back, dripping, and let herself feel the emptiness where the ache used to be.

Kai was last. He hesitated before hurling his bundle with more force than the others, sending it beyond the break where it bobbed and spun, and vanished in the glare. He watched until it was gone and looked at his mother.

For a while, they stood there, the three of them, watching the water. Naalei was first to speak, not a chant this time, but a song, almost a lullaby, the kind she'd used to sing when Leilani was too fevered to sleep. The melody was round and soft; the syllables drifting into the wind, but when it ended, Kai knew not to break the quiet.

They stood side by side, arms linked, and their faces towards the rising sun. Leilani felt the warmth go all the way through. She reached for her son, pulled him close, and was surprised to find he didn't resist, but leaned in, solid and so much lighter than she remembered.

She looked at Naalei, who had her own arm around them both. The woman's hair glowed silver in the sun, the lines in her face deeper but softer now, like folds in a well-worn sheet.

"We face whatever comes next together," Leilani said, not as a promise, but as a fact.

Naalei nodded. "Always."

They watched the water until the sun climbed high enough to make the sand almost too bright to look at. Kai pointed out a sailboat far offshore, and the way the waves spread behind it, all smooth and open. They made their way back across the beach; the tide chasing their heels, their footprints stretching in a line that grew shorter with every step.

Leilani squeezed her son's hand one more time, then let it go, knowing he would always find his way back.

The walk home was slow, nobody rushing, nobody trying to fill the silence. Once on the bluff, they stopped to look back, watching as a new set of waves crashed over the spot where their offerings had vanished, the foam glimmering gold in the fresh light.

Leilani smiled for no reason at all.

CHAPTER TWENTY

New Horizons

The gold badge felt heavier than its last incarnation. A fraction more brass, a new number etched in the curve, but most of all the gravitas. That was the thing nobody warned you about when they handed you a command.

Leilani stood in Chief Mori's office, the door closed behind her, its hinges drawn taut like a line of muscle across a fighter's neck. She planted her feet, squared her hips, and rolled her shoulder once to signal that, yes, she was ready.

Mori's desk was an altar to the institution. Mahogany, the surface so polished it reflected the ceiling's fluorescent light in a thin white band. On the walls, a collection of antique paddles, sepia photographs of beat cops in short sleeves and long socks, and two framed commendations so dense with bureaucratic font that a detective couldn't parse the full meaning without a magnifier and half a day. Over everything, the smell of coffee and the citrus of floor wax.

"Have a seat, Detective," Mori said. Her voice was the same as always, as though nothing had happened in the last six weeks but another stack of paperwork.

Leilani took the chair without the usual hesitation, matching Mori's posture, shoulders back, gaze level, and not a hint of apology in the line from crown to spine. The bruises had faded from yellow to ivory. The aches from the cliff and the fights had receded to background noise, like the radio static in her mother's kitchen.

Mori steepled her fingers, then reached for a slim blue folder resting on the desk. The logo on the front was embossed in silver: Special Investigations Task Force. The acronym was unfortunate, SITF, but Leilani was already drafting how she'd convince the rank and file to call it anything but Sit Down and Shut Up.

Mori slid the folder across the desk. "Your mandate," she said. "You'll note the terms are broad."

Leilani opened it, eyes skimming. Two pages, one a chart of the initial funding, the other a legalese breakdown of jurisdiction. The names in the margin were interesting: two assistant DAs, three city auditors, and a single line for an investigator to be named. The authority was total, but the budget had training wheels.

She didn't blink. "You want me to start with the brass," she said.

Mori raised an eyebrow. "I want you to start where the blood is brightest, but if you're asking, yes. We need a cleansing, not a scapegoat. The Mayor has authorized you to go wherever the evidence leads. You are not Internal Affairs. Your mandate is the entire city government. There will be resistance. They'll throw you to the press and call you a traitor, but that's nothing new."

She picked up the badge next, new from the shop, the number barely dry. The weight rested on her palm, cool and hard, with the HPD spiral in the middle, the arms curling but now interrupted by a star instead of a void. She thought of Kai's notebooks, every map a spiral unwinding, never folding in on itself but always pushing outward.

Leilani pinned the badge to her lapel, right where the old one had left a faint blue ghost of itself, and said, "Thank you, Chief. I won't let you down."

Mori's expression softened a fraction, enough to make Leilani wonder how many times the woman had sat here, making the same bet on a different horse. "This task force is independent," she said. "But the accountability is yours. If you find the rot, you pull it, no matter who it is. Understand?"

"Understood." The old paranoia tingled up Leilani's arms. There would be traps, and the first would be waiting by the time she made it to the bullpen.

Mori set her own hands on the desk, palms down. "Your partner from the Bureau is being reassigned, but you have the authority to request outside support. Use it. Also, take some time to review the resumes in the folder. You'll need a top-notch investigator on your team. There are some good people in there, but the decision is all yours. No one in that folder is aware they are there, so there will be no hard feeling no matter who you choose. This city deserves better than another decade of coverups."

Leilani nodded. In her head, she was already sorting the cases. Palu's scandal reopened after the warehouse raid. The missing years from the Kahana case, now with the full timeline exposed but leave loose ends for every week of silence. The retired captain who'd taken a job with the water authority, and whose phone now pinged in the same building as one of last week's indicted councilmen. She could taste the next arrest before the ink was dry on her new orders.

Mori watched her for a long beat. "You're not here to make friends."

"I don't think I've ever been good at that," Leilani replied, and it was almost a joke.

"Good," Mori said. "Because you'll make enemies. Make sure they fear you for the right reasons."

She stood and offered her hand across the desk. Leilani stood as well and shook it. Her grip was firm, no nonsense, but not in the alpha dog contest of most men who'd held the office before.

"For the record," said Mori, her voice low, "I am sorry for what you lost."

Leilani didn't answer right away. There was no way to say, It's all right, when the losses kept compounding.

She nodded instead, once, as if it were the last piece of a deal already done.

As she left the office, the light in the hallway seemed brighter than before, every detail sharper, every line drawn clean. She glimpsed herself in the glass; the badge shining in the sun, and a new uniform already forming around the old one.

She raced up the stairs, her hand tight around the blue folder, her mind already spinning with the names she'd pursue first. The old captain, the judge, the city auditor whose voice had never quite matched his expense reports. All of them waiting, the spiral unwinding, every loop drawing tighter.

She passed the squad room, the air alive with

rumors and questions. Nobody called out her name, but nobody looked away, either. They all knew the new world had arrived. She stepped out onto the front steps, where the city fanned out in waves of sunlit street and humid haze, and paused for a long moment to let it all settle in. She started forward, her feet steady, the future a live current buzzing beneath every step.

Isaac waited in the conference room, counting the holes in the ceiling tiles. There were exactly one hundred and twenty, spaced in a grid so perfect it made his eyes ache. The air was too cold, filtered through ducts older than the field office itself, and the glass pitcher on the credenza sweated onto a coaster like it had something to be nervous about.

He clicked the lid of his Bureau laptop, leaving the afterimage of his unfinished case file on the inside of his eyelids. He was supposed to be writing a summary report, but every sentence read like an accusation. The cursor blinked. He let it.

The door opened with the pop of a seal breaking. In came Agent Morgan, his direct supervisor, her shoes shined and suit was so precisely tailored that the shadow it cast was a straight edge. Morgan carried a folder, the off-white of recycled copy paper, thick with forms. Her face was neither angry nor pleased. Merely clinical. The way career agents could do.

"Agent Torres." Morgan didn't sit but hovered at the table. She let the folder land with a thud, deliberate. "You know why we're here."

Isaac nodded, having nothing to say. The room had a faint scent of whiteboard marker, the residue of the last ten briefings on opioids and counterterrorism.

Morgan opened the file, leafed through it with a finger. "Your work on the Kahana corruption takedown is exemplary. Your hours, your informant management, your closing tactics, all above expectations. But—" She didn't look up, but let the word sit, fat and ugly, between them.

Isaac finished it for her. "But I made the Bureau look like a joke on national TV."

Morgan's mouth twitched. "You did not follow established lines of communication. You partnered off-book with a local detective whose history of insubordination is a matter of public record. You failed to report a direct threat to your own life until after the case broke. And you put the agency at reputational risk."

Isaac folded his hands, his forearms flush against the table. "And yet you called me in to say thank you."

Morgan looked at him, the lines around her eyes as sharp as a gaff hook. "I called you in to give you a choice. You can go back to protocol, desk duty for six months, then phased in as liaison, or you can opt for reassignment. The Director will have your transfer through by the end of the quarter. I don't recommend testing her patience."

Isaac considered it, just long enough to make it look like he hadn't already decided. He reached for the badge on his hip, snapped the leather open, and slid it across the table.

"I'm good, ma'am," he said. "Consider this my two-week notice, or less if you'd rather."

Morgan didn't touch the badge. "You know you're wasting your best asset, Torres."

Isaac stood, gathering his laptop and the thin manila folder he'd brought for effect. "There are other ways to make a difference," he said. "And this city needs more than protocol."

Morgan didn't rise. "There's no coming back from this."

Isaac shrugged. "There wasn't before today."

He turned, left the badge exactly in the middle of the table, and walked out without waiting for a formal dismissal.

The cubicle they'd given him was barely bigger than the holding cells down the hall, but it had a view of the ocean and a little shelf of potted plants left over from the last occupant. He swept the plants into a cardboard box, along with his framed certificates, the Newton's cradle that had never worked, and a half-used pack of American Spirits. He did it all methodically, the way his mother had taught him to clear out a house after a death.

His colleagues passed, some glancing into his cubical, others staring straight ahead. One agent from the white-collar squad looked at him with open envy. Another, an admin who'd once made him coffee on a morning when he looked like death, nodded and mouthed good luck.

Isaac smiled and turned to the one thing left on the desk. A four-by-six photo, in an acrylic frame, of himself and Leilani outside the burned-out warehouse, jackets dusted with ash, both grinning like kids on a field trip. It was taken by a beat reporter, probably intended as evidence of collusion, but he kept it because it was the one shot of either of them looking happy in the last three months. He set it in the box, then closed the lid.

He took the back stairs, past the agents who pretended not to recognize him, out the loading bay where the city hummed and a faint breeze cut through the stink of diesel and copier toner. He walked, box in arms, toward the line of city buses that would take him anywhere but here.

He didn't look back.

The new office was technically a conference room, but Leilani had claimed it before Facilities could wheel out the folding tables. The back wall was already three-quarters whiteboard, a patchwork of flow charts and maps, with a thick margin of sticky notes in four colors and a running tally of names along the bottom. Most of them were crossed out; a few, circled in red.

Boxes littered the space, stacked two high in the corners, some labeled in block print, KAHANA CASE, WAREHOUSE FIRE and others in the careful cursive of the records clerk who always wrote as if someone would frame her notes for posterity. The room was still bland. Neutral carpet, long LED fixtures, and a lingering trace of mildew from the two decades it spent as a hurricane shelter during budget shortfalls. She liked the honesty. Nothing to hide.

It was midafternoon, and the city outside the tinted window was a glaze of white light, cars crawling up Beretania in one endless loop. Leilani set a fresh marker to the board, then stood back to check the geometry of her notes. It was perfect, if a diagram built on six years of trauma and city politics could be called that.

A rap at the door. Isaac, already half inside, balancing a battered banker's box on his hip. He wore jeans and a loose blue button-down; the sleeves rolled to the elbow and the ink from a morning's paperwork still visible on his wrist. He looked tired, but in a way that meant he was no longer pretending otherwise.

"Nice setup," he said, scanning the room with a practiced cop's eye. "You spring for the premium markers?"

Leilani capped the one in her hand and tossed it his way. "Only the best. I want the old guard to taste the color when we take them down."

He caught it, spun the cap, and set the box down on the nearest chair. "You're not wasting any time."

"I've got years to make up for," she said. "You want a desk, or are you here for moral support?"

He tapped the HPD badge sitting in front of him. "I hear you're hiring."

She didn't miss a beat. "Thought you were an FBI lifer."

He made a face. "It turns out I'm allergic to meetings and authority. Who knew?"

She motioned to the stack of folders closest to him. "I should send you for a background check, but I already know what you did last summer."

He picked up a file and thumbed through the

first couple of pages. "You're starting with the judges?"

"The ones who didn't get arrested. Or the ones who made sure no one ever did." She leaned on the table, arms folded. "Do you mind being the bad guy for a while?"

Isaac shrugged. "I was born for it."

She caught his eye and let the silence hang long enough to register. "So. Are you in?"

He looked down at the table, at the badge. "I'd follow you anywhere, Leilani."

It was the first time he'd said her full name in months, and it landed with a weight that didn't need a follow-up.

She slid the detective badge across the table along with his police department ID card; the laminate was still warm from the press in HR, and the plastic edges a little rough where she'd cut the sheet herself to avoid the wait. "Already processed the paperwork," she said. "You're official as of this morning. Welcome to the HPD, Detective Torres."

He reached for the badge, but their hands collided. She pulled back, and he took the badge, turning it over in his palm.

They let the business of it settle in before starting again.

"So, what's on the agenda?" he asked.

Leilani gestured at the board. "Judge Perry. He's got connections to three cases that vanished from evidence, and his daughter's married to the guy who torched the records at City Hall."

Isaac smirked. "Are we using Bureau protocol or going HPD style?"

She grinned. "Neither. We make our own."

He nodded, already reaching for the next folder. "There's an ADA in here, too. Martel. She's cleaner than most, but I don't buy that she missed the operation. Want me to start with her?"

"Absolutely." Leilani checked the clock, then made a note in her pad. "You'll have to go easy on her. The DA's office is still tender from last week."

"I'm always gentle," he said.

She rolled her eyes. "That's what they all say."

He set the file aside and spoke, not as a partner, but as something more. "How's your son?"

Leilani's defenses appeared, then disappeared. "He's good. He made a map of our neighborhood's escape routes. For security, he says, but mostly to prove he's smarter than me."

"Is he?"

She smiled. "Not yet. Give him a few years."

Isaac returned the smile, the fatigue on his face softening. He glanced around the office, and back at her. "It's nice. The space. Feels like a new start."

"Don't get used to it," she said. "We're gonna move fast."

He popped the lid off the marker she'd thrown him, uncapped it with a flourish, and added a note to the margin of her whiteboard. Root it out before you replant. He stepped back and admired his handiwork. "You think it's possible to fix all this?"

She took a breath, steady and deep. "Not in one year. But in a lifetime."

He nodded. "Good. Gives us something to do."

They stood side by side, arms nearly touching, the energy around them more electric than any of the city's summer storms, and the world receded. There was the board, the task, and the shared certainty that whatever came next, they would face it together.

She picked up her own marker, circled the first name on their hit list, and smiled at him, enough to say. "Let's go."

The cliffs were different this time. No storm, no war, only the endless hush of the north shore wind and the orange flattening of sunlight on the water below. The scent of wet iron and crushed naupaka drifted up from the rocks, laced with the faintest sweetness from someone's backyard plumeria. The sky was so clear it made the ocean seem deliberate, every ripple and crash a kind of punctuation.

Leilani watched the waves from the bluff, her toes pressed into the eroded red dirt, and hands stuffed deep in her jacket. Isaac stood beside her, less than a foot away, still in his too-new HPD windbreaker, the badge peeking out enough to catch the last rays. They'd walked up from the trailhead without a word, content to let the birds and the wind take up all the space between them.

Below, the sea thundered against the volcanic shelf, each swell sending plumes of white up into the wind. Some of the mist found its way to the top, dampening Leilani's hair and spattering Isaac's sunglasses, which he'd worn despite the sun being nearly gone.

He wiped the lenses on the hem of his shirt. "Never thought I'd be back here without a witness or an evidence kit," he said, the tone light but not empty.

Leilani didn't answer right away. She let the sound of the water work its way through. "I almost forgot what it looked like in daylight," she said.

He nodded. "It's not so bad. You could get used

to it."

She laughed, the sound riding up and out, past the brittle grass and the last bits of the old caution tape still tangled in the brush. "If I get used to this, they'll have to fire me. There's too much to do."

He stepped close enough for his shoulder to brush hers. "The task force?"

She nodded. "It's a start. If we can keep the heat on, perhaps we can fix things before Kai's in high school."

He grinned. "Or he fixes them for us."

She looked sideways at him, then out at the horizon, where the gold faded into violet and the clouds stacked like paper lanterns. "He's got more sense than I ever did."

Isaac let the silence roll on for a while. The sea below them was relentless, unsentimental, and still alive with the possibility of both drowning and salvation. He let his hands hang loose, flexed them once, as if about to reach for something, but stopped.

"So, what's next?" he asked.

Leilani let her hair loose from its tie. The wind caught it, whipped it around her face until she was forced to smile. "Now? We do the work. Day by day, no shortcuts. We follow every trail, especially the ones that make us look stupid.

Especially those."

He reached into his pocket, fished out a wrapped chocolate, and set it on the flat rock between them. "You want a bribe?" he said. "I'm told it's a good way to get things done around here."

She laughed, but pocketed it anyway. "Don't think I don't know where you keep the stash."

He grinned, and this time, the laugh between them was real. It lingered as the sun dropped into the water and the sky lost its edge. They stood there, not talking, breathing and letting the wind do what it always did. The city behind them was another world; here, the future felt possible, or at least not doomed.

She turned to him, her hair wild and her eyes as clear as the sky. "We've got our work cut out for us," she said.

He didn't try to sound cool. "Good thing we've got the right team."

The light faded, but the shape of them together on the cliff, two bodies, not quite touching, held against the dark. Below, the sea kept up its music, ancient and stubborn and full of stories nobody had written yet.

They watched the sun go all the way down. When only the outline of the island remained, they stood, faces to the wind, and waited for the stars to show.

Acknowledgments

A special thank you to my daughter Christina J. Morgan, my unofficial collaborator.

Special thanks to my daughter Stephanie Morgan, my beta reader. Stephanie has read every novel in its rough stages and rarely gets to see the completed product. Her insight and critique have been critical in making sure the stories make sense.

Also, I would like to thank my family for their encouragement. I have been telling them stories since they were little, and I always told them that someone should be writing this stuff down. I decided to write it down myself.

I want to thank my closest friend, Trish Moakler-Herud. She has been encouraging me for years to write my stories down. I hope this will make her proud.

A special thanks to my late wife, Jane. She pushed me for years to become a writer, and my biggest regret is that she didn't live long enough to see it happen. I love her with all my heart and miss her every day. I think she would be pleased.

Finally, thanks to the readers. Without you, none of this would be important.

About the Author

2019 Pacific Book Awards Best Mystery Finalist . . . *Crime Delayed*

2020 Pacific Book Awards Best Mystery Winner . . . *Crime Denied*

2020 Chanticleer International Book Awards: 1st Place Blue Ribbon, CLUE Book Awards for Suspense, Thriller Fiction . . . *Crime Denied*

2021 Chanticleer International Book Awards Finalist, CLUE Book Awards for Suspense, Thriller Fiction . . . *Crime Conspiracy*

2021 Chanticleer International Book Awards Finalist, Book Series, CLUE Book Awards for Suspense, Thriller Fiction . . . Crime Series, The Buck Taylor Novels

2022 Chanticleer International Book Awards Finalist, CLUE Book Awards for Suspense, Thriller Fiction . . . *Crime Exploded*

2022 Chanticleer International Book Awards Finalist, CLUE Book Awards for Suspense, Thriller Fiction . . . *Crime Spree*

2023 Chanticleer International Book Awards Finalist, CLUE Book Awards for Suspense, Thriller Fiction . . . *Crime Scene*

2023 Chanticleer International Book Awards Series Finalist, Mystery & Mayhem Book Awards . . . *Crime Series*

Chuck Morgan attended Seton Hall University

and Regis College and spent thirty-five years as a construction project manager. He is an avid outdoorsman, an Eagle Scout and a licensed private pilot. He enjoys camping, hiking, mountain biking and fly-fishing.

He is the author of the Crime series, featuring Colorado Bureau of Investigation Agent Buck Taylor. The series includes *Crime Interrupted, Crime Delayed, Crime Unsolved, Crime Exposed, Crime Denied, Crime Conspiracy, Crime Unknown, Crime Exploded, Crime Spree, Crime Family, Crime Scene,* and *Crime Victims.*

He is also the author of *Her Name Was Jane,* a memoir about his late wife's nine-year battle with breast cancer. He has three children and four grandchildren. He resides in Lone Tree, Colorado.

Other Books by the Author

Dear Reader, thank you for reading this novel. Please enjoy the other books in this series and follow Colorado Bureau of Investigation Agent Buck Taylor and his team as they investigate new and sometimes unusual crimes in the Colorado mountains. Each novel is a separate story, and they can be read in any order, but you might find it more enjoyable to read them in order.

Happy Reading,

Chuck Morgan

"Crime Interrupted: A Buck Taylor Novel by Chuck Morgan is a gripping, edge-of-the-seat novel. Right from page one, the action kicks off and never stops, gaining pace as each chapter passes." Reviewed by Anne-Marie Reynolds for Readers' Favorite.

Finalist . . . 2019 Pacific Book Awards Best Mystery

"This crime novel reads like a great thriller. The writing is atmospheric, laced with vivid descriptions that capture the setting in great detail while allowing readers to follow the intensity of the action and the emotional and psychological depth of the story." Reviewed by Divine Zape for Readers' Favorite.

"Professionally written in the style of a best-selling crime novelist, such as Tom Clancy, Crime Unsolved: A Buck Taylor Novel by Chuck Morgan is a spellbinding suspense novel with an environmental flair. Intriguing subplots of fraud, survivalist paranoia, and murder weave their way through the fabric of the plot, creating a dynamic story. This is an action-filled, stimulating tale which contains fascinating details that are relevant in our present climate." Reviewed by Susan Sewell for Readers' Favorite.

"*Chuck Morgan has a unique gift for plot, one that makes Crime Exposed: A Buck Taylor Novel a hard-to-put-down book.* From the start, readers know what happens to Barb, but they become curious as they follow the investigation, wondering if the characters will find out what happened to her. The descriptions are filled with clarity, and they offer readers great images. The prose is elegant, and it captures both the emotional and psychological elements of the novel clearly while offering vivid descriptions of scenes and characters. This is a fast-paced thriller with memorable characters and a criminal investigation that is so real readers will believe it could happen.*" Reviewed by Romuald Dzemo for Readers' Favorite.

Winner . . . 2020 Pacific Book Awards Best

Mystery

2020 Chanticleer International Book Awards: 1st Place Blue Ribbon, CLUE Book Awards for Suspense, Thriller Fiction

"It's really progressive to see a female serial killer portrayed with such intelligent writing and depth of character, and the cat and mouse chase dynamic is thrown off nicely by the switching of genders. What results is a really enjoyable thriller and crime mystery novel, and overall Crime Denied is certain to please fans of both hard-boiled detective tales and action/adventure crime novels." Reviewed by K.C. Finn for Readers' Favorite.

2021 Chanticleer International Book Awards Finalist, CLUE Book Awards for Suspense, Thriller Fiction . . . *Crime Conspiracy*

"This makes for a truly dynamic story where anything is possible, and a hero you can root for even when it looks like all is lost." Reviewed by K.C. Finn for Readers' Favorite.

"This is a book you can't put down, which will entertain you on many levels, and at times make your skin crawl; the kind of book that remains in your

thoughts long after you finish reading." Reviewed by Steven Robson for Readers' Favorite.

"I read Crime Unknown in one sitting. The plot is intense and the main character, Agent Buck Taylor, is a hero like no other. This book has everything a thriller needs to be and more. I thought I knew the story at the beginning. Buck will solve a tricky murder case, I thought. But Chuck Morgan adds a twist to this story that expands it and makes it one of the most enjoyable books I've read in this genre. I loved that the lead was such an awesome well-rounded fellow but that he also had a support team who were just as important to the story." Reviewed by Maureen Dangarembizi for Readers' Favorite.

"Crime Unknown is a thoroughly enjoyable read and I would not hesitate to recommend this book to fans of the crime genre and those looking for a gateway in." Reviewed by K.C. Finn for Readers' Favorite.

2022 Chanticleer International Book Awards Finalist, CLUE Book Awards for Suspense, Thriller Fiction . . . *Crime Exploded*

"Action-packed and fast-paced, I was sucked into the story the moment I opened the novel. The author built the story to perfection. Chuck Morgan gave just the right amount of suspense, mystery and action to keep readers' attention on Buck and his team. There was never a dull moment in the story. The narrative ran smoothly until the end; it followed the development of the story and the pace set by the characters. I enjoyed the twists and turns. What I loved more than anything else in the plot was how calculating Buck was. He was smart; he didn't let the FBI discourage him and kept his head in the game. The action gave me an adrenaline rush. Absolutely brilliant!" Reviewed by Rabia Tanveer for Readers' Favorite.

2022 Chanticleer International Book Awards Finalist, CLUE Book Awards for Suspense, Thriller Fiction . . . *Crime Spree*

"It is one of the best crime novels I have read in a long while, with real characters developed in a way to let you get to know them intimately, understand them, and appreciate their strengths and weaknesses. The plot is tight, exciting, and tense, with plenty of action, and it will grip you from the start. The bizarre storyline is enthralling, written in descriptive prose that lands you right in the middle of the action. Forget sleep; once you pick this book up, you won't want to put it down until it's finished. Fantastic story, and highly recommended for fans of high-octane crime thrillers." Reviewed by Anne-Marie Reynolds for Readers' Favorite.*

"Crime Family is the tenth book in the Buck Taylor series. Chuck Morgan had me hooked from the first page until the end. There was never a dull moment with all the action; one chapter flowed into the next. The story was fast-paced and kept me on the edge of my seat. I kept turning the pages to find out what would happen next. I was intrigued, and with all the twists and turns, I could not predict what was looming. The characters were well-developed. Each had a background description, and it was fun getting to know some of them. The story was excellently written with a fitting ending." Reviewed by Alma Boucher for Readers' Favorite.*

"Crime Scene is a must-read for lovers of mystery sleuth and murder tales with a touch of conspiracy." Reader's Favorite review.

"Crime Scene has a carefully designed intrigue that deepens with every unforeseeable turn of events, and a dynamic narrative." Reader's Favorite review.

"This is a great book. Holds your attention and you don't want to put it down. I would recommend this book to anyone who loves a good crime novel." Amazon review.

"Spellbinding, gripping, powerful, and relevant are just a few words that come to mind after turning the

last page of Crime Scene: A Buck Taylor Novel, book 11, by Chuck Morgan." Amazon Review.

"*A riveting plot and good pacing keep the reader in suspense as Buck Taylor and his team establish evidence beyond a reasonable doubt. The author sustains interest by skillfully showing the art and intuition involved in crime investigation and the science behind it, as well as the elements that can delay or confound it. There are a lot of quirky characters in the novel and the author gives them mannerisms, voices and descriptions that make them distinctive and realistic. The details and descriptions of the work and everyday life of the players are both pleasantly appealing and revolting, depending on the scenario. What's most captivating and intriguing about the character development is the backstory of the unhinged characters and how the author uses them as part of the perplexing trail of a horrendous crime. Themes of sadism, cruelty, grief, forensics, police procedures, and even a little bit of romance can be found in this installment of the Buck Taylor series. Highly recommended for crime story fans who especially enjoy the information as well as the twists, turns, and the untangling of intricate and cold case crime sprees." Reviewed by Carmen Tenorio for Readers' Favorite.*

www.ingramcontent.com/pod-product-compliance
Lightning Source LLC
Chambersburg PA
CBHW070633180626
46817CB00006B/2107